Guiding Star

Augusta

Cornucopia

Twin Star

Star of the Magi

Providence

Also by Jennifer Chiaverini

The Lost Quilter

The Quilter's Kitchen

The Winding Ways Quilt

The New Year's Quilt

The Quilter's Homecoming

Circle of Quilters

The Christmas Quilt

The Sugar Camp Quilt

The Master Quilter

The Quilter's Legacy

The Runaway Quilt

The Cross-Country Quilters

Round Robin

The Quilter's Apprentice

Sylvia's Bridal Sampler from Elm Creek Quilts: The True Story Behind the Quilt

More Elm Creek Quilts: Inspired by the Elm Creek Quilts Novels

Return to Elm Creek: More Quilt Projects Inspired by the Elm Creek Quilts Novels

Elm Creek Quilts: Quilt Projects Inspired by the Elm Creek Quilts Novels

A Quilter's Holiday

An Elm Creek Quilts Novel

JENNIFER CHIAVERINI

Doubleday Large Print Home Library Edition

Simon & Schuster
New York London Toronto Sydney

This Large Print Edition, prepared especially for Doubleday Large Print Home Library, contains the complete, unabridged text of the original Publisher's Edition.

Simon & Schuster
1230 Avenue of the Americas
New York, NY 10020

Manufactured in the United States of America

ISBN 978-1-61523-547-6

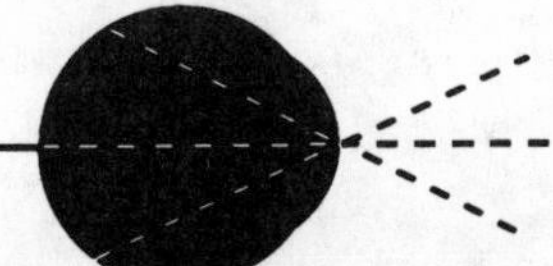

This Large Print Book carries the Seal of Approval of N.A.V.H.

To Nic and Heather

Acknowledgments

MANY THANKS GO to Maria Massie, Nicole De Jackmo, Dina Siljkovic, Kate Ankofski, Mara Lurie, Kate Lapin, and Melanie Parks, for their contributions to *A Quilter's Holiday* and their ongoing support of the Elm Creek Quilts series.

I also offer thanks to Tara Shaughnessy, the world's best nanny, for giving me time to write; to my teammates from Just For Kicks for providing me with great workouts, camaraderie, and crucial stress relief when I needed them most; and to Janet Miller for permitting me to use her beautiful quilt *Thankful Harvest,* on the jacket of this book.

My warmest appreciation goes to Denise Roy, for her generous advice and encouragement, and to Steven Garfinkel, for the lovely new author photo.

I would not have been able to complete *A Quilter's Holiday* without the friendship and insight of Brian Grover, who offered help at a crucial time, read several early drafts, and provided the essential constructive criticism I needed to improve the story.

I am very grateful for the friends and family who supported and encouraged me during the difficult months in which this book was written, especially Geraldine Neidenbach, Heather Neidenbach, Nic Neidenbach, Leonard and Marlene Chiaverini, and my boys, Marty, Nicholas, and Michael Chiaverini.

CHAPTER ONE

Sarah

ON THE DAY after Thanksgiving, Sarah woke to discover her unborn twins apparently engaged in an in utero kickboxing match to the accompaniment of her growling stomach. Propping herself up on one elbow, she reached for the crackers her husband had left on her nightstand beside a glass of water. She gently stroked her abdomen as she nibbled, taking care not to drop crumbs on the bed, and thought about the busy day full of friendship and fun awaiting her. It would be a quilter's holiday at Elm Creek Manor, and as soon as Sarah satisfied her hunger pangs, she would drag herself out of bed and seize the day.

"Morning," Matt said sleepily, propping himself up to kiss her cheek and then her tummy, twice. His curly blond hair was flattened against his head on one side and his brown eyes were still half closed. "Honey, I've been thinking . . ."

"How have you had time to think? You just woke up."

"I've been awake for a while, lying here watching you nibble your crackers."

Sarah held out a saltine. "Want one?"

"No thanks. I'll wait to see what Chef Anna's fixing for breakfast. Yesterday Jeremy mentioned that he was going to drop her off early on his way to Chicago."

"I'm afraid you're on your own." Sarah carefully sat up against the headboard, drew her long, reddish-brown hair over one shoulder, and muffled a grunt as she leaned over for the glass of water. "Jeremy's dropping Anna off for our quilter's holiday—not for kitchen duty. Sylvia insisted she take the morning off."

"After preparing that Thanksgiving feast yesterday, she deserves a day of rest."

Sarah sighed happily, remembering. Although she had toasted the holiday with ginger ale rather than the California cabernet sauvignon her friends and family had enjoyed, for the first time in her adult life, she had indulged in a Thanksgiving feast without giving calories a second thought. "I'm eating for three," she had responded cheerfully when her mother cautioned her against taking such generous helpings of Chef Anna's succulent roast turkey and savory cranberry cornbread dressing. Green beans and butternut squash had never seemed more flavorful, and best of all, she didn't have to choose between pumpkin pie and apple cake for dessert but took modest slices of both.

"Matt's going to have to roll you upstairs to bed tonight," her mother had remarked. "You won't need to eat for a week." Carol had gained only twenty pounds in her pregnancy, or so she claimed, but Sarah had left that number behind long ago.

"Anna earned the time off," Sarah agreed, "so it's oatmeal or cereal for you this morning, honey."

"I'll make up for it at the potluck lunch." Matt propped himself up on his elbows, motioned for her to scoot forward, and slipped his pillow between her back and the cold brass bars of the headboard. "Husbands are allowed at the feast, right? Even though we aren't participating in the quilting bee?"

Sarah smiled, but her gaze traveled past Matt to the window, where the light peeking below the curtains was thin and November gray. The weather forecast called for snow, but not enough to keep her friends away. "You know the rule. Everyone who brings a dish to pass will have a place at the table, quilter or not."

That wasn't the only rule defining the Elm Creek Quilters' post-Thanksgiving tradition. On the Friday after Thanksgiving, while others throughout their rural central Pennsylvania valley were sleeping in or launching the Christmas shopping season, their circle of quilters would gather at the manor for a marathon of quilting to work upon holiday gifts or decorations. At noon they would break for a potluck lunch of dishes made from leftovers from their family feasts the previous day. Agnes, Sylvia's sister-in-law, called their dinner a "Patchwork Potluck" and said the meal befit quilters, whose frugality inspired them to find creative uses for leftover turkey, stuffing, and vegetables just as they created beautiful and useful works of art from scraps of fabric.

Matt rolled onto his back, tucking his hands beneath his head. "Do you think I can get away with bringing the leftover rolls as my dish, even though that wouldn't involve any actual cooking?"

"That's a step up from the bowl of corn you reheated in the microwave last year, so I'm going to say yes."

"Watch it, sweetheart, or I'll say something I'll regret about how we're lucky there are any leftovers to work with, the way you kept cleaning your plate."

"You sound like my mother." Usually that rebuke brought a swift end to Matt's criticism, whether it was in jest or in argument. "I'm eating for three, remember?"

Matt held his hands apart about six inches. "Yes, but two of you are only this big. If you were feeding yourself and a pair of three-year-olds, I could understand the need for five helpings, but since it's one woman in her thirties and two fetuses in their sixth month—"

"Five helpings?" Sarah protested. "I stopped at thirds."

"Three helpings of dinner plus two of dessert equals five plate-cleanings." Then Matt seemed to think better of proving his point. "But you ate healthy food and you're taking great care of little Barnum and Bailey. They're lucky to have you for a mother."

Sarah laughed. "Barnum and Bailey?"

Matt grinned up at her. "Why not?"

They didn't know whether the twins were boys or girls or one of each, and they didn't want to know until the moment the babies were born. Most of their friends understood and respected their decision, but some of the Elm Creek Quilters hoped they would change their minds because, they said, it would be easier to make quilts and other gifts if they knew whether the babies were girls or boys. Diane was the most persistent in her complaints, as she was about most things. She was certain that Sarah and Matt had glimpsed the truth during one of Sarah's ultrasounds but were concealing the secret just to be contrary, so she scrutinized the couple's words and actions for clues. If Sarah preferred a pink fabric for a new quilt project, Diane triumphantly declared that the babies were surely girls. If Matt referred to one of the twins as "he" because "he or she" became annoying after frequent repetition and he hated to refer to one of his children as "it," Diane gleefully teased him about giving away the secret. Always ready to give as good as he got, Matt began calling the babies various paired names, usually nonsensical duos that amused Sarah and drove Diane crazy. Sarah's favorites included "Sugar and Spice," "Zig and Zag," "Needle and Thread," and "Bagel and Schmear." The joke became even funnier when Carol began to worry aloud that Sarah and Matt might seriously consider one of those alarming combinations. Perhaps she was right to worry. Maybe it was the hormones, but Sarah thought "Barnum and Bailey" had possibilities.

"Well, this ringmaster thinks it's time to get this circus on the road." Sarah picked cracker crumbs from her nightgown and threw back the covers. "I have to get started on my turkey Tetrazzini."

"Now?"

"I want to get as much prepared ahead of time before my friends show up." Sarah's stomach rumbled and one of the twins kicked. Apparently the crackers had made little impact. "But I guess it can wait until after breakfast."

It was only later, after she had showered and dressed and returned to the bedroom to find the bed made and Matt absent that she realized she had not given him a chance to tell her what he had been thinking about upon waking.

ELM CREEK MANOR wasn't the best place to raise children, Sarah reflected as she descended the oak staircase to the grand, three-story front foyer. The elegant balusters on staircase and balconies were too far apart for government safety standards and the gleaming black marble floor would offer a toddler unsteady footing and hard landings. Baby proofing would be a nightmare, but Matt assured her he would take care of everything. Sylvia Bergstrom Compson, Master Quilter and cofounder of Elm Creek Quilts, often reminded Sarah that generations of Bergstrom children had safely reached adulthood on her family estate, but Sarah found that small comfort. Once upon a time lead paint had been acceptable and seat belts optional, and although countless numbers of children had escaped injury, Sarah had no intention of repeating past generations' mistakes.

In many other important ways, Elm Creek Manor was an idyllic place to raise a family. The estate offered acres of forest to explore; a creek for wading, fishing, and tossing stones; a thriving orchard with trees to climb and apples to pluck; gardens for picnics and games of make-believe; and a broad expanse of lawn for running and playing, for crunching through fallen leaves in autumn, and for building snow forts in winter. Even when guests filled the manor, a quilters' retreat throughout the spring and summer, there was plenty of room for playing hide-and-seek and many private nooks for curling up with a book or paper and crayons. Most important, the manor was home to Sylvia and other dear friends who would offer the children unconditional love and affection, and what helped children thrive more than that?

She and Matt had so much to be thankful for in that season of Thanksgiving, Sarah thought as she crossed the foyer and turned down the older, west wing of the manor. Perhaps that was what he had wanted to tell her.

Appetizing aromas wafted down the hallway from the kitchen, lingering scents of cinnamon, nutmeg, and fresh-baked bread and something new that Sarah didn't recall from their Thanksgiving feast. She found Anna Del Maso at the stove stirring something in a large copper stockpot, her long, dark-brown hair in a neat French braid, a crisp white apron tied about her neck and waist.

"Good morning, Anna," Sarah greeted her from the doorway. "You'd better not be making breakfast! Sylvia strictly forbade it."

Anna threw her a quick smile over her shoulder. "Don't worry. This is for lunch. I'm only here early because the bus is running a limited holiday schedule, so Jeremy dropped me off on his way to Chicago."

Sarah nodded. "Yes, I heard. He's going to see Summer."

Anna nodded and turned back to the stockpot. "She was too swamped with grad school work to come home for Thanksgiving, so he went to her."

"I thought Gwen said she'd made plans with her roommates."

"He's her boyfriend, isn't he? Wouldn't he be welcome to join them?"

"I can't speak for Summer's roommates, but I can't imagine why not." Sarah watched a thin wisp of steam rise from the pot and inhaled deeply. "That smells wonderful."

"It's our soup course. Ginger pumpkin bisque."

Sarah glanced into the pot at the simmering golden liquid as she took a paper sack of bagels from the breadbox. "Made with leftover pumpkin pie? Because I didn't think there was any."

Anna laughed. "No, not leftover pie. Left-over pumpkin that didn't make it into the pie." She set down her spoon, turned down the flame, and wiped her hands on her apron. "Would you mind keeping an eye on this while you have breakfast? I still have a few more seams to go on my quilt block for the cornucopia. This is my first day-after-Thanksgiving as an Elm Creek Quilter and I want to get it right."

Sarah nodded, but not without misgivings. No matter how often Anna assured her that she was a fine cook, Sarah was reluctant to risk ruining one of the talented chef's marvelous culinary creations. "The quilt block cornucopia is new to all of us," she reminded Anna. "I don't think you can go wrong."

Anna smiled as she untied her apron, the dimple in her right cheek deepening and a sparkle lighting up her dark brown eyes. Sarah knew Anna considered herself too plump to be pretty, and she often wondered how her friend could be so blind to her own beauty. "Even so, I'm not leaving that up to chance. You Elm Creek Quilters set high standards."

"You mean *we* Elm Creek Quilters set high standards," Sarah called after her as Anna left the kitchen. Too often Anna forgot to include herself when she spoke of them, though as far as Sarah was concerned, she was no less a member of their circle than the founding members. Sarah hoped Anna would begin to feel less like an outsider as the Elm Creek Quilters forged new traditions, such as this one, inspired by a discovery Anna and Sylvia had made while remodeling the kitchen a few weeks before.

The kitchen in the west wing of Elm Creek Manor had been built in 1858, and when Anna was offered the chef's job in August, she couldn't hide her concern regarding its condition. Sarah didn't have to be a professional chef to understand her dismay. Not a single appliance was post-1945 except for a tiny microwave on the counter, possibly the first ever invented by the look of it. Poor lighting, battered utensils, broken stovetop burners—the list of necessary repairs went on and on. The Elm Creek Quilters had managed to feed an entire quilt camp three meals a day by adapting to what Sylvia referred to as the kitchen's "charming quirks," but none of them expected someone with Anna's experience to endure such conditions happily, and no one was surprised when Anna made the promise of a total remodel a prerequisite for accepting the post. Fortunately, Sylvia agreed that drastic improvements were long overdue, so after the camp season ended, contractors transformed the kitchen by knocking out a wall and expanding into an adjacent sitting room, then hauling away the old appliances, counters, and cabinetry, and replacing them with everything on Anna's wish list. Privately Anna had confided to Sarah that she had not expected Sylvia to do half of what she had requested and she would have settled for less. Sarah had laughed and told Anna that as she would soon discover, Sylvia never did anything by half measures.

Before the contractors could begin, Sylvia and Anna had been obliged to clear every cabinet, cupboard, drawer, and pantry shelf, sorting useful items from clutter that should have been discarded long ago. As they worked, they discovered cherished Bergstrom family heirlooms: an old gingham tablecloth, a great-aunt's collection of feedsack cloth aprons, Sylvia's mother's favorite cut glass serving dish, and a Thanksgiving cornucopia Sylvia's sister, Claudia, had woven of straw as a schoolgirl.

As Sylvia told it, the cornucopia, dilapidated from years buried under a pile of tablecloths in the back of a cupboard, had been the centerpiece of the Bergstrom Thanksgiving table every year from the time Claudia had brought it home from school. When the Bergstroms gathered for the holiday feast, each member of the family placed something in the cornucopia—a small object, a drawing, a letter, anything small enough to fit inside would do as long as it represented what that person was most thankful for that year. Sylvia's mother had always placed a picture of her family inside the centerpiece, while Sylvia's father had usually selected something like an apple or a horseshoe to signify the abundance of their farm. The children's choices were often more amusing if no less heartfelt—trinkets, toys—but everyone from the youngest toddler to the eldest grandparent added something. After the meal, the family removed the items from the cornucopia one by one as the person who had chosen each one explained what it symbolized and what he or she was most grateful for that year.

Upon discovering her late sister's long-forgotten craft, Sylvia had been inspired to revive the tradition, but with an important change appropriate for a gathering of quilters. Where the Bergstroms had used pictures, letters, or small trinkets, the Elm Creek Quilters would create quilt blocks, each stitching one that either by name or imagery represented something for which she wished to give thanks. As they enjoyed their Patchwork Potluck, they would share their stories of gratitude, the inspiration for their handiwork.

For Sarah there had only been one possible choice.

SARAH FINISHED HER breakfast and started putting together her perennial contribution to the potluck, turkey Tetrazzini, occasionally stirring Anna's ginger pumpkin bisque and glancing out the window over the sink to the back parking lot for the arrival of her friends. She was grating the mozzarella when Gretchen entered, her black cardigan buttoned over a crisp white blouse, the formality of her plum corduroy skirt offset by her comfortable fleece slippers, their size exaggerated by her thin ankles. "Nothing that smells so yummy could possibly be made from leftovers," Gretchen exclaimed, savoring the aroma. "Is Anna here?"

"Of course. You don't think I'm responsible for something so complicated as ginger pumpkin bisque, do you?"

"I'm sure you could whip up something just as tasty if you had the recipe," said Gretchen loyally, opening the refrigerator.

She was in her mid-sixties, with steel-gray hair cut in a pageboy and a slender frame that Sarah thought seemed chiseled thin by hard times. Still, Sarah had noticed that Gretchen's careworn look had improved considerably since she had accepted the teaching position with Elm Creek Quilts and had moved into the manor with her husband. Joe, who endured lingering effects from a serious injury he had suffered years before as a steelworker in Ambridge, enjoyed restoring antique furniture in the woodshop he had set up in the barn and occasionally assisted Matt with his caretaker's duties.

"It would take more than a recipe or an entire collection of recipes to put me in Anna's league," said Sarah, filling a pot with water, setting it on a back burner, and turning on the flame.

"It's true that Anna has a gift." Gretchen searched through the refrigerator, taking out plastic containers and lifting the lids to check the contents. "I've been feeling quite spoiled ever since I came to live here, having so many of my meals prepared by a professional chef. You weren't going to use the leftover green beans and stuffing, were you? I thought I'd make a three-bean casserole."

"Mmm, sounds yummy. They're all yours." Sarah thought wistfully of Summer, a vegetarian, who often brought a three-bean salad to their potlucks but would not be joining them for the first time since they had begun their day-after-Thanksgiving tradition. Summer was closest in age to Sarah of all the original Elm Creek Quilters and her best friend among them except for Sylvia, who would always hold a unique place in Sarah's heart. Probably the only Elm Creek Quilter who missed Summer more was Gwen, her mother.

Sarah kept her ears tuned for the sound of cars approaching as she and Gretchen worked on their dishes. After a few moments, Gretchen broke the silence by saying absently, "I wonder what everyone else will contribute?"

"Gwen will bring a dessert because she always does," said Sarah, draining the cooked pasta in a colander in the sink. "Diane will bring something healthy or something that looks suspiciously new, and then she and Gwen will spend ten minutes debating what percentage of the dish has to be leftovers in order for it to meet the requirements."

Gretchen smiled as if she had no doubt Sarah's predictions would prove true. "I was thinking aloud," she said. "I should have been more clear. I was wondering what quilt blocks everyone has made for the cornucopia, and what they're most thankful for. I had so much to be grateful for this year I had a difficult time choosing only one. And that, I think, is the sign of a very good year."

Sarah agreed, but privately she wondered if Gretchen's trouble selecting a single quilt block said more about her indomitable spirit and appreciation of life's simplest gifts than about the year.

ONE BY ONE, the residents of Elm Creek Manor came to the kitchen for breakfast and to prepare their contributions for the potluck. Sylvia put together a casserole from the leftover butternut squash and cranberry cornbread dressing, which she promised tasted much better than it sounded, and then left to take freshly washed linens from the laundry room to the banquet hall. Sarah's mother, Carol, who was visiting for the holiday, delighted Sarah by using leftover sweet potatoes to prepare one of her grandmother's favorite recipes, a baked dish of sweet potatoes, apples, and cranberries. Matt stopped by on his way in from the barn to have a quick breakfast of cereal, a bagel, and coffee, as well as to hide the leftover rolls in the back of the pantry so that no one else would claim them.

Sarah found him in the back hallway as he was putting on his coat and gloves before returning to work. "What was it you wanted to tell me this morning, honey?"

Matt frowned thoughtfully as he laced up his sturdy boots. "What do you mean?"

"This morning, in bed. You said, 'Honey, I've been thinking,' You never told me."

"Oh, that. It was nothing."

She caught him by the sleeve as he opened the back door. "It must have been something."

Matt hesitated and ran his gloved hand over his jaw. "I was thinking about growing a beard. What do you think?"

Sarah folded her arms and studied his stubble, blond flecked with red. "I think you might look like a mountain man, but it's your face."

"True, but you're the one who'll have to look at it."

She reached up to place her right hand on his left cheek. "Bearded or clean-shaven, there's no face I'd rather see every day for the rest of my life."

"Wow." Matt paused as if stunned. "The most I was hoping for was, 'You can always shave it off if you don't like it.' "

"Sometimes in life you get more than you hoped for."

"That's only fair, because too often you get less."

She drew her hand away. "What do you mean?"

"Nothing." He grinned and kissed her. "Save me a seat beside you at lunch, okay?"

She agreed and closed the door behind him after he left, troubled. Something more than a beard weighed on his mind, but he clearly no longer wanted to discuss it. Maybe later she could catch him at a more forthcoming moment, but in the meantime . . . she would try not to worry.

She returned to the kitchen. Andrew,

Sylvia's husband, who had cooked for himself for years after his first wife's death but nonetheless seemed ill at ease in Anna's spotless, modern kitchen, stood with his hand on the refrigerator door studying the contents so apprehensively that Sarah was moved to assure him that he could consider the remaining bottles of wine and sparkling cider his contribution to the potluck.

Relieved, Andrew accepted the offer. "I thought I'd have to go hungry," he confessed. "Matt told me the rules."

"We'd make an exception for you," said Sarah. "But don't tell Matt."

"You still have time to make a block for the cornucopia, too," remarked Carol as she deftly cut the peel from an apple in one long, shiny, red strip. She had finished her block late the night before, but not without chiding Sarah for not informing her of the ritual sooner. Sarah hadn't thought to tell her. Her mother was only a novice quilter, not that her beginner's status would have excluded her, but it hadn't occurred to Sarah that her mother might want to participate.

"I'll stick to bringing the drinks and admiring the quilt blocks you ladies make," said Andrew. He poured coffee into a thermos and said he'd be out in the woodlot cutting logs if anyone needed him.

"He is an absolute gem," Carol declared after he had gone. "Sylvia's lucky to have him."

"I think their luck is mutual," said Gretchen, and they all agreed. Sylvia and Andrew had known each other since childhood, but their lives had taken them down different paths. They had reunited decades later after each had lost a beloved spouse, never expecting that they would fall in love and marry.

It was not quite nine o'clock when Gwen's hybrid pulled into the parking lot. Within minutes they heard the back door open and close, followed by a bustle of boots and coats in the hall closet. Then Gwen appeared in the doorway carrying a glass cake pan covered in foil, her cheeks rosy from the cold, her long, wavy, auburn hair streaked with gray, a quilted knapsack on her back. "Did you hear the forecast?" she greeted them cheerfully, setting the pan on the counter. "We're expected to get hit with a nor'easter today."

"What?" exclaimed Sarah. "The last I heard, we were only expected to get some light snow showers."

"How much snow are they predicting?" asked Sylvia, returning from her errand to the laundry room and banquet hall, her arms full of freshly washed dish towels.

"Ten to twelve inches," said Gwen, strolling through the kitchen to peek at her friends' creations. "We all might have to spend the night."

"With quilt camp closed for the season, we have plenty of rooms," said Sarah, settling into a booth in the breakfast nook with a cup of decaf coffee. "As long as everyone makes it to the manor before the storm hits, it shouldn't spoil our plans. We could have an all-night quilt marathon like the old days."

"The front isn't supposed to reach our county until this afternoon," said Gwen, apparently the only one among them who had spared time for the news that morning. "It was over Ohio last time I saw the weather radar."

"I hope Jeremy doesn't get stuck on the interstate," said Anna, who had returned to the kitchen smiling and lost in her own thoughts, but whose smile faltered when she heard the updated forecast. "He's probably near Cleveland right about now."

"I'm sure he'll be fine," said Sylvia. "He's a resourceful young man, smart enough to know when he should pull off the road rather than press on."

"Maybe usually," Anna murmured, and she looked no less worried as she put on a fresh pot of coffee and filled the kettle for tea.

The manor's permanent residents finished preparing for the potluck lunch and were tidying the kitchen when the last two Elm Creek Quilters arrived together, the taller, younger Diane driving petite white-haired Agnes, as was their longtime custom. Blond, enviably slender Diane was the mother of two sons in college, although she didn't look it. "Make way for the main course," she warned as she entered the kitchen, still clad in her tailored red wool coat and black leather gloves and carrying a large white casserole dish with a glass lid.

"Hold on," said Gwen, her beaded necklaces clinking softly as she put her head to one side, studying the casserole dish, which thudded heavily when Diane set it on the counter. "A main course means effort. You just dumped a bag of frozen veggies in there and stirred in a can of cream of mushroom soup, didn't you?"

"Shut it, hippie," said Diane breezily, taking off her gloves and tucking them into her coat pockets. "This is Agnes's deep dish turkey pie. We swapped. She's carrying my cinnamon bread. It's lighter."

"One would hope so," said Gwen. Sarah exchanged a knowing look with Sylvia. Gwen and Diane bantered so habitually that an outsider would never guess they were dear friends.

Just then, Agnes, who had paused to leave her winter garb in the hall closet, entered the kitchen. "Good morning, everyone!" She set a plastic bag holding a round loaf of marbled bread on the counter beside the casserole. "Who's ready for a quilter's holiday feast?"

As the others happily chimed in that they were ready, Gwen studied the bread skeptically. "Did you stop at the bakery on your way in? That's cheating."

"Of course not, Gwen," chided Agnes,

her blue eyes mild behind pink-tinted glasses.

"See? I have a witness," Diane retorted over her shoulder as she left the kitchen to put away her coat and boots. "I made it in my bread machine this morning."

"Well, to be fair," said Agnes, glancing after her, "I can only verify that we didn't stop at the bakery on the way. I didn't witness any actual baking."

"I'm sure we can take Diane's word for it," said Gretchen just as Diane returned.

"You don't know her as well as we do," said Gwen. "Tell us, Diane. Exactly what part of this bread qualifies as a leftover?"

"Almost all of it," said Diane, searching the cupboards for her favorite coffee mug. "The flour, the salt, the cinnamon—I bought every ingredient for other recipes."

Gwen shook her head. "Kitchen staples aren't the same as leftovers."

"I didn't use them up earlier, and therefore, they're left over." Diane filled the large pink cappuccino mug with coffee and sipped it, black. "Anyway, I have two young men home from college. It's a Thanksgiving miracle I have any food left in the house."

Suddenly Gwen turned wistful, and Sarah knew she was thinking of her daughter, Summer, hundreds of miles away at the University of Chicago. "Now, that's a problem I'd like to have."

Diane eyed her over the rim of her coffee mug. "You'd like to have two young men home from college in your house? Why, Gwen, this is a side of you I haven't seen before."

"Shut it, cheater," said Gwen.

Before Diane could argue that she hadn't cheated, Sylvia stepped in and suggested they coordinate the cooking and reheating times and temperatures for their assorted dishes so that everything would be ready to serve as close to the same time as they could manage. Anna took charge and quickly wrote up a schedule, and with the kitchen details sorted out, the Elm Creek Quilters gathered their supplies and reconvened in the ballroom to begin their daylong quilting marathon.

The ballroom took up almost the entire first floor of the south wing of the manor, added on to the original home in the early 1900s after the Bergstrom family had made its fortune raising champion horses. A carpeted border roughly twenty feet wide encircled the broad parquet dance floor, most of which was subdivided into classrooms by tall, white, moveable partitions. Three crystal chandeliers hung high above from a ceiling covered with a swirling vine pattern of molded plaster. A dais on the far side of the room served as a stage from which teachers could offer a seminar to the entire camp at once or where musicians or other performers entertained the campers during evening programs. On the opposite wall was a large fireplace flanked by a rack of fire tools and a newly filled log holder, evidence of Andrew's hard work. Ever thoughtful, he had arranged chairs nearby and had laid a fire for them, awaiting only the touch of a match. Tall, narrow windows topped by semicircular curves lined the south, east, and west walls. The heavy drapes had been drawn back, and through the glass Sarah saw a few large, white flakes swirling in a light wind.

Though the ballroom was too grand and vast to be called intimate, it was the perfect place for the Elm Creek Quilters to spend a day quilting. The classrooms provided every quilting tool or notion they could possibly need, from sewing machines to irons to rotary cutters and mats, and the chairs pulled up to the fireplace gave them a sense of warmth and coziness. Earlier, Matt and Joe had rolled wheeled work-tables from the classroom area closer to the fireside and had set up workstations for cutting fabric, sewing, and ironing so that no one would have to venture far from the camaraderie and conversation to attend to those tasks. Fortified by coffee or tea, mindful of the time and tasks remaining in the kitchen, the quilters settled down to work, threading needles and unfolding fabric, arranging quilt blocks on the parquet dance floor, and admiring one another's projects.

"There's no better way to kick off the quilting season than with a quilter's holiday," said Diane with a satisfied sigh as she settled back into an armchair, propped her feet up on a padded stool, and paged through a holiday-themed craft magazine.

"The quilting season?" echoed Anna, searching through Sarah's thread box for a shade of gold that more closely matched the scrap of fabric on her lap. "Isn't it always the quilting season at Elm Creek Manor?"

"Of course, but the day after Thanksgiving marks the official start of the official quilting season."

Gretchen looked dubious. "I've never heard of an official quilting season, and I've been quilting for a very long time."

"It's only official in Diane's mind," said Gwen. "She's lobbied the National Quilter's Association to have it declared a holiday, but to no avail."

"I have not," retorted Diane, but she looked as if she thought it might be a good idea.

Gwen threaded a needle with a long strand of cream-colored thread. "Then stop tossing around the word *official* like it means something."

Sarah glanced up in surprise from arranging patchwork blocks on the parquet floor. She had become accustomed to the banter between Gwen and Diane, but Gwen seemed relentless in her pursuit of a conflict that morning.

"We all miss Summer," said Sylvia, pinning a forest green rhombus to a mirror image piece cut from scarlet. "And Bonnie, and Judy, and all our friends who couldn't be here today. But of course, Gwen, we understand that the absence of a daughter aches more keenly."

"What she's trying to say is that we understand why you're so grumpy, but stop taking your bad mood out on me," said Diane, rolling up her magazine, "or I'll be forced to swat you."

"Your kind always resorts to threats of violence in the end," said Gwen, but she allowed a small smile.

"Official or not, this does feel like the start of the quilting season," remarked Agnes, and all, even Gwen, agreed. Although quilters pieced and sewed throughout the year, when the weather turned colder and forced them indoors, it was especially appealing to layer a quilt sandwich in a lap hoop, curl up on the sofa, and snuggle beneath the soft folds. While the winds blew and snow fell, quilters could enjoy the comforting softness and stimulating color of fabric as they cut and sewed and created objects of warmth and beauty for those they loved. The arrival of the day after Thanksgiving also meant that the Elm Creek Quilters had about a month left to complete all the quilts, table runners, garments, ornaments, and other quilted items they intended to give as Christmas gifts. A day devoted to quilting in the company of friends, free of other distractions, would allow them to make good progress on their homemade gifts—and hold off the frenzy of the holiday season one day more.

Some of the Elm Creek Quilters hoped to finish their current works-in-progress before the end of the day, but Sarah knew she would need at least another two weeks to finish the quilt she was making for Matt's father. The block pattern, her own original design, was a Log Cabin variation with a burgundy star in the center and dark blue, tan, and ivory diagonals instead of the traditional two-part, dark-and-light divisions. She had pieced forty-eight blocks, enough for a queen-size quilt, and was on her hands and knees on the floor laying them out in a Barn Raising setting. Placing the last in the lower left corner, she huffed and pushed off with her hands and managed to get on her feet, then stood back to inspect her work. The design had looked stunning on her computer screen, but sometimes the difference between pixels and fabric could be profound.

"Beautiful," proclaimed Agnes, who had

left her appliqué handwork on her chair and had come closer for a better look. "Matt's father is going to love it."

"I hope so," said Sarah, nudging an errant block into place with the toe of her slipper. "He's said on several occasions that he has no interest in quilting."

"Quilting, not quilts," noted Carol. "He might like quilts, but have no interest in taking up the art himself."

"I'm not so sure. His eyes glaze over every time Matt or I talk about what goes on at quilt camp." Sarah walked around the arrangement of blocks, studying it from all sides. Yes, the Barn Raising setting was definitely the way to go. "I thought perhaps if he had a quilt of his own, he might take more of an interest in our work."

She meant in Matt's work as well as that of the Elm Creek Quilters. Years before, when Matt had earned his degree in Landscape Architecture from Penn State, Hank McClure had hoped his son would put his training to use with Hank's successful home building company in southwestern Pennsylvania. Matt had worked for his father ever since he was old enough to hold a hammer, whenever he was not in school.

Even while in college he had often driven home on the weekends to help with projects running behind schedule, but he had never intended to take over the family business, or so he had always assured Sarah.

For years, Hank had let Matt go his own way without complaint, but the closer he came to retirement, the more often he hinted that he hoped Matt would change his mind. On their last visit, in early September, Hank had told Matt that with two babies on the way, he had to think more seriously about his future. "A partnership with your old man is as secure a job as you're going to get in this world," he had said, clapping Matt on the back and grinning. Matt hadn't defended his career choice, just smiled in return while Sarah bit the inside of her lower lip to keep herself from informing Hank that Matt's job at Elm Creek Quilts would be secure even if he weren't married to the cofounder. He was essential to their operations, as essential as Sarah herself, but Hank seemed to think Matt's skills were going to waste.

In all the years Sarah and Matt had lived and worked at Elm Creek Manor, Matt's father had come to visit them only twice.

Matt made excuses for him, saying that he couldn't get away from work as easily as they could, so it made more sense for them to visit him. Sarah knew this was true, but she also realized—even if it had not yet occurred to the men—that it wouldn't be so easy to drop everything and drive halfway across the state after the twins were born.

That year, Matt's father had agreed to spend Christmas at Elm Creek Manor. Sarah didn't expect the quilt he would find under the tree on Christmas morning to work miracles, but the quilt and a pleasant visit combined might encourage him to reconsider his doubts about Elm Creek Quilts and Matt's choice to work as the caretaker there. Not too long ago, Sarah's mother had been skeptical that a quilt camp could provide a good living, Sarah reminded herself as she glanced at Carol, who sat near the fireplace chatting with Diane and rummaging through her sewing basket. Sarah didn't expect Matt's father to sign up for quilt camp as Carol had done, but perhaps a quilt of his own would spark his appreciation, maybe even his curiosity, for the art form that the Elm Creek Quilters fostered within the gray stone walls of the manor. If he thought that Matt was contributing to something worthwhile, something with a strong tradition that continued to thrive, perhaps he would stop pressuring Matt to take over his construction firm. Sarah hoped so, because if Hank kept it up, Matt might be persuaded, and the last thing Sarah wanted to do was leave Elm Creek Quilts—

"What are you going to call it?"

"Hmm?" Sarah said, startled from her reverie.

"Your new quilt block," said Agnes. "You have to name an original design."

"I haven't thought of a name yet," Sarah admitted. "Maybe something with the word *cabin* or *star* in it."

"Cabin Star?" said Anna, admiring Sarah's blocks. "Star Cabin?"

"Stars over the Cabins?" suggested Agnes.

"Maybe." Sarah wasn't sure. The name should evoke elements of the design, but it should also reflect the person and the occasion for which she had created it. It was meant to be a Christmas gift, but she had chosen Hank's favorites rather than traditional holiday colors. Cabins could be homes, and Hank had spent his life building homes for others. The Barn Raising setting suggested Hank's profession as well. Contractor's Star? No. Definitely not.

A name would come to her, she decided as she retrieved her pincushion from her sewing kit and settled down to pinning the blocks into rows. If not, she could count on her friends to test ideas and debate their merits until together they hit upon the perfect name. It was how they had often found solutions to problems, in sharing and in collaboration, and Sarah was not about to give that up.

"Found it," Diane cried so unexpectedly that Sarah almost stuck herself with a pin. "And it only took me three magazines. I knew it was in one of these."

"Found what?" asked Carol.

"The pattern for this Advent calendar." Beaming, Diane held up the magazine, but Sarah couldn't see the pages from her seat on the floor. "It's a holiday scene, and the numbered appliqués are actually pockets. You can tuck a coin or a piece of candy inside."

Gwen glanced at the pictures. "It's cute,

but it seems better suited for younger children, don't you think?"

Diane dismissed that with a wave of her hand. "The boys will understand. We used a cardboard Advent calendar almost exactly like this one for years when they were younger, but it's too dilapidated to display anymore. Half of the little paper pockets have fallen off and some of the numbers are so faded you can't read them anymore."

Carol nodded her approval. "Your sons will remember your tradition and they'll appreciate that you're replacing the worn out calendar with something more enduring. It'll be something their own children can enjoy when they come to visit you at Christmas in years to come."

"Let's not get ahead of ourselves. I'm not ready to be a grandma just yet." Glancing between the magazine and her sewing supplies, Diane began collecting the necessary fabric and notions. "Anyway, I'm not really replacing mine. I'm going to make two, one to give to each of them."

"Wait. You've just now found the pattern?" Gretchen's brow furrowed. "Does this mean you haven't started yet? And you plan to finish two before Christmas?"

"This is Diane's way," explained Sylvia, amused. "It's become a tradition."

"And yet I always manage to finish in time, don't I?" Diane defended herself. "There's plenty of time until Christmas."

"Not as much time as you seem to think," said Gwen. "And to get the most out of the calendars, you really ought to give them to your boys on the first day of Advent. If they receive them on Christmas, they'll only have the pocket for December twenty-fifth to open, right?"

Diane looked perturbed for a moment, but then she shrugged. "So they'll have them for next year's Advent rather than this one. I'll tuck something special into the last pocket to make up for any disappointment they might feel at missing out on the other twenty-four pockets."

"Like what, a hundred dollar bill?" Gwen loosened the bolt on her lap hoop and adjusted the layers of fabric and batting. The colors were more muted and the pattern more traditional than her usual work, but if it was a gift, Gwen had likely designed it for the recipient's tastes rather than her own. "It would take something on that order to interest most college kids I know in an Advent calendar."

"Gwen," Agnes rebuked gently, but Sarah shared Gwen's misgivings. If she had two college guys on her Christmas shopping list, her first thought wouldn't be to make them quilted Advent calendars. Wasn't it right for a friend to tactfully suggest other, probably better gifts, especially since Diane hadn't cut a single piece of fabric yet?

"This isn't all that Tim and I will have under the tree for them," said Diane, unconcerned. "This is just a bonus. A little memory from Christmases past."

"And a lovely idea it is," declared Sylvia, with a warning look for Gwen, who held up a hand in a small gesture signifying that she wouldn't debate the matter—and no one loved a good debate more than Gwen.

As Gwen slipped on her thimble to begin hand-quilting, Sarah craned her neck to get a better look at her work-in-progress. "What's that you're working on?" she asked. "I can't remember the last time I saw you hand-quilt anything."

"I'm finishing this for a friend," said Gwen,

eyes on her work. "She hand-quilted most of the top before passing it on to me, so naturally I'll continue in the same style."

Agnes studied the draped layers of top, batting, and backing concealing Gwen's lap and most of her chair. "And you hope to have it done by Christmas?"

"Sooner, actually, since I'll need time to ship it."

"You'll have to quilt day and night from now until Christmas Eve to meet that deadline," said Diane.

Gwen made the barest of shrugs. "If I have to. Whatever it takes."

"But you'll have classes until the end of the semester and exams to grade," protested Agnes. "And I assume you might want to sleep every once in a while. Why don't we put it in the quilt frame and we can all help you finish it?"

Gwen looked up from her work, smiling fondly. "That's very thoughtful of you, but take a look around. If you all help me, when would you work on your own projects?"

"She's right," Diane quickly interjected. "Sorry, Gwen, but you're on your own."

"Not a problem." Then Gwen added, as

if thinking aloud, "I want to finish it myself, anyway."

"It's a beautiful design," said Sarah, admiring it from a distance. In each block, four isosceles triangles flared outward toward the corners from a central square set on point. Each triangle was flanked by two long, narrow isosceles triangles so that they seemed to split into two, creating an unusual eight-pointed star. Four additional squares, each touching one corner of the central square and cut from the same fabric, created the illusion of one larger square behind the more prominent star. The meeting of the star points created a secondary pattern of stars overlapping in a striking, almost circular fashion. The muted colors—browns, greens, and pinks in an array of floral prints—provided a welcome, softening balance to the sharp points and corners of the triangles and squares.

Even if she had not been told that someone else had pieced the top, Sarah would have guessed it was not her friend's work, for Gwen usually worked with a bold, jewel-toned palette. Also, Gwen's creations tended toward the contemporary and experimental whereas this top was traditional, despite its complexity. And yet the design carried some essence of Gwen in a way Sarah could not quite determine.

"I should have the last of these Christmas stockings finished by the end of next week," said Agnes firmly, apparently unwilling to see Gwen exhaust herself to meet a deadline. "At least let me help you with the binding."

"I might take you up on that," said Gwen.

"Agnes," Diane broke in, "if you're that eager to help others . . ."

Agnes smiled. "If I finish my grandchildren's Christmas stockings before Gwen is ready to bind her quilt, I'd be happy to help you too, Diane."

"Thanks," said Diane cheerfully, as if she had expected Agnes's answer.

"This too happens every year," Sylvia told Anna and Gretchen. "It's our resident procrastinator's secret to completing her projects by Christmas. If not for Agnes's help—"

"Diane would be in serious trouble," Gwen broke in.

"Tis the season for giving," said Agnes

cheerfully. "Not just the giving of gifts, but of our time and talents."

"I couldn't agree more," said Gretchen from the ironing board, where she was pressing small blocks pieced from bright rainbow hues, colors so clear and vivid that they must be meant for a child's quilt. But which child? Gretchen had no children of her own, no grandchildren. A young grandniece or nephew perhaps? Pondering the possibilities, Sarah recalled Gretchen's cryptic response earlier that day when Sylvia had asked her about her project as she unpacked her tote bag. Gretchen had said that she was working on dozens of Swamp Patch blocks—the design was fortunately much prettier than its name implied—and she had not yet met the children to whom she intended to give the finished quilts.

Suddenly Sarah understood. Bright, cheerful colors for children Gretchen had not yet met—that could only mean she was making baby quilts for Sarah's unborn twins. Quickly Sarah averted her gaze, hiding a grin. She must not seem too interested in Gretchen's project or she would ruin her friend's surprise.

Sarah carried the pinned blocks to one of the available sewing machines Matt had set up, changed the bobbin and top thread from Gretchen's bright blue to taupe, and sewed the first pair of blocks together. As she sewed more blocks into pairs and then into trios, and the trios into rows, her friends worked alongside her, their conversation flowing and darting and laughter ringing out. By the time the Elm Creek Quilters set aside their sewing to prepare for the Patchwork Potluck, Sarah had completed all eight rows and had begun pinning them together.

Anna organized the cooking and reheating of dishes while Sarah and Sylvia set two round tables in the banquet hall with tablecloths, crystal, and the fine Bergstrom china bearing the family emblem, a rearing stallion. Matt, Andrew, and Joe pitched in as well, setting up a single buffet table, one of many they used to serve the campers during the season. The smells from the kitchen were richly fragrant—baked apples, cinnamon, cornbread, and roast turkey—making Sarah's stomach rumble in anticipation. None too soon, she and the other Elm Creek Quilters carried their creative dishes patched together from Thanksgiving leftovers to the serving table while Sylvia and Andrew lit candles, giving their small corner of the banquet hall a festive, intimate air.

As the friends gathered around the table, Sylvia placed her late sister's woven cornucopia in place as the centerpiece. Laughter broke out as one by one the quilters placed their quilt blocks into it, taking elaborate measures to prevent their friends from seeing what they had made. The laughter redoubled when first Andrew, and then Matt, and then Joe each furtively contributed something of their own.

"You sewed a quilt block?" Gretchen asked her husband, astonished. "In all our years of marriage, I've never seen you pick up a needle except to help me tidy the living room."

"Not exactly," said Joe. "It's fabric, but that's all I'm going to say."

"We took an oath of secrecy," explained Matt, indicating all three men. "You'll find out after lunch."

"You ladies aren't the only ones with a reason to give thanks," said Andrew. "We didn't want to sit around waiting for dessert and looking ungrateful while you talked about thankfulness."

"We were remiss not to invite you to participate." Sylvia patted her husband's lined cheek with a blue-veined hand. "I'm glad you took it upon yourselves not to let us leave you out. But now, let's all give thanks for this bountiful meal so that we may enjoy it properly."

Standing, they joined hands and bowed their heads as Sylvia led them in a blessing, and then, with compliments for one another's cooking spiced with good-natured teasing, they filled their plates from the buffet table, taking at least a small helping of everyone's dish. The one exception was Gwen, a vegetarian, who passed on the turkey sausage dressing and Agnes's turkey pie and sighed tolerantly when Diane tried to tempt her by describing their succulent flavors in mouth-watering detail.

Sarah was not the only one to go back for seconds. Before long, not a drop of Anna's ginger pumpkin soup remained, and only a few bites of her own turkey Tetrazzini clung to the edges of the pan. When everyone had eaten their fill and some had filled their cups with coffee or tea, Sylvia began what she declared she hoped would become a new tradition. She reminded them of her family's custom, brought the cornucopia to her place at the head of the table, and removed the first quilt block, a pink-and-blue Grandmother's Delight.

"Oh, that's mine," said Carol, flustered, as Sylvia handed the block to Sarah, seated at her right, and indicated that she should admire it and pass it around the table. "I didn't think I'd have to go first."

"Someone has to," said Sarah, passing the block on to Matt, but not before noticing that her mother had chosen a more complex pattern than Sarah would have expected and had met the challenge to her sewing skills admirably. "Go on, Mom. Tell us what you're most thankful for this year because your choice is a little ambiguous, I think."

Everyone else around the table grinned, but Carol needed a moment longer to figure out that Sarah was only teasing. Their relationship had been strained for so many years that simple, friendly teasing had long been impossible between them.

"I'm very thankful that I'm going to become a grandmother soon," Carol began.

"At long last, after years of waiting and almost giving up hope—don't roll your eyes, Sarah, you and Matt certainly took your sweet time about this. And I'm very thankful that my daughter is in such good health and strong spirits, and I'm very, very glad she has such a wonderful husband by her side every day to support her and encourage her. Matt, you're blushing."

"No, I'm not," he said, and it was true that he had barely reddened, but the praise must have caught him off guard because he looked uncomfortably startled, almost wary.

"A lovely thought, Carol," praised Sylvia as she reached into the cornucopia again. This time she brought out a square of floral print fabric, folded into quarters. "Diane, I know you're busy, but you were supposed to stitch a block."

"Scofflaw," Gwen teased. "Corner cutter."

"I didn't put that in the cornucopia," Diane protested. "I sewed a block, and a very nice block, too. Why would you assume that was mine?"

No one wanted to answer that, but fortunately they didn't have to because Joe spoke up. "That's mine," he said sheepishly. "I can't sew a stitch so I just scrounged through that bag of scraps you keep in the parlor. I chose this because it reminded me of my wife." As Sylvia passed the fabric square to Sarah, Joe turned to Gretchen. "Every year I'm more thankful for you and your love and our family. I know it's a small family, just us, but it's all I ever needed all these many years. To me you're everything that's good and kind and generous in this world. I picked out a piece of fabric that had flowers on it, for all the bouquets that I wish I could give, except there's no garden with enough flowers to show you how much I adore you, not even at Elm Creek Manor."

He kissed his speechless wife on the cheek to a round of applause.

"Nice going, Joe," said Matt, with mock annoyance. "Way to set the bar for me and Andrew."

"Yeah, thanks a lot." Andrew tried to scowl, but couldn't quite pull it off. "For the rest of the year it's gonna be, 'Why can't you be romantic like Joe?' "

"Oh, stop," scolded Sylvia, but she smiled too. When she reached into the cornucopia for the next block, Sarah recognized her own even before Sylvia unfolded it and held it up. "I don't know this pattern, but this looks like your handiwork, Sarah."

"It's called Twin Star," said Sarah, taking it from her and passing it on to Matt. She didn't need to linger over it and discover mistakes she had missed before. "I found the pattern on the Internet, and I picked it for obvious reasons." She patted her tummy and one of the twins kicked in response. "I'm going to echo my mom and say that I'm thankful that the babies are healthy, and that everything's coming along as expected—"

"Except for that little surprise that you're having twins," Diane interjected.

"Maybe *expected* was the wrong word. Everything's coming along *well*," Sarah amended, "and I'm hopeful that if anything else unexpected happens, it will be an equally wonderful surprise. Oh, and as my mom said, I'm also very thankful that Matt's been by my side every day showing me constant support, through morning sickness to attending childbirth classes with me to tying my shoes since I can't reach to do it myself anymore." As her friends laughed, Sarah reached for Matt's hand and squeezed it. "Thank you, honey. I couldn't manage without you, and the babies aren't even here yet."

He smiled weakly back, perhaps embarrassed by the attention, or Sarah would have gone on praising him.

Sylvia watched Matt speculatively as she drew another block from the cornucopia, an unusual eight-pointed star design with an octagon in the center, triangles in the corners, and narrow rectangles separating the star points. "Oh, that's mine," said Gretchen, with a guilty glance at her husband. "I'm afraid my story isn't even a tiny fraction as romantic as Joe's."

"That's all right," said Joe. "This isn't Valentine's Day. It's Thanksgiving."

"Thanksgiving was yesterday," said Diane, pouring herself another cup of coffee. "We're celebrating the first day of the quilting season. Am I the only person here who remembers that?"

"There is no official quilting season," Gwen reminded her.

"Killjoy."

"It was in the spirit of Thanksgiving that I made my block," said Gretchen quickly, to forestall an outbreak of bantering. "It's called Prosperity. I chose it because out of all the blessings I received in the past year, I am most thankful for my wonderful new job with Elm Creek Quilts." Her fond gaze traveled around the circle of friends. "A year ago, I never could have imagined myself so happy and secure in my livelihood. Thanks to you, Joe and I have a beautiful new home here in the manor, and I can teach and quilt and enjoy the work that I love. In all my life I've never felt as prosperous as I do now, blessed by the riches of fulfilling work and precious new friendships."

When Gretchen smiled, Sarah detected tears of happiness in her eyes, but she quickly blinked them away.

"You've earned your newfound prosperity, my dear," said Sylvia, "with your talent and hard work. Don't thank us. Thank yourself."

"I should and I will. Thank you, Self," said Gretchen so comically that everyone laughed.

Next Sylvia took another square of fabric from the cornucopia, a theme print of men fishing and trout leaping that Andrew explained represented not only the great trout stream that ran through the estate but all of its bounty, which provided for each of them, Elm Creek Quilters and husbands alike. "I love my wife as much as Joe loves his, and I was going to put a piece of flowery fabric in there and use even more flowery words to talk about Sylvia, but Joe stole my idea, and now anything I say is going to look like I copied him." Shaking his head in mock dismay, Andrew sat down amidst a ripple of laughter.

Turning to Matt, Sarah said in an undertone, "When it's your turn, you really don't have to go on and on about how thankful you are for me—unless that's what you really planned to say all along."

"You know I'm thankful for you," protested Matt just as quietly. "Every day, not only Thanksgiving."

"I know." Still, it would be nice to hear it every once in a while, but not now, not when he might be saying it only to keep up with the other men.

"I made that one," Diane declared as Sylvia held up a simple red-and-white Nine-Patch block. "See? I didn't just take the easy way out and stuff a solid piece of fabric in there. No offense, guys."

"None taken," said Joe.

"Enlighten us, Diane," Sylvia prompted. "What does this pattern represent to you? What are you thankful for this year?"

Diane looked genuinely baffled. "It's obvious, don't you think?"

"No," said Gwen.

"'A stitch in time saves nine,'" quoted Gretchen. "Perhaps she's grateful for an early action that prevented trouble down the road?"

"Our resident procrastinator?" Gwen shook her head. "Doubtful."

"A cat has nine lives," said Carol. "Did your cat survive an illness in the past year?"

"I don't have a cat," said Diane.

"Baseball," said Andrew, inspired. "Nine players on the field, nine innings."

"I'm not thankful for baseball," said Diane, incredulous. "You really don't get it?"

"Perhaps you're thankful for simplicity?" guessed Agnes. She had baby-sat Diane as a child and had never broken the habit of coming to her rescue. "For the simple things in life?"

"You're close," said Diane. "The Nine-Patch is a traditional block. I'm thankful for tradition. Traditions hold a family together and guide us when we leave home and step out into a dangerous world. Now that both of my boys are in college, I'm grateful for the traditions that will keep them safe."

"Safe in the dangerous worlds of the campuses of Princeton and Waterford College," said Sarah, suppressing a smile.

"When your twins head off to school, you won't treat those dangers so lightly," Diane retorted, and Sarah—who was already sufficiently anxious about baby proofing the manor and entirely unprepared to contemplate binge drinking and unsafe sex—raised her palms in an appeasing gesture, deferring to her friend's superior experience.

"I don't recognize this quilter's handiwork," said Sylvia, holding up another block, a five-patch in blue and gold reminiscent of a Bear's Paw but with subtle alterations. "By the process of elimination, I deduce it must be the work of one of our newer quilters, and since Gretchen and Carol have already taken their turns, it must be Anna's, although it doesn't look like her usual work either."

"It could be Matt's," said Gwen. "You've never seen his quilting."

"And you never will," said Matt.

"It's mine," said Anna. "And you're right—I'm not one for quilt block style quilts." Anna preferred abstract, whole-quilt appliqué designs that despite her original artistic vision always ended up resembling food. Sarah would never forget how, as the Elm Creek Quilters had passed around Anna's sample quilt block during her job interview, Diane had loudly declared that it looked like a tossed salad.

"Let's give Anna a round of applause for stretching her boundaries," said Sarah.

As everyone clapped, Anna rose and waved them to silence. "Oh, come on, it's not like I've never made a regular quilt block before. This is a new pattern for me, though. I found it in Sylvia's huge book of quilt blocks and I thought the name suited me, or rather, what I'm most thankful for this year."

"And that name is?" Diane prompted, sipping her coffee.

"The Best Friend." Anna seemed to blush ever so slightly, but perhaps it was the candlelight. "Without Jeremy, I never would have heard about the job opening at Elm Creek Quilts, and without his encouragement and the fact that his girlfriend worked here, I might not have applied. Since I took the job, he's given me countless rides to work to save me time and bus fare, and although he'll say otherwise, the trips weren't always on his way. He's been a true friend to me, and his kindness and generosity brought me into this wonderful circle of quilters and friends. I just hope I can be half as good a friend to him and to all of you as he's been to me."

As Anna sat down, Agnes remarked, "It's a shame he's not here to hear himself praised so highly."

"You should tell him how you feel, Anna," said Carol.

Anna, who had just sipped from her water glass, coughed, pressed a hand to her lips, and shook her head. "Oh, I don't think so," she said, after clearing her throat. "I'm sure he knows."

"Make him a quilt, then," said Gwen. "That's the standard quilter's response to any situation meriting praise, comfort, or commemoration. Wrap 'em in a quilt."

"I'm sure Summer's made Jeremy lots of quilts. He wouldn't have room for one of mine."

Gwen frowned thoughtfully and shook

her head. "I don't think she's made him any. She's been very busy with work, and grad school applications, and then the move to Chicago, ever since they met."

"Well—" Anna seemed to search for something to say. "I'd be surprised if she hasn't, and if she hasn't she probably will eventually."

"You can't have too many quilts," said Gretchen.

"Not if you live in a place with as much space as Elm Creek Manor, but if you have a small apartment—" Anna shrugged and pulled a face to suggest that it was hopeless. "Who's next, Sylvia?"

Sylvia reached into the cornucopia and held up another block, a pastel green-and-rose four-pointed star with split squares in the corners that Agnes identified as her rendition of the Signs of Spring pattern. "Even with winter upon us, there are signs of the coming spring," she said, glancing out the window at the falling snow. "What I'm most thankful for is hope in difficult times."

Another solid piece of fabric followed, a landscape print of green trees on rolling hills that everyone easily guessed Matt had contributed. "I'm most thankful for my wonderful, beautiful wife, Sarah," he began emphatically and not unexpectedly, to a chorus of laughter and friendly jeers. "Since I didn't want it to look like I was copying the other guys, I thought I would expand my answer to include my whole family. I'm thankful for their support, their loyalty, their understanding, and most of all, their love. I owe my family everything, and it's a debt I doubt I'll ever be able to repay in full, but that doesn't mean I won't stop trying."

"I don't get it," said Diane.

"What don't you get?" said Matt, lacing his fingers through Sarah's and kissing the back of her hand.

"That fabric. What's it supposed to symbolize, the landscape of your loyalty?"

"Trees," said Matt. "You know, family trees. Family."

"That's a bit of a stretch," remarked Gwen. "Oh, wait, did I just accidentally agree with Diane? On second thought, that's an excellent choice, Matt, especially on such short notice. Very creative."

Matt accepted her praise with a grin as Sylvia took another block from the cornucopia. The vivid colors and dramatic prints told Sarah at once that this was Gwen's handiwork. "A Guiding Star block?" said Sylvia, holding up the unequal nine-patch block for all to see. Triangles of different sizes combined to form kites that together created a four-pointed star on the horizontal and vertical axes. In each corner square, two dark triangles flanked a lighter kite, giving the illusion that the star threw off radiant beams.

"That's right," said Gwen. "Recently I've been reflecting upon the teachers and mentors I've had throughout my life, and how indebted I am to them. They pushed me when I thought I couldn't take another step, led me by the hand when I didn't know the way, and sent me on alone when they knew I was ready, even when I didn't."

"What a lovely tribute," said Gretchen, who had once been a middle school teacher. "I'm sure your former teachers would be pleased to know that you've become the mentor to so many young people at Waterford College."

"Not to mention all the quilters you've taught," Anna added. "The roles have been reversed."

"I don't know if they've been entirely reversed," said Gwen. "In many ways I'm still a student."

"And there she goes, dancing off into the land of metaphor," said Diane.

"The last block is mine," said Sylvia, reaching into the cornucopia. She inspected her work with a critical eye and removed a stray thread. To Sarah the green-and-red patchwork pattern resembled a Sawtooth Star overlaying a cross. "This is a traditional block, Providence, and I thought it summed up my feelings best. This year I'm particularly thankful for the Lord's protective care, even though I confess I don't always recognize it for what it is."

"We've all been very blessed," Gretchen said.

"Yes, but sometimes I'm so preoccupied with what I don't have that I neglect to properly appreciate what I do have." Sylvia looked around the table, her gaze warm and affectionate. "You're my family and my dearest friends, and I'm ever thankful that you've enriched my life by allowing me to be a part of yours."

"You've enriched our lives, too," said Sarah, wondering why Sylvia thought she ever neglected them even for a moment.

No one was more generous or staunchly supportive than Sylvia, although Matt ran a close second.

"As the best of friends do." Sylvia glanced into the cornucopia, but they all knew it was empty. "Unless anyone wants more dessert, should we ladies return to our quilting, and you men to your puttering in the barn or whatever it is you were doing?"

All agreed, and after the blocks and fabric squares had made their way around the table and back to Sylvia, everyone pitched in to clear away the dishes and tidy the kitchen. As Sarah was leaving the banquet hall with an armload of carefully stacked plates, Matt caught up to her. "Let me help you with that," he said, taking the plates. "You shouldn't be carrying so much weight."

"You're sounding like my mother again," Sarah teased, but she stopped short as she took in Matt's worried frown and furrowed brow. "What is it? What's wrong?"

"Can we talk for a minute? In private?"

She nodded and waited in the hallway as he hurried to the kitchen with the plates, then returned and guided her to the laundry room, where they could speak without being overheard. "What's going on?" she asked him as he shut the door. "You're starting to scare me."

"It's nothing that serious." He ran a hand over his jaw, stubble scratching his callused palm. "You know I had a long talk with my dad yesterday."

"Yes, you called to wish him a happy Thanksgiving."

"That's not all we talked about." Matt took her hands. "His old back injury has been acting up, but with the housing market down, he can't afford to turn down any work."

"Can't he find workers to hire?"

"Yes, that's not the problem. He needs someone on-site to supervise them, someone he can trust." Matt took a deep breath. "He needs me."

"Well, he can't have you," said Sarah without thinking. "Right?"

Matt hesitated. "With the orchard and gardens dormant for the winter and the campers away, this is a slow season for me at the manor."

"You've already told him you'd do it." Sarah pulled her hands free from Matt's, pressed a hand to her brow and another to her lower back. "Without even talking to me."

"I thought you'd understand."

"Matt, I need you here. The babies—"

"Won't be here for another few months, and I'll be back by then." He brushed her cheek with his fingertips. "You know I wouldn't miss that."

"What about our childbirth classes?" What about the back rubs, the foot massages, the encouragement, the decorating the nursery, the childproofing the manor, the choosing of names, the holding her while she slept at night and kissing away her worries? "What if something goes wrong and I need you?"

"Nothing's going to go wrong," he told her firmly, wrapping her in a hug. Despite her anger, she was too sick at heart to push him away even though he was the cause. "But if something does, call me and I'll jump in the truck and be here in three hours. It's not like we won't see each other. I'll come back from time to time, whenever my dad feels well enough to handle things on his own."

And if Hank didn't feel well enough, or if

he claimed not to? Matt might stay away all winter. A few occasional visits would not be enough. Slow season or not, Matt was needed at Elm Creek Manor. Sarah needed him even if the orchards and gardens didn't.

"Sarah, listen." Matt put his hands on her shoulders and tried to look into her eyes. When she dropped her gaze, he put a hand under her chin and gently lifted it until their eyes met again. "I wouldn't ask if this wasn't important. My dad's close to retirement but lately his savings have taken a huge hit. If he doesn't keep the business running steadily, he might not be able to restart it later. He's put his whole life into that company, and I can't stand by and do nothing when he needs me."

She nodded, tears filling her eyes. She understood. Matt was a good and loyal son, and he had to do what he thought was right. But what would she do without him, and where would it lead? What if Hank and Matt together decided that Elm Creek Quilts needed him less than Hank did?

She thought of what Matt said about the fabric he had placed into the cornucopia and his words earlier that morning in bed, and she knew that he had weighed his decision carefully. If she asked him not to go, he would probably stay, but he would blame her if his father's business failed, and she would, too.

"Don't stay away too long," she told him, blinking away her tears and forcing a smile. "You're not getting out of diaper duty that easily."

Matt smiled, and the strain in his expression turned to relief. He held her close—as close as he could with her ample midsection between them—but she felt as if he were already far away, far beyond her reach.

CHAPTER TWO

Diane

UPON RETURNING TO the ballroom, Diane peered out the windows warily. It was not her imagination; the snow was falling far more thickly than before.

"How much snow did you say we might get?" she asked Gwen, who had removed her quilt from the lap hoop and spread it upon the floor, the better to adjust the layers as she moved the slender rings to a new, unquilted portion.

"Ten to twelve inches," replied Gwen cheerfully, as well she might. She probably didn't care if they were snowed in at Elm Creek Manor, unable to return home. On an ordinary day Diane wouldn't mind either, but Michael and Todd had come home for the long holiday weekend and were probably at that moment watching football on television with their dad and looking forward to the home-cooked supper she had promised them. She had almost canceled on the Patchwork Potluck rather than miss so much of their visit, but she had kicked off the start of the quilting season with the Elm Creek Quilters for years and she hated to break tradition.

Matt's truck had four-wheel drive, she reminded herself as she unfolded a kelly green fat quarter on the cutting table. If the storm worsened, perhaps he would drive her and Agnes home. She could return to dig her car out from beneath the snowdrifts another day.

"So much snow, and it's still November," she mused aloud. "What do you think it means?"

"Climate change," said Gwen promptly. "It seems counterintuitive, but global warming can bring on harsher winters."

"Perhaps it means that we'll get all our nasty weather out of the way now and enjoy an early spring," suggested Agnes, who could always find the bright side of things even when blizzard clouds obscured the sun.

"It's just something we have to get through," said Sarah, her voice strangely distant. She hadn't sewn a single seam since the quilters returned to the ballroom, but had sat at the sewing machine staring out the windows at the falling snow, one hand resting on her abdomen. "It probably seems worse than it is."

"Easy for you to say," retorted Diane. "You live here. You won't have to drive in this."

"Yes, but Matt will, all winter long, and anything could happen to him."

At that, Diane raised her eyebrows at her friend, but Sarah didn't notice, for she had roused herself and had begun feeding pinned quilt blocks beneath the needle of her sewing machine. "Oookay. Understood," Diane murmured under her breath. Apparently asking Matt for a ride home if the storm worsened was not an option.

Glancing from her work to the window so frequently that she risked a serious scissors accident, Diane cut a piece of freezer paper from the large roll left over from the summer camp season and traced templates from the magazine. An heirloom project such as her sons' Advent calendars called for hand appliqué, and despite her rapidly approaching deadline, she couldn't resort to machine appliqué. In her haste her hand stiches might turn out larger than usual, but from a few paces away no one would notice the difference. Her sons certainly wouldn't subject them to such scrutiny.

A worry tickled at the back of her mind, but she dismissed it and gathered up her fabric and freezer paper templates.

"Are you done with the cutting table?" Anna asked, rearranging the order of the folded bundles of blue and gold fabrics in her arms, studying the contrast between one and another.

"It's all yours," said Diane, clearing the rest of her supplies out of the way and heading for the ironing board. "What are you making, anyway? You never said."

"You never asked." Laying out her fabrics on the cutting mat, Anna shifted ever so slightly, her back to Diane, almost as if she were hiding her work.

"Everyone else volunteered the information." Curious, Diane left her things on the ironing board and returned to the cutting table for a better look. This time she was sure Anna was fighting the urge to fling a yard of fabric over her work so Diane couldn't see it. She glimpsed gold stars on a deep blue background, nothing that Anna should want to hide from friends, nothing that would inspire anything worse than constructive criticism. "It doesn't resemble food," Diane said helpfully, knowing that this was quite an accomplishment for Anna—unless this time she was actually *trying* to create images of food, a still life in fabric. "Come on, let's have a look. No tossed salad jokes this time, I promise."

As Diane attempted to peer over her shoulder, Anna spun around and held out her arms, touching the edges of the cutting table. "Diane, a little space, please. I want this to be a surprise."

"I promise I won't breathe a word to your Aunt Mabel or Cousin Bob or whoever this is for."

Anna smiled, but held up her hands as Diane stepped forward. "That's close enough. I can't have you spoiling the surprise."

"Spoiling it for whom?"

"Allow me to refer you back to her aforementioned concern about spoiling the surprise," Gwen called out, tightening the bolt on her lap hoop and gathering the folds of fabric and batting.

"She can at least tell us who it's for, can't she?" protested Diane, and then turned back to Anna, whose smile had turned apologetic, and a little wary. "What's the harm? This can't be a gift for any of the Elm Creek Quilters or you wouldn't be working on it in front of us."

"That's not necessarily so," remarked Sylvia. "Remember the year Bonnie gave us those lovely homespun plaid table runners for Christmas? She worked on them right here in this ballroom throughout our quilter's holiday, and none of us suspected she was making them for us."

"She hid them in plain sight," Agnes chimed in, but then she sighed. "I hope Bonnie's having a wonderful time in Hawaii, but I do miss her so."

"I'm sure she's not missing this weather," said Carol, nodding to the window just as a sudden gust of wind scoured the pane with icy crystals.

Diane forgot Anna's inexplicable secrecy as her concerns about the storm returned. She resigned herself to leaving early, but at least she had fulfilled the quilter's holiday tradition even if she would not accomplish as much sewing as she had hoped. The traditions she kept at home were equally important as those she observed with her friends, and she would miss out on several if she were snowed in at Elm Creek Manor over the Thanksgiving weekend. And if she didn't keep the family traditions going, who would? Not her husband, she thought with reluctant certainty, and not the boys.

It wasn't that Tim, Michael, and Todd didn't enjoy marking important occasions as a family. They did, at least most of the time, as long as she handled all the preparations and reminded them where to show up and when. Sometimes, during those difficult years when Michael had struggled in school, glowering sullenly in the shadow of his popular younger brother who excelled academically and athletically and every other way it was possible for a teenager to excel, Diane had thought that their traditions were all that held the family together. The family dinners Diane had insisted upon every night, even if it meant dining at nine o'clock to accommodate a school event, prevented the boys from withdrawing too much into the world of their peers and leaving Diane and Tim utterly unaware of how they spent their time and with whom. Weekly Mass taught the boys the importance of faith and instilled in them a moral code that would last a lifetime, even if its immediate results were not apparent. Or so Diane had told herself, sometimes while clenching her teeth when Michael vandalized the middle school, or when he was arrested for skateboarding in a marked zone downtown. Throughout the years when she had held her breath, hoping that Michael would surpass his guidance counselor's predictions and graduate from high school, and through the long months when she questioned Todd's choice of friends, arrogant boys whose sense of entitlement rendered them void of humility, she had found strength in ritual and faith.

Through it all, their traditions, both religious and secular, had held the family together, and every prayer and lesson seemed justified when she reflected upon the fine young men her sons had become.

Michael flourished at Waterford College, on his own even though he was never more than a few miles away from his childhood home. He shared a rented house downtown with a few friends and came home almost every Sunday to do laundry and have dinner with his parents, moments of reconnection Diane cherished. Todd had started at Princeton only a few weeks before, and although he didn't stay in touch as often as Diane wished, when he did call or email, he sounded happy, excited, and involved, reveling in the first real challenge to his academic gifts. Though separated by distance that would perhaps increase after the boys graduated, they would not fragment as a family. Their love would unite them, and the practice of their traditions would draw them together in spirit, despite the miles that might separate them.

And yet—

Diane sighed, frowning. Without her as the impetus for maintaining their traditions, she doubted they would endure. Their traditional pumpkin patch trip and scary movie night the Saturday before Halloween had gone the way of the tooth fairy in middle school when Todd's basketball practices took precedence. It had been ages since she and Tim had taken the boys to the Pancake Café before visiting Santa at the Elm Creek Valley Mall on the first day of Winter Break. Diane accepted these changes as the sad but inevitable consequence of her sons' journey toward adulthood, and her nostalgia was tempered by the introduction of new, more age-appropriate activities. But Diane believed some traditions should not fall away as children grew. Some should have become so essential to their identity as a family that Michael, Todd, and Tim should look forward to them and nurture them as much as Diane did.

And yet sometimes it seemed as if they didn't care.

Only two days before, Diane had gone out for coffee with some friends after their Pilates class and, upon realizing that she had completely lost track of time, had raced home to get dinner in the oven. Any other night and she would have pulled a made-ahead casserole out of the freezer, but on that night only one meal would do. Ever since she was a newlywed, Diane had made lasagna for supper the Wednesday night before Thanksgiving. On that day in that first year of their marriage, she had asked Tim what he wanted for supper, and he had said anything but turkey. Diane had interpreted that to mean that he wanted the least Thanksgiving-ish meal she could devise, and she couldn't think of anything that reminded her less of Thanksgiving than lasagna. As she shopped for noodles and ground beef, it occurred to her that salad was even less Thanksgiving-ish in that it was the opposite of a feast, so she added salad to the menu. Asparagus was a spring vegetable and thus likely not served by Pilgrims in an autumn of the days of yore, so into her grocery cart went a bag of frozen asparagus.

Tim delighted in her explanation of the meal, and so it became a tradition: a supper with no logical connection whatsoever to Thanksgiving to cleanse their palates for the harvest feast to come the next day. Sometimes she varied the recipe—adding spinach or mushrooms to the sauce, substituting whole-wheat noodles for semolina—but it was always lasagna on Thanksgiving Eve. She enjoyed the whimsy of the tradition, and she thought the boys did, too.

But that year she had lingered too long with her friends at the Daily Grind, chatting about their holiday plans and how the predicted storm might interfere with their travel. It was after five o'clock when a glance at her watch sent her racing to her car. She had prepared the lasagna earlier that day and had left it in the fridge, and if she had left instructions on the counter for Tim, it could have been on the table piping hot by six. If she had remembered to charge her cell phone, she could at least have called to have someone preheat the oven, but with her cell phone spent and useless in her purse, all she could do was hurry home and hope no one minded that supper would be a little late.

But when she arrived home, she found Tim at the stove, spatula in hand, Todd setting the table, and Michael rooting around in the refrigerator. "Did you put the lasagna in?" she asked, still in her coat and boots, gym bag and purse slung over her shoulder. The smells wafting through the kitchen suggested ground beef and frying fat, without the least note of tomato or oregano.

"Oh, hi, honey," Tim greeted her, glancing over his shoulder before quickly returning his attention to the stove. "You didn't answer your cell."

Diane set her bag on the floor and purse on the counter, taking in the scene warily. "The battery died."

Michael shut the refrigerator door with his shoulder, his arms loaded down with ketchup, mustard, a jar of pickles, and a plastic bag of buns. "See, Mom, there's this really cool thing called a cell phone charger. You plug one end into the wall outlet and the other end into your phone, and after a while, your battery is recharged and you can use it again."

"Yes, thank you dear. I'll remember that." Hamburgers. Tim was definitely flipping hamburgers. "What are you guys thinking? You're going to spoil your supper."

"This *is* supper," said Todd, grinning, his hair flopping in his eyes. He had never worn it so long but he kept laughing off Diane's offers to schedule an appointment with the barber while he was home from school.

Diane opened the refrigerator. Sure enough, the glass dish of lasagna was exactly where she had left it. "Why didn't you heat up the lasagna?"

Tim glanced at her, wary. He knew her well enough to realize they had done something wrong. "We didn't know whether you were saving that for something special."

"I was." Diane shut the refrigerator. "Tonight's dinner. We always have lasagna on Thanksgiving Eve."

"You weren't home, honey, and we couldn't reach you." Tim lifted hamburger patties from the pan to a platter on the counter. "You're going to spend hours cooking for us tomorrow, so we thought we'd cook supper tonight."

They were trying to help, Diane reminded herself, and they were clearly pleased with themselves. She knew she should thank them, but she couldn't help pointing out, "You could have heated up the lasagna. That would've been just as helpful with much less effort."

"We felt like hamburgers," said Michael. "And Todd thought maybe that pan was something you'd made for your lunch with the quilters."

"It couldn't have been. Our recipes have to be made from Thanksgiving leftovers." Honestly. How many years had the Elm

Creek Quilters celebrated their quilter's holiday with the potluck, and her family still didn't grasp the simple rules?

"We can have the lasagna Friday," said Todd. "It'll still taste good and that'll give you more time to quilt with your friends."

Their faces were clouding up with uncertainty that could easily become disappointment. Only moments before they had been cheerful and industrious, expecting her to welcome their surprise with delight and appreciation. Instead, she kept harping on about the lasagna, as oblivious to their helpfulness as they had been to their tradition.

The most important part of the tradition was that they were gathered together for a family meal. Did it really matter what they ate?

She took a deep breath and forced a smile. "There's sliced cheddar in the deli drawer if anyone wants to upgrade to a cheeseburger."

Tim's hamburgers were tasty and filling, the company welcome, and the conversation full of the boys' amusing stories from school. It was a pleasant meal, and Diane tried to drive away her lingering disappointment that they apparently didn't care about the lasagna as much as she did.

But it was just lasagna, after all, and she knew she should get over it and save her righteous dismay for the passing of far more important traditions—such as her sons' waning interest in attending Mass. They could fill their bellies with an endless variety of meals but only church would nourish their souls.

Though neither of her sons had ever bounded out of bed early on a Sunday morning declaring that they greatly preferred hard, wooden pews to soft, warm quilts, from the time they were babies they had attended Mass week after week without too much grumbling or complaint. As they grew, they had prepared for the sacraments and had been proud to receive them. Still, they were boys, and Diane had always suspected that without her prodding they would have slept in; if it had been up to them, they would have been contentedly reading the comics over a sugary bowl of cereal while the priest delivered his homily.

Even so, on the first Sunday after Michael moved into the freshman dorm at Waterford College, she had expected him to join the rest of the family at church. She had called him the day before and asked if he wanted a ride, and when he said he didn't, she assumed he intended to walk the few blocks from campus. Through the first reading, the second, and the Gospel, she kept turning around in her seat to scan the pews for her son, until Tim patted her knee and told her to relax. Michael had overslept, she told herself, an excusable one-time mistake considering it was his first week of college. Or perhaps he had attended Mass with friends the night before in the campus ministry chapel.

Mindful that he was officially an adult, she held off asking him where he had been that morning, reluctant to appear overbearing. When he didn't show up the next week or the next, her resistance broke down. She called him, and after a few perfunctory questions about his classes and professors, she inquired, as casually as she could manage, how he had spent the past three Sunday mornings.

"Sleeping as late as I could," he told her drowsily. She could picture him lying in his loft, eyes closed, feet dangling over the wooden safety rail Tim had insisted Michael and his roommates add to the design. "We stay up late Saturday night."

"Maybe you should go to bed earlier so you won't miss church the next day," she suggested. "We've been saving a seat for you."

"Even if I wanted to go to bed early, everyone else's partying would keep me awake." Michael paused. "Mom, you don't need to save that seat in the pew for me anymore. Unless, you know, I'm home on break or something, and you want us to all go to church together."

Diane's heart caught in her throat. "You go off to college and three weeks later you've lost your faith?"

Michael let out a dry laugh. "I haven't lost my faith. I still believe in God."

"Then why not come to church?"

"Why, to prove it to everyone?"

"You know better than that," she retorted. "To pray. To give thanks."

"I can do that anywhere."

"But do you? Are you spending your Sunday mornings in prayer and reflection?"

"I mostly spend them asleep." She heard

him sigh heavily despite the hollowness that indicated he had covered the mouthpiece with his hand in an attempt to hide it. "Mom, don't be mad."

"I'm not mad," she told him, and it was mostly true. "I'm disappointed."

But what could she do? She couldn't force him to go to church any more than she could force him to believe. He was an adult and responsible for his own decisions, his own faith. At least when he was home on school breaks, he came and sat on the pew beside his brother as he had always done, perhaps to set a good example, perhaps to avoid a scene. She knew he was doing this more for her than for himself, and although this troubled her, she didn't push the matter because at least he was getting himself to church.

When it came time for Todd to go off to college, she resolved to handle things differently. On every campus tour she had made a point of collecting brochures from campus ministries, locating chapels with Masses for students, and stopping by the offices of Catholic student groups. Despite her efforts, Todd soon followed his older brother's example and took Sunday mornings as an opportunity to catch up on his sleep.

Troubled, she discussed her worries with her parish priest and found some comfort in his assurances that she had done her duty by her children. Often young people let their attendance wane in their late teens and twenties, he said, but they usually resumed their participation when they had children of their own. "But this is when they need the guidance of the church the most," Diane had lamented, sniffing into a tissue. She had heard enough harrowing stories from Tim and Gwen, both professors at Waterford College, to know what dangers lay in wait to tempt and ensnare her sons. For that matter, her own college years served as warning enough.

Gently, Father Doug had encouraged her to pray and to continue to offer a strong example of faith to her sons, but that she should not demand more of herself—or them—than that. Reluctantly, she agreed to try. She hated to sit and wait and hope that everything would work out all right in the end, preferring to take action and steer matters toward the end she desired. But she couldn't bring herself to argue against a priest's advice to have faith—not to his face in his own church, anyway.

"Does anyone else smell that?" Carol's voice broke into her reverie. "It's like something's burning or scorched."

"It's me," said Diane irritably, peeling a strip of brown fabric meant to be the wall of a log cabin from the bottom of the iron.

"You're on fire?" inquired Gwen.

"Not me, my appliqué." Diane flung the piece onto the ironing board and blew on her fingertips to cool them. The brown rectangle circled into a tube and gave off a thin wisp of white smoke, the freezer paper on the back scorched to a burnt toast black that matched the waxy residue stuck to the bottom of the iron. Berating herself, she unplugged the iron and waited for it to cool. If she didn't get that gunk off the iron, the smell would fill the ballroom and the stickiness and scorch marks would get all over her fabrics as well as the ironing board.

Perfect. Just what she needed: something else to go wrong with her project, as if being ill-conceived and behind schedule weren't bad enough.

"White vinegar will take those scorch

marks right off," said Agnes from the fireside, quickly deducing the mishap.

"We have some in the kitchen," said Anna. "Top shelf of the pantry, on the right."

As Diane was leaving the ballroom, Andrew passed on his way in carrying a cordless phone handset. "Bonnie's calling all the way from Hawaii," he said, handing her the phone. "She wants to talk to everyone."

"Aloha," Diane greeted her friend, welcoming the distraction. "How do you say 'Happy Quilter's Holiday' in Hawaiian?"

"I have no idea," said Bonnie, so lighthearted that Diane could vividly imagine her tan and relaxed, lying in the sand beneath a beach umbrella, lazily dipping her toes in the Pacific. As Diane went to the kitchen and returned with the bottle of vinegar and a half-roll of paper towels, she and Bonnie swapped stories of their Thanksgiving celebrations. Bonnie had enjoyed what sounded like a fabulous backyard luau complete with a pig cooked in a traditional underground oven and a band playing Hawaiian songs on a ukulele and slack-key guitar. Diane was genuinely happy for her, without the slightest twinge of envy. If anyone deserved a holiday in paradise, it was Bonnie, who had lost her quilt shop and was going through a nasty divorce. Bonnie's family always celebrated Thanksgiving at her mother-in-law's home in Scranton. Diane guessed Bonnie would not have been welcome that year, so it was just as well that she was thousands of miles away. But Thanksgiving was only the beginning. Bonnie would have to create new traditions for all the holidays to come—and perhaps, since her ex-husband would surely demand his turn, she would not always be able to spend the holidays with her grown children and grandchildren. It was unfair that Bonnie would lose her beloved traditions on top of her marriage, business, and everything else, and Diane felt for her.

But maybe Bonnie didn't mind. Maybe she welcomed a fresh start, and her decision to winter in Hawaii with a college friend was only the beginning. Out with the old and in with the new seemed to be the guiding principle for everyone Diane knew, everyone but herself.

"Have some pineapple and a mai tai on the beach for me," Diane told Bonnie, and then she passed the phone to Sarah. Sarah and Bonnie chatted for a while before Sarah handed the phone to Sylvia, at which point the friends realized they were repeating the same stories so they put Bonnie on speakerphone. Bonnie seemed intrigued by the new tradition they had introduced to their quilter's holiday feast and sounded almost sorry that she had not been there to contribute a patchwork block of her own to the cornucopia—not sorry enough to regret that she was enjoying sunshine and tropical breezes on Maui instead of a snowstorm, but sorry all the same.

After Bonnie wished them all a happy quilter's holiday and hung up, Diane wet a paper towel with vinegar and scrubbed the bottom of the cool iron until the scorch marks disappeared and the stainless steel gleamed. Now she could resume her work, but as she rearranged the appliqués on the snowy-white background fabric, she wondered why she bothered. Folk art Advent calendars for college men? What a dumb idea. Her sons wouldn't remember the Advent calendar from their childhood. When they unwrapped their gifts Christmas morning, they would study them in bemusement and offer her perplexed thanks. They probably didn't even observe Advent anymore.

Maybe when they had children of their own they would enjoy tucking coins or candies with the Bible verses into the pockets and allowing their kids to open one each day. Someday her sons would teach their children with these small daily joys the meaning of Advent, that not only were they preparing to celebrate the birth of Jesus on the Feast of Christmas but also anticipating his glorious return in the fullness of time. When Michael and Todd had children of their own, they might care about the small rituals that reminded them of greater mysteries. Until then, Diane was wasting her time in a futile effort to continue a tradition that meant nothing to them.

In the meantime, the storm was worsening, the snow falling in icy flakes that whirled in gusty winds. If she waited much longer, she would be stuck at the manor overnight and would miss precious hours of her sons' visit home, and really, what was the point of staying at the manor to work on unwanted gifts? A home-cooked meal on a cold winter's day was something her sons understood, and that was what she ought to give them.

Diane gathered up her appliqués into neat piles, but when that wasn't fast enough, she snatched up her tote bag and swept the pieces of her project into it. "I'm calling it a day," she announced. "I'm sorry, Agnes, but do you mind if we leave now?"

"You're going to drive in that?" said Sarah, gesturing to the whirling white outside the window. "You know the county never plows that back road, and I don't think Matt's hooked his plow to the pickup yet. He'll have to, to clear the parking lot, but he probably thought he wouldn't need to until tomorrow morning."

Diane wished Matt—and Sarah and everyone else for that matter—had not been so quick to assume that everyone was eager for a slumber party. "It's not far from the parking lot to the woods, and there the trees block most of the snowfall. Once I get to the main road I'll be fine." Diane zipped her tote and hefted it to her shoulder. "Agnes, are you coming?"

Agnes peered at her worriedly through her pink-tinted glasses, glanced out the window, and shook her head. "I don't think leaving now is wise, dear. Let's wait until the storm passes. Stay, and I'll help you with your Advent calendars."

"I don't care about the stupid calendars," said Diane. "The storm probably won't pass until morning, and I can't wait until then. I want to get home while I still can."

"There's no need to risk life and limb," Sylvia assured her. "You're welcome to spend the night. We keep plenty of new toothbrushes and other necessaries on hand for campers who forget to pack them. Sarah can lend you a nightgown and you can have your pick of rooms."

"My sons are home for only a few days." Diane inched toward the door, throwing Agnes pleading glances for understanding and forgiveness. It wasn't fair to drag her from the party, but a strange urgency had seized her and she couldn't bear to wait another moment.

"I suppose I can finish these at home." Reluctantly, Agnes rolled her unfinished Christmas stockings into tidy bundles and tucked them into her bag.

"Agnes, you can stay," said Gwen. "I think you both should stay, but if Diane's determined to go, I'll drive Agnes home in the morning. When it's safer," she added, shooting Diane a look of pure exasperation.

Diane ignored her. "Would that be all right, Agnes?"

"Of course that's fine," said Agnes, her blue eyes worried. "It's a horse apiece, your car or Gwen's. But won't you reconsider? Spend the night here, safe and sound, and you can still see the boys by midmorning tomorrow. They won't begrudge you a few hours when your safety's at stake."

Diane shifted her weight from one foot to the other, glancing from her friends' concerned faces to the snow whirling outside. "And if the storm lasts longer than that?"

"Your house has TV and Internet," said Gwen. "Michael and Todd might not even realize you're gone."

Gwen's teasing jab hit too close to home. "The longer I stand here debating it, the deeper the snow gets. I've lived in Pennsylvania all my life and I've driven in storms worse than this. The sooner I leave, the safer I'll be."

"That doesn't necessarily follow," said Gwen, but Diane couldn't bear to waste any more time discussing it. She bade her friends a hasty good-bye, offered one last apology to Agnes, and hurried off, pausing at the back door to throw on her coat and boots and gloves, and wrap her scarf around her head and neck. The wind swept her breath away the moment she stepped out the back door, but she clutched the collar of her coat shut, put her head down, and struggled through the ankle-deep snow and occasional knee-deep drifts to her car. She left her bag and purse in the back seat and found an ice scraper in the trunk, forgotten for months under a picnic blanket and collapsible beach chair. Matt must have spied her laboring to clear the roof and windshield of snow, for within minutes he was at her side shouting over the wind for her to come back indoors. When she refused, he offered to drive her home in his truck, but she pointed out that Sarah wouldn't like it if he got snowed in at her place.

Matt either realized that she was determined to go or he had grown weary of shouting over the wind, for he shook his head and helped her clear the car. "Call me if you get stuck on the way and I'll come get you," he said as he scraped the last bit of ice from her windshield.

She agreed, thanked him for his help, and quickly climbed into the car. A thin layer of snow had already accumulated on the windows she had first cleared, so she turned the key and flicked on the wipers. The wheels fought for traction on the snow-covered pavement, but suddenly the car lurched forward and spun awkwardly until she managed to straighten the axel. In the rearview mirror she glimpsed Matt, hands thrust in his pockets, shoulders braced against the storm, shaking his head as he watched her slowly pull out of the parking lot and inch her way across the bridge over Elm Creek. Then, on her way at last, she sighed with relief, sat up straighter, flexed her gloved hands around the steering wheel, and gradually increased her speed.

The gravel road was almost completely obscured by drifts, but past experience had taught her that the conditions would improve once she reached the sheltering forest. After that she would come to the highway, which had surely been plowed and salted, and then the familiar streets of her own neighborhood, a few blocks from campus and backing up to the Waterford Arboretum. Soon she would be home, and even if the trip took twice as long as usual, everything would be fine. She had left cooking instructions on the kitchen counter, so even though her cell phone was out of reach in her purse on the back seat, Tim would know to preheat the oven and remove the foil and bake the lasagna at the appointed time if the storm slowed her down so much that she couldn't do it herself. She knew it meant more to her than to Tim, Michael, and Todd combined, but that evening they would all sit down to a hot, nourishing meal together. That was one tradition she was unwilling to let go.

She passed the banked barn on her left, its usually solid form blurred and insubstantial behind the veil of snow, crouching against the hillside, huddled against the storm. She pumped her brakes as the car half-rolled, half-slid downhill, past the apple orchard, bare limbs lifted in supplication to the gray sky, branches coated in ice and shuddering in the wind. At the bottom of the hill, the brakes did nothing to slow the car; an alarm beeped and a light flashed on the dashboard as she skidded toward the trees. She gasped as the car struck a snow bank and came to an abrupt halt, a shower of ice chunks falling upon the hood of her car, shaken loose from the tree limbs above.

Heart pounding, she sat for a moment, unsure whether backing up or plowing forward would be more likely to free her from the snow bank. It occurred to her that trying to drive home under these conditions was probably one of her less brilliant ideas, but now that she had set forth, she would press on. She took a deep breath, put the car in reverse, and gradually eased backward onto the road, then forward into the woods.

There, her breathing eased. The trees sheltered her from the worst of the winds, and the roads, while not as clear as she had hoped, were free of the drifts and slopes that had made the short trip from the manor so treacherous. Now she was at last truly on her way and she could make up for lost time. As long as she made it safely home, she didn't care if Tim remembered to heat up the lasagna or if he opened a few cans of chicken noodle soup. All that mattered was that they would be together—she, her husband, and their sons. It didn't matter what they ate, only that they gathered around the table out of love and respect for one another. It was the same with the Elm Creek Quilters. Each of them could quilt alone and usually did, but there was something important to be gained by gathering in community to work together, to support one another, to celebrate accomplishments, or to help a struggling friend find her way.

Another flashing light on the dash, another shrill warning beep, another moment of breathless fear as the car skidded ahead and sideways and shook to a stop as the brakes finally took hold. The snow cover was not as deep in the woods as in the open fields, but the bare branches had not held off the morning's freezing rain, and the rustic gravel road was covered in a sheet of ice. Diane wrenched the wheel, pointed the car toward home, and gave the gas pedal a tentative push. Inching forward, she spotted the second bridge over Elm Creek some distance ahead, barely visible in the unnatural twilight. Beyond it, not yet visible up the hill and around the bend, was the road to the front entrance of the manor.

Relief flooded her. She had another choice. She could admit the hazards were greater than she had imagined, turn onto the front road, spend the night with her friends—surely that was what Tim and the boys would want her to do. She would still have most of Saturday and Sunday with her sons before they returned to school, time enough to tell them the thoughts she had been piecing together all that day. Some traditions were not meant to last a lifetime, only a season, and those she could let fade away. Others were far too important to fall by the wayside, and those traditions were worth fighting for. It didn't matter what the family ate on Thanksgiving Eve, but it did matter that they shared a family meal, if they could. It didn't matter if her sons cherished an Advent calendar inspired by the one they had enjoyed in childhood, but it did matter that they observed the season, thoughtfully and respectfully. And it didn't matter if they attended Mass at the parish where they had first received the sacraments or—Father Doug forgive her—if they attended a Catholic service at all or another denomination's, but it did matter that they attend, not only to express their love for God but also to receive the essential spiritual nourishment that only worship offered and to experience it within community. She could not force her sons to attend church, nor would she wish to, no more than she could or would have their love and respect come compulsorily. But she could tell them what worship meant to her, how it enriched her life, how through her presence in that community she hoped to enrich the lives of others. And then, when she had shared her truth with them, they could adopt her traditions as their own or set them aside, an unopened gift, but at least she would know that she had offered it. Perhaps they would hear her, perhaps not. Perhaps not now but later.

Patience did not come naturally to her but she would try. And that meant spending the night at the manor instead of risking her life or at least the car in that howling fury of a storm.

"Across the bridge, up the hill, and onto the front road," she said aloud, steeling herself as a gust of wind shook the car. The drifts would surely be deep across that broad, open expanse, the road perhaps completely obscured, but if the car got stuck, she would trudge along on foot the rest of the way. Gwen would say "I told you so," and Diane would shock her by agreeing, but after that Sylvia would fix her a bracing cup of coffee and Agnes would insist she take the chair closest to the fire. Diane would leave her Advent calendars in her bag—for that matter, she might as well leave them in the car—and when she had warmed herself she would help her friends with their Christmas projects for a change. For once she would celebrate a quilter's holiday by offering help instead of seeking it.

She steered the car across the narrow bridge, her thoughts full of the warmth awaiting her within the gray stone walls of the manor. On the other side, the car balked at the rising slope and slid backward, wheels churning up ice and gravel. Cautiously Diane gunned the engine and flushed with relief when the car climbed another few feet up the hill, only to halt a few yards short of the summit, wheels spinning forward uselessly as the car fell back.

Without thinking, she slammed hard on

the brake and the car jerked to a stop. Sand—she should put sand under the wheels for traction. But she had no sand in the trunk except for a few summer grains dusting the beach chair. She could call Matt to bring her some, but she was reluctant to compel him outdoors now that she understood just how treacherous the road had become. Ruefully, she realized that she might not have a choice, but she would try one more time on her own before digging her cell phone out of her purse and begging for a rescue.

She eased her foot off the brake and pressed the accelerator. At first the car did not budge, but then it inched forward, then slipped backward, crawling up the hill and falling back, making slow but steady progress toward the summit, and once she reached it she would be able to coast downhill all the way to the front road if that's what it took, a bit more gas and another inch more—

But then the car was sliding backward. Instinctively she hit the brakes hard, but the car continued its sickening backward slide toward the bridge. She abandoned the brake and pounded the accelerator but the engine roared impotently as the car picked up speed. Frantically she wrestled with the wheel, fighting to straighten the car, to slow it, to stop it before it struck the guard rail or worse yet, missed the bridge and plummeted into the creek, a thick black slash beneath a thin crust of ice below. A sudden impact made her cry out—but at last the car was still, off the road and halfway down the embankment.

Heart pounding, she turned off the engine and sat for a moment, stunned, until a thin dusting of snow covered the windshield. Then she took a deep, shaky breath, turned the key, switched on the wipers to clear the windshield, and tentatively pressed the accelerator. The wheels spun and shrieked, but the car only shuddered in place.

Shutting down the engine again, Diane gingerly climbed out of the car, neck and shoulders aching from the impact, gasping as the icy wind drove snow into her face and down the collar of her coat. Clutching it closed at the neck with one hand and touching the side of the car for balance with the other, she picked her way alongside it, every step confirming what her first glance had warned: The rear of her car was stuck fast, the undercarriage pinned in place by a fallen log buried beneath the snowdrift. Nothing less than a tow would free it. Unless—Matt had a chainsaw and a pickup truck with a hitch. If he could cut the log and free the car, he might be able to tow it back to the road. After that, she would follow him to the manor, and as long as she could sit by the fire beneath a warm quilt with a hot cup of coffee in hand, she would gladly endure her friends' teasing.

Shivering, Diane brushed as much snow from her coat and hat as she could before climbing back into the driver's seat. She reached into the back seat for her purse and retrieved her cell phone, cursing herself when she saw that she had a strong signal but only eight percent of her battery left. Why could she never remember to charge it?

She called the manor first, but no one answered and she was sent to voicemail. "Okay, okay, you told me so," she said for the benefit of whoever heard the message. "My car's trapped on the forest road and I need a rescue squad. Please send Matt with his pickup and a chainsaw so I don't have to spend the night out here. And a thermos of coffee. And ask him to hurry. Please."

She had barely hung up when the phone rang—Tim, calling from home. "Honey?" she said quickly, mindful of the low battery. "I'm afraid I'm going to be a bit late."

"You shouldn't try to drive in this," protested Tim. "I was calling to tell you to spend the night at the manor."

Diane glanced at the windshield, once again covered in snow. "An excellent suggestion. Thanks, honey."

"Stay inside and stay safe. I know you're probably tempted to drive home so you can spend more time with the boys, but don't do it. You're smarter than that."

"Yes, I'm a genius. Listen, my battery's about to die but I should tell you—"

"Just tell me you love me and you'll be careful."

"I love you," said Diane. She had bypassed careful the moment she pulled out of the parking lot.

Her phone beeped three times and fell silent. Sighing, Diane returned the dead phone to her purse, let her head fall back against the headrest, and vowed to plug in her phone every night before going to bed even if the indicator insisted she had hours of charge left. How many minutes would pass before someone at Elm Creek Manor realized a message waited on the voice-mail? She knew from the outgoing message that it was the voicemail, not the answering machine, so she was not merely waiting for someone to pass by the answering machine and notice the blinking light. She needed someone to make an outgoing call, hear the stutter tone that indicated voicemail, and enter the code to hear the message. Why hadn't she called Anna's cell phone instead? Anna carried her phone with her everywhere and was always texting one friend or another. If only Diane had some other way to get their attention. If only she had a flare to send up—not that they would see it in the storm—

Chastising herself for not thinking of it sooner, she pressed hard upon the horn, shattering the silence, pausing to listen for an answering shout. She turned on the headlights and sounded the horn again, one long beep followed by a series of short bursts. But she knew it was unlikely that anyone would pass on the road to the manor until after the storm. The Elm Creek Quilters, warm and happy, would not venture out and their families, secure in the knowledge that they were safe, would not come seeking them.

No one would hear the horn through thick stone walls and windows shut tight against the cold. She switched off the lights to save the battery, and then reluctantly shut off the engine to save gas. She would have to wait until someone received her voicemail.

Resigned to a long wait, Diane reached into the back seat for her tote bag, stuffed full of the sewing tools and the pieces of the Advent calendars she had meant to make for her sons. Maybe her choice had not been so foolish after all. If Michael and Todd didn't appreciate the calendars this year, they might someday, and in the meantime she could make one for herself to replace the dilapidated paper version she would always remember fondly.

Besides, she had nothing better to do while awaiting rescue.

She lost track of time as she cut out the fabric appliqués and basted down the seam allowances, occasionally pausing to sound the car horn. The cold crept into her skin, seeping through her boots and slipping beneath her scarf. Shivering, Diane started the car and ran the heater full blast. As she packed up her project, having proceeded as far as she could in the car, she realized it could be hours more before anyone heard the message she had left what felt like ages ago.

Snow scoured the windows, covering the glass, leaving her in darkness. Her breath came in short, quick, white puffs. She closed her eyes. Her ears rang and waves of exhaustion washed over her. Later that evening Tim might call the manor to bid her goodnight, knowing that her cell was dead, and then her friends would realize that she had not made it home, but they would not know where she was; it was equally likely that Tim wouldn't call.

No one was coming for her, and she couldn't spend the night in the forest in the storm. She would have to set out on foot for the manor. Her high-heeled boots were not meant for a long hike, but she had no choice.

She wrapped her scarf more snugly around her neck and tucked the ends across her chest beneath her coat. She pulled her hat down to cover as much of her ears and cheeks as it would, and she slipped on her sunglasses in the faint hope of keeping the stinging snow out of her eyes.

She slipped the strap of her purse over her head and glanced around the car. Was she forgetting anything, leaving behind anything that might be useful? Her gaze fell upon her tote bag, stuffed full of the sewing tools and the pieces of the Advent calendars she had meant to make for her sons. She couldn't afford the additional burden of the tote bag, so she resigned herself to leaving it behind.

Taking the keys from the ignition, Diane braced herself for an icy blast as she left the car, locking it behind her out of habit, tucking the keys into her pocket. Wading through drifts, she made her way to the road and paused only a moment to consider whether the road ahead to the front of the manor would be the easier path, or if she should turn back the way she came. Turn back, she decided, and set forth. The wind howling across the open meadow in front of the manor would be brutal, the driveway entirely snow covered and impassible. If she backtracked, she would have the limited protection of the forest, and the barn would offer her shelter where she could rest before continuing on.

If she made it that far.

Bending almost double against the wind, she thrust her hands into her pockets and set off into the storm.

CHAPTER THREE

Sylvia

WITH MISGIVINGS, SYLVIA watched Diane dash out of the ballroom, tote bag slipping off her shoulder. Perhaps Diane had indeed driven through worse storms in the past, but that was no reason to take unnecessary chances now. Still, Sylvia thought she understood her friend's urgency. If she had been blessed with children, she would not want to be snowed in apart from them either, even if they were almost grown, almost on their own. She supposed good mothers never lost that sense of longing for their children, that instinct to protect and nurture, to preserve the family at all costs.

Of course, this was only conjecture based upon her experiences as a daughter and sister and her observations of friends. Though Sarah was like a daughter to her and she was glad to be stepmother to Andrew's grown children, she would never be so brash as to assume she truly understood what it felt like to be a mother. As she watched Diane rush off into a snowstorm rather than be parted from her sons, or when she observed Agnes contentedly stitch Christmas stockings for her grandchildren, she longed for family ties of her own, for a niece or nephew who shared the same roots and branches of the family tree, for a cousin to reminisce with about the same shared memories of holidays from years gone by. She had told stories of those long ago celebrations to her friends—and she had even revived some of her favorite traditions, such as placing symbols of gratitude into the Thanksgiving cornucopia—but although that was worthwhile and gratifying in its way, it was not the same as celebrating with people who knew those traditions as their own, people with whom she shared a common heritage.

Since returning to Elm Creek Manor after

her sister's death, Sylvia had first denied then eventually come to accept that she was the last living descendant of Hans and Anneke Bergstrom, her great-grandparents and the founders of Elm Creek Manor. The private detective she had hired as she put her sister's affairs in order and wrote her own will confirmed the sad news, but even then she could scarcely believe it. She mourned the end of her proud family line but resolved not to become so trapped in grief that she took for granted the new family she had created for herself through cherished friendships and marriage to Andrew. Still, she never stopped wondering what had become of all those dear aunts and uncles and cousins, how it could be that they had left behind not a single descendant. Most of all she wondered about her favorite cousin, Elizabeth Bergstrom Nelson, who lived on so vividly in Sylvia's memory that it seemed impossible she had departed this earth without leaving her mark upon it.

Elizabeth illuminated Sylvia's earliest memories of holiday celebrations at Elm Creek Manor, and she could not ring in a New Year without reflecting upon Elizabeth's last New Year's Eve at Elm Creek Manor. Sylvia had been scarcely five years old when the family decided to revive a New Year's Eve tradition that Hans, Anneke, and Gerda Bergstrom had brought to America from Germany. The last time the Bergstrom family had celebrated the night of Holy St. Sylvester with a ball for family and friends had been before Sylvia was born, so Sylvia listened, entranced, as Great-Aunt Lucinda described the dancing, singing, and delicious things to eat and drink. Sylvia's mother promised that she and her sister, Claudia, could stay up until midnight to welcome the New Year as long as they napped beforehand.

Sylvia and Claudia passed the morning of December 31 sledding and building snowmen until their mother called them inside for a nap. Claudia promptly complied, but Sylvia pretended not to hear until her mother called out that no nap meant no Sylvester Ball for naughty little girls. At that, Sylvia reluctantly came inside and tugged off her coat and boots and mittens, leaving snow to melt in a puddle on the mat. As she dragged herself upstairs, Elizabeth passed her on the landing, her golden curls bouncing, her eyes alight with pleasure and mischief. “Hello, little Sylvia,” Elizabeth greeted her. “Where are you off to on this last day of the year?”

When Sylvia glumly reported that she had been sent to bed even though she wasn’t the slightest bit tired and naps were for babies, Elizabeth declared that the time would be much better spent preparing Sylvia for her first big dance. She took Sylvia by the hand and quickly led her upstairs to the nursery on the third floor, where she shut the door and slid a chair in place beneath the doorknob. “That’ll give you time to hide should anyone come snooping,” said Elizabeth. “We’ll have to keep our voices down. Take off your shoes and show me what you know.”

Sylvia took off her Mary Janes and bravely demonstrated the few ballet steps her mother had taught her and Claudia, half-afraid that Elizabeth would laugh and send her off to take a nap after all. “Well, you’re not a lost cause,” said Elizabeth after Sylvia finished, “but that’s not the kind of dancing we’re doing tonight. You have a lot to learn and not a lot of time.”

Elizabeth took her hands and, over the

next two hours, introduced Sylvia to grown-up dances called the foxtrot, the quick step, and the waltz. When Sylvia proved to be an apt pupil, Elizabeth praised her and taught her the tango and the Charleston. Dancing hand in hand with her cousin, gliding over the wood floor in her stocking feet, smothering laughter and asking questions in stage whispers, Sylvia happily rehearsed the new steps until suddenly Elizabeth noticed the time and sent Sylvia off with a warning not to let anyone see her on the way. Giggling, Sylvia crept downstairs to her bedroom, where she rumpled her quilt, opened the blinds, and woke her unsuspecting sister, mere moments before their mother arrived to help them dress for the party.

Face scrubbed, hair brushed, and neatly attired in her best winter dress, Sylvia nearly burst with excitement as she awaited the moment she and Elizabeth would dance together at the ball. First she had to sit through a traditional New Year's feast of lentil soup, followed by pork and sauerkraut, foods meant to bring good luck. Afterward, the party resumed in the ballroom, where musicians struck up a lively tune that beckoned couples to the dance floor. Sylvia looked around for Elizabeth, but Claudia dragged her off to play ring-around-the-rosie just as she spotted Elizabeth on the arm of her fiancé, Henry Nelson. When the song ended, Sylvia slipped away from her sister and wove through the crowd to Elizabeth, but her cousin was already waltzing with her father.

Her turn would come, Sylvia told herself, but dance after dance went by and always Elizabeth was with Henry, or her father, or Henry's father, or one of her uncles. Mostly she was with Henry. Hours passed, and just as Sylvia reluctantly concluded that her cousin had forgotten her, Elizabeth smiled at her and said, "Are you ready to cut a rug?"

Her happiness restored, Sylvia nodded and took her cousin's hand. Elizabeth led her to the dance floor, counted out the first few beats, and threw herself into a jaunty Charleston. Sylvia struggled to keep up at first, but she stoked her courage and persevered, kicking higher and broadening her smile as if she believed herself as beautiful and admired as her cousin. Soon the other guests stopped dancing to gather in a circle around the two cousins as they danced side by side. Sylvia mirrored her graceful cousin's spirited steps as closely as she could, praying her family and the guests wouldn't notice her mistakes.

All too soon the song ended. Breathless and laughing, Elizabeth took Sylvia's hand and led her in a playful, sweeping bow. She blew kisses to the crowd as she guided Sylvia from the dance floor while the musicians struck up a mellow foxtrot and the couples resumed dancing. Henry promptly claimed Elizabeth as his partner, but for once Sylvia didn't mind. She and Elizabeth had shown everyone what Bergstrom girls could do, just as Elizabeth had promised as they practiced in the nursery.

They danced together again at Elizabeth's wedding a few months later, but soon afterward the newlyweds left for Southern California. Heartbroken, Sylvia took little comfort in Elizabeth's letters, despite her enchanting tales of splashing in the Pacific Ocean, strolling down the streets of Hollywood, and plucking apricots and oranges from her own groves on the rolling, sun-drenched hills of Triumph Ranch in the Arboles Valley. Over the years, perhaps as Elizabeth's responsibilities as ranch wife and mother grew, her letters became fewer and further between, until they stopped coming. Sylvia never saw her cousin again and never stopped wondering what had become of her.

The distant thud of the back door closing tugged Sylvia from her reverie, and Agnes's sigh echoed her own. Sylvia realized then that she was not the only Elm Creek Quilter who had hoped Diane would change her mind before she put on her coat and boots.

Hand on her abdomen, Sarah rose from her sewing machine and went to the window. "Diane's car is almost completely buried," she said. "It looks like an igloo. I think I'll go outside and try to talk her out of leaving."

"Send Matt," Sylvia advised, worried that Sarah might lose her footing and fall, injuring herself or the twins.

"That might not be wise." Sarah's voice had a brittle edge. "He probably thinks this is a perfect day for a drive and won't do anything more than help her clear the snow from her roof. He can be completely oblivious to hazards sometimes."

Gwen raised her eyebrows inquisitively and looked as if she might speak, but Sarah strode from the ballroom before Gwen had the chance. She returned only a few minutes later looking none the chillier, which implied that she had taken Sylvia's advice and sent Matt in her place.

"I don't know why Diane insisted upon going," fretted Agnes. "I should have offered to help her with those calendars. I could finish my stockings at home another day."

"Diane seemed perfectly happy working on the calendars on her own," said Carol.

"I'm not so sure about that." Agnes turned a slight frown on Gwen. "You could have been more considerate, you know."

"Me?" protested Gwen. "What did I do?"

"You could have encouraged her when she showed us the magazine picture, but instead you called it 'cute' and said it would be more suitable for younger children."

"I still think that's true," said Gwen. "Should I have lied? She hadn't started yet so I thought I'd give her an opportunity to reconsider and choose something more likely to please them. Anyway, she ignored my advice as she always does, so what does it matter?"

"I don't think Diane left because of anything Gwen said," said Anna. Suddenly she jumped in her seat and took her furiously buzzing cell phone from the back pocket of her jeans as if she had forgotten it was there. She read something on the screen, bit her lower lip, and painstakingly typed a response with both thumbs.

"Of course you shouldn't have lied, dear," Agnes told Gwen contritely, just as a car started up in the parking lot, the sound of the engine almost drowned out by the wind. Apparently Matt had not convinced Diane to stay.

Sarah sighed heavily and settled back down at the sewing machine, joining rows of blocks at a brisk, determined pace. One by one the Elm Creek Quilters resumed their work, pausing to cast anxious glances at the window, turning as one at the sound of the ballroom door opening.

Red-cheeked, hair standing up in wild disarray as if he had yanked off a stocking cap moments before, Matt blew on his hands and shook his head as he entered the ballroom. "She wouldn't listen," he said, joining Sarah at the sewing table. "She's on her way home."

"We heard the car," said Sarah without looking up.

"Did you watch to make sure she made it out of the parking lot?" asked Gwen.

"I kept an eye on her until she rounded the barn and went out of sight. She was doing fine, taking it nice and slow."

"She has a cell phone on her, right?" asked Anna.

"Yes," said Sarah, "but it's fifty-fifty odds whether the battery's charged."

"She has a terrible habit of letting it run out." Sylvia watched as Matt bent to kiss Sarah's cheek, but Sarah was so intent on her work that she did not respond until Matt stroked her hair. Even then, the smile she offered seemed a bit forced.

Sylvia wished she had thought to ask Diane to call the manor when she reached home so that they would know she had arrived safely.

Sighing to herself, she settled back down to work, finishing the final seam of the last Star of the Magi block she needed to complete her quilt top. She had finished the complementary Chimneys and Cornerstones blocks in October, knowing that she wanted to make the focal point blocks from a star pattern but uncertain which would look best. It wasn't until later that it had occurred to her that she might have unwittingly chosen the Chimneys and Cornerstones blocks in memory of a quilt Great-Aunt Lucinda had made for Elizabeth as a wedding gift. Simple in design and pieced from scraps, it nonetheless seemed as precious to Elizabeth as her official bride's quilt, an elegant Double Wedding Ring embellished with floral appliqués made by all the women of the family. Both had been lovingly packed into Elizabeth's trunk before she left Elm Creek Manor for the last time.

Sylvia wondered if those quilts still graced a cozy home somewhere in California or whether, like so many other heirlooms created from fabric and thread, they had been lost to time. A few months before, inspired by the success of other searches into her family's past, Sylvia had enlisted the help of Summer Sullivan, the official historian and Internet guru of Elm

Creek Quilts, and Grace Daniels, a long-time friend, quilter, and museum curator. When Sylvia told them how she longed to discover what had become of her cousin, Summer offered to search her favorite genealogy databases for the Nelson family, while Grace took on the more daunting challenge of attempting to find Elizabeth's quilts. Elizabeth would never have parted with such precious wedding gifts, and if they had not worn out or suffered another sad fate, she surely would have passed them down to her children. If the quilts were found, their provenance could trace a path back to Triumph Ranch and Elizabeth.

While Summer worked online, Grace contacted all the quilt museums, appraisers, historians, and private collectors she knew in Southern California. Unfortunately, even though Sylvia had provided sketches of the quilts, the Chimneys and Cornerstones block was so common that the prospect of finding one particular scrap rendition seemed impossible. The Double Wedding Ring pattern had also been popular for more than a century, but the floral appliqués set Elizabeth's version apart, perhaps distinguishing it enough to fix it in a viewer's memory. On this slight chance, Sylvia had pinned her hopes.

Grace had spared her the day-by-day account of the false leads traced and disproved, but then, the day after Halloween, she had phoned with intriguing news. A colleague had shown Sylvia's sketches to a friend at UCLA who specialized in Southern California history. He was convinced that he had seen the floral Double Wedding Ring quilt in a book about the development of coastal stagecoach routes, but he couldn't remember the title.

"How many books on that subject can there be?" Sylvia had asked Grace, who laughed and said that she suspected there weren't many, which gave them an advantage. One of the UCLA professor's graduate students was writing a dissertation on the subject, and he was certain he had seen the photo while helping her prepare for her candidacy exam. He promised that he would have the student page through the books in question and locate the photo as soon as possible, but it was a busy semester and they might not get to it right away.

"I understand," Sylvia had said, and she

asked Grace to offer the professor and his student her heartfelt thanks. "But remind them that I'm a senior citizen and I can't wait forever."

"Sylvia!" Grace had scolded, bursting into laughter. "You're as fit as a woman half your age."

"Hardly," Sylvia had said dryly. "And don't tell your friend that. Let him think time is of the essence."

Grace had agreed, and as Sylvia had hung up the phone, she had felt a flutter of cautious anticipation, a familiar sensation she remembered from her search for five of her mother's long-lost heirloom quilts that Sylvia's sister had sold off decades earlier. In the quest for a missing quilt, fresh leads often appeared when one least expected them, but sometimes the answers, once finally discovered, proved disappointing. Sylvia had prepared herself to expect the same from this new quest. The quilt from the photograph might not be Elizabeth's at all, and even if it were, the trail might end there, with its appearance in an obscure academic text.

Sylvia finished the last seam, tied a knot in the thread, and snipped the trailing end.

Then she smoothed the Star of the Magi block on her lap and inspected it critically. The eight-pointed star in the center lay perfectly flat, seams carefully pressed in a spiral on the back to eliminate an unsightly lump where the diamonds met. The eight irregular pentagons that pointed outward from the central star enhanced the design's radiance. The unusual shapes and angles lent themselves to hand piecing, but now that the blocks were complete, Sylvia intended to assemble the top by machine to save time. If Diane were there to see Sylvia embark upon the next stage, she would have given Sylvia an earful for mixing hand and machine piecing in the same quilt top, an inconsistency she abhorred.

Sylvia would have gladly endured her protests to have Diane there, safe and sound in the manor rather than fighting her way home in a snowstorm that seemed to have intensified since her departure.

She must have sighed aloud, for Agnes caught her eye and smiled encouragingly. "Whatever flaws you think you've found, I assure you, you're imagining them."

"Oh, the block is fine." Sylvia rose and brushed stray threads from her lap. "I simply don't relish crawling about on my hands and knees as I arrange the blocks into rows." That was certainly true, so it wasn't a lie, although it wasn't the reason for her troubled sigh either.

"Is this quilt your annual contribution to the Holiday Boutique?"

"Why, yes," said Sylvia, all innocence. "Would you like to place a bid?"

"And deny your fellow parishioners the chance to own one of your masterpieces? And deny *you* the pleasure of watching the bidding go higher and higher?" Agnes feigned horror at the very thought. "I couldn't live with myself."

Sylvia smiled and gathered up her pile of completed blocks, her worries about Diane momentarily subsiding. Agnes knew her too well. It was perhaps a sin of pride to take so much delight in knowing that she never failed to provide one of the most sought-after items for her church's annual sale, but since the proceeds went to a noble cause, she figured she would be forgiven. "It's not for myself that I want my donations to fetch a good price," she reminded her sister-in-law, "but for the county food bank. You know the proceeds from the boutique provide almost a third of their annual budget."

Gretchen looked up from her work, impressed. "That must be quite a sale."

"Or quite a small budget," said Gwen with a naughty grin.

"It would be wonderful indeed if the food bank required only a small budget, but the need is greater than that," said Agnes. "People don't go hungry only in the big cities but also in rural towns like ours, especially in times like these, when even working families are struggling to make ends meet."

"Preachin' to the choir, darlin'," said Gwen with a trace of her old Kentucky accent. "I give my undergrads extra credit if they volunteer to sort donations at the food bank."

"Can you do that?" asked Carol, concern cutting a furrow between her brows. "Is that fair to the students who don't have time to volunteer?"

"I firmly believe that every college student can find a spare hour once a week," said Gwen. "They may have to cut back on their beer bong time, but they can do it. Anyway, I don't give them enough extra credit to change a failing grade to passing, but it's enough to make the difference between a B-plus and an A-minus. I've also found that once young people start volunteering and learn how good it feels to contribute to the community, they often continue on their own and draw their friends into it, even without the reward of a better grade dangled in front of them."

"Can anyone donate a quilt for the boutique?" asked Gretchen, admiring Sylvia's quilt with keen interest. "Or is it members only?"

"I don't think participation is restricted to church members, and in any case I can't imagine they'd turn down one of your lovely creations," said Sylvia. "The Holiday Boutique isn't limited to quilts either, but all manner of handmade gifts, jewelry, Christmas ornaments, knitted scarves, baked goods—"

"Baked goods?" Anna broke in from the cutting table. "In that case I could probably whip up something, too."

"I'm sure the committee chair will be delighted," said Sylvia, pleased. "I don't know why I never thought to ask you for donations before."

"A better question is why we never volunteered," said Gwen, eyes on her needle as she worked it through the layers held fast in her hoop. "Anna and Gretchen have a good excuse since they didn't join us until recently, but the rest of us have watched you work on quilts for the boutique on every quilter's holiday year after year, and yet we never thought to ask if we could pitch in."

"I'm sure you all support your own favorite charities," said Sylvia. Gretchen promptly nodded and Gwen shrugged as if that went without saying, but Sarah allowed the sewing machine to stop its cheerful patter and the rest exchanged contrite glances. "Well, if you haven't in the past I hope you'll consider it in the future."

"Who has time to take on another task during the holidays?" said Carol, but she looked as if she regretted her words even as she spoke them.

"What better time than the holidays?" asked Sylvia. Using one's gifts in the service of others and caring for those in need figured so prominently in the Bergstrom family's Christmas traditions that Sylvia couldn't imagine the holidays without them.

Her mother had set an admirable example, teaching her children that they were called not to give from their surplus, but to give their all. Sylvia had often thought that the Elm Creek Quilters should do more as a group to lend their talents to worthy causes, but she had never found a moment to sit down and plan a project for the entire circle of quilters. Until Sylvia could get herself organized, she must do more to encourage her friends to support worthy causes on their own, leading by example as her mother would have done.

"As Gwen said, it feels good to contribute to the community." Sylvia carried her blocks to an open spot on the parquet dance floor and began to arrange them medallion fashion, starting with the center blocks and working outward to the edges. "Especially in this season of giving. We're all very busy, but we should never become too preoccupied with our own concerns to help those in need."

"Hear, hear," said Gwen, shifting in her chair and unfurling the quilt so that the soft folds draped over the armrest. The floral Augusta blocks had been carefully pieced, each triangle tapering to a perfect point, but the quilt's soft colors and traditional setting were so unlike Gwen's more avant-garde creations that Sylvia had to smile at the incongruous sight. It occurred to her that in finishing her friend's quilt in time for Christmas, Gwen, too, was helping someone in need in that season of giving. Not all needs were material, and some worthy causes were as close as one's own circle of friends.

Sylvia had benefited from the generous gifts of her friends' time and talents more often than she could count. If not for Grace and Summer, she never would have learned so much about her heritage, and thanks to their tireless efforts on her behalf, she stood to learn more.

How Summer had found time away from her graduate school studies to investigate historical records for her, Sylvia had no idea, although Summer had always been an admirably capable young woman. Only a week before, she had called the manor with startling news: She had discovered census records from 1930 for a Nelson family living in the Arboles Valley.

"The names seem to fit, but other details don't," Summer had said, with an odd note in her voice that could have been puzzlement or caution or both, as if something about the evidence made her suspect it might disappoint Sylvia. "There's no mention of Triumph Ranch, for one thing, but the census form doesn't really have a place for the names of individual farms. Did you have any relatives named Jorgensen?"

"Not that I recall," Sylvia had said, "unless they're distant relations by marriage. Why do you ask?"

"You'll understand when you see the forms."

Summer had promised to put them in the mail that afternoon, and sure enough, they had arrived a few days later. Sylvia's excitement gave way to uncertainty as she opened the envelope and studied the first page, a printout from a microfilm taken of the original government documents. Two-thirds of the way down the page she discovered Henry Nelson, a twenty-seven-year-old white male, born in Pennsylvania as his parents before him had been. Living with him was his wife, Elizabeth, age twenty-six and also from Pennsylvania, and their two-year-old daughter, Eleanor, born in California. The names, birthdates, and birthplaces were a perfect match for Sylvia's cousin and her family, but not only was the name *Triumph Ranch* absent, Henry was not even listed as head of the household. That title went to Oscar Jorgensen, a California-born farmer married to Mary Katherine Jorgensen, the mother of his two daughters. Other members of the household included Oscar Jorgensen's mother and a number of men identified as hired hands. Henry was listed as the last of these, his relation to the head of household noted as *lodger* and his occupation as *foreman*. Like the other adult women on the page, Elizabeth had no occupation listed, as if the census taker had considered their roles as wives and homemakers so obvious that he need not record it.

This Elizabeth had to be Sylvia's long-lost cousin, her daughter Eleanor the namesake of Sylvia's mother, but how could Henry be lodger and foreman rather than landowner and rancher? At first Sylvia had wondered if Henry had lost the ranch in the onset of the Great Depression and had stayed on as the new owner's employee, but a second form Summer had included quickly disproved her theory.

A printout of the census from 1920, five years before Elizabeth and Henry moved to California, indisputably proved that the land had belonged to the Jorgensen family even then.

Gradually, almost against her will, Sylvia had come to accept the inescapable truth: She had not found Triumph Ranch because there had never been such a place. Henry had spent his life savings on it and had carried the documents of sale around in his coat pocket as a talisman for months leading up to his wedding, but despite Elizabeth's cheerful accounts to the contrary, the newlyweds had not settled down to a happy and prosperous life as the owners of a thriving cattle ranch. Sylvia could only imagine what misfortune had befallen the couple, but it surely explained Elizabeth's silence.

After pondering the census forms and the mystery of Elizabeth's long-held secret, Sylvia had called Summer to thank her and to ask her to find her cousin's family in the 1940 census. Perhaps over the decades their fortunes had improved. To her disappointment, Summer had told her that census forms fell under a seventy-two-year privacy law, so the 1940 census records would not be released to the public until 2012. "That doesn't mean we've hit a dead end," Summer had added. "We may find other sources with much of the same information. Voter registration lists, public directories, county court records—but that would probably require a trip to the Arboles Valley and some digging through primary sources."

"I'll have Andrew add a trip to the Arboles Valley to our summer travel itinerary," Sylvia had told Summer. She couldn't abandon the search after acquiring such tantalizing new information, even though it seemed the most difficult part of her quest still lay before her.

Then, not two days later, Grace had sent her an email, a forwarded response from her colleague at UCLA with an attached document and the promising subject line, "Eureka!" "If this is indeed the quilt in question, I owe my friend an expensive dinner," Grace had added before the quoted text, a paragraph offering the book's title and apologizing for the imperfect quality of the scanned-in photo. Holding her breath and trying to keep her expectations grounded,

Sylvia had opened the document, hoped for the best, and prepared herself to settle for somewhat less than that.

She had adjusted her glasses and leaned closer to the screen, scrutinizing the image. The grainy, black-and-white photo of what appeared to be a small hotel room had not been improved by its transformation from printed page to pixels, but it was clear enough to make out a Double Wedding Ring quilt with a different floral appliqué gracing the center of each ring. Overcome, Sylvia had hardly dared to believe she gazed upon a picture of Elizabeth's wedding quilt, lovingly stitched by three generations of Bergstrom women. Even Sylvia and her sister had added a few, shaky, imperfect stitches rather than be left out of the creation of such a precious gift. But although Sylvia had wanted to believe the quilt in the photo was Elizabeth's, the image was too unclear, her last glimpse of the real quilt too long ago, for Sylvia to conclude unquestionably that the quilts were one and the same.

A caption below the photo noted, "In the late eighteen hundreds, the Grand Union Hotel in the Arboles Valley served travelers on the stagecoach route that connected Los Angeles to Santa Barbara. The guestrooms, cramped by modern standards, boasted luxuries such as a single bed, a window, pegs for hanging clothes, a bureau with wash basin and pitcher, and, after 1902, indoor plumbing in the form of a common bathroom. Photo circa 1930."

Sylvia had sat back in her father's leather chair, her gaze traveling around the library but seeing none of the shelves, the well-read volumes, the sepia-toned family photographs, the artifacts of four generations in a family of collectors. The photo placed the quilt in the Arboles Valley after Elizabeth had moved there. But why on earth would her cousin's wedding quilt be spread upon a narrow bed in a hotel instead of one in her own home?

The newlyweds had struggled through hard times, Sylvia reminded herself. Elizabeth had likely been forced to sell the quilt, and perhaps the Chimneys and Cornerstones quilt as well, just as Sylvia's sister had sold their mother's cherished heirlooms. Sylvia knew it must have broken her cousin's heart to part with her wedding quilt, and she hoped that Elizabeth had demanded and received an outrageous sum for it.

Suddenly she had snapped on her glasses and opened her web browser to her favorite search engine. A historic hotel, important and relevant enough to be included in a book of scholarly research on the region, might still exist, and if it did, perhaps, perhaps . . .

There were Grand Union hotels in New York City, Saratoga Springs, Fort Benton, Montana, and Ljubljana, Slovenia, on the first page of 34,000 hits, but none of the first twenty were in Southern California. Undaunted, Sylvia had refined her search to "Historic Hotels Arboles Valley" and was rewarded with a far more manageable list of less than 4,000 hits—the first of which was for the Arboles Valley Stagecoach Museum.

Eagerly Sylvia had read the history of the museum, learning of its founding on July 4, 1876, and its storied history as an oasis for weary stagecoach travelers until a railroad line constructed through an adjacent valley diverted its clientele. The museum *was* the hotel, Sylvia had discovered, relocated during the construction of the

101 Freeway, restored to its late–nineteenth century appearance, and awarded a spot on the National Register of Historic Places.

Sylvia had admired a bright, full-color photo of the museum with its broad, wraparound porch, tall windows, and a second floor balcony with a railing of turned spindles. A grainy photograph from 1898 showed the inn at the end of a cobblestone drive lined by tall, leafy oaks with an orange grove in the background, and Sylvia had imagined how restful and charming the sight must have seemed to men and women peering through the windows of the jostling coach, weary from the long, dusty, uncomfortable ride. Clicking on a link to additional photos, her gaze had skimmed past images of the restored dining room and close-ups of remaining pieces of the original owner's china service—and fixed on the same picture of a guest room that Grace's colleague had scanned in from the book.

The contact page had provided a phone number, so Sylvia had called and spoken to a docent. The docent knew of the guest room photo, noting that the framed original was displayed in the hallway outside the room, which had been refurbished to match the photo as closely as possible.

"Is that same Double Wedding Ring quilt on the bed?" Sylvia had asked, but the docent had explained that the museum staff could not find the original, so a local quilter had created a similar version based upon the photo. The museum's collections boasted other antique quilts of local historic interest, including a few that had belonged to some of the first families to settle in the Arboles Valley, but not Elizabeth's Double Wedding Ring.

Although the photo proved that the wedding quilt had once warmed guests of the Grand Union Hotel, it was not there now, and as the museum staff's exhaustive search had not uncovered it, Sylvia had little hope that her own efforts would prove more successful.

Sarah's voice abruptly drew Sylvia back to the present day. "Did anyone else hear that?"

"Hear what, dear?"

"It sounded like a car horn, a few long blasts."

"I'm afraid I've been lost in my own thoughts," Sylvia admitted as she set the last Star of the Magi block in place on the dance floor. "I didn't hear anything."

Leaving the cutting table, Anna set her blue and gold fabric pieces on the table next to a free sewing machine and went to one of the windows overlooking the back of the manor. "The only cars in the parking lot are ours, and they're buried in snow. I don't see any headlights approaching, either."

"It must have been my imagination," said Sarah.

"Maybe audio illusions are a pregnancy symptom," offered Gwen.

"When I was pregnant with Sarah, I would wake up at night thinking I had heard a baby crying in the other room." Carol shuddered. "It was positively eerie, like living in a haunted house."

"Now I understand why I never had any younger siblings," said Sarah.

"That's not the only reason," said Carol dryly, but Sarah let the comment pass unchallenged rather than demand her mother explain herself and offer what would probably be an unflattering account of her early months. Silently Sylvia commended her young friend, who in the past would have bristled at the slightest hint of criticism from her mother.

Sylvia studied the blocks she had arranged on the floor, frowning thoughtfully. The rich greens, reds, and golds she had taken from her fabric stash harmonized well while still offering a rich palette of varying hues and contrasts. The layout looked almost as she had imagined it, but the balance wasn't quite right. She needed something more to enhance the single block set on point in the center of the quilt. Perhaps a row of squares at each of the star tips would emphasize it and set it apart from the other Star of the Magi blocks as a focal point. The careful arrangement of the light and dark halves of the Chimneys and Cornerstones blocks surrounding them created a subtle layered effect that gave the quilt an added dimension Sylvia found quite appealing. She hoped the customers of the Holiday Boutique would agree.

Gretchen and Carol wandered over to admire her work-in-progress, and soon Agnes joined them. Gretchen almost apologetically suggested that Sylvia switch a few of the blocks to distribute the darkest of her green fabrics more evenly so that they wouldn't seem to clump together and weigh down her quilt. Carol shot Gretchen a look of startled amazement and declared that the quilt was perfect as it was, but upon reflection Sylvia understood exactly what Gretchen meant and rearranged the blocks.

"This is why it's essential to seek out another perspective," remarked Sylvia, inspecting the new layout. "Thank you, Gretchen."

"It's the least I could do. You've helped me more than I could ever repay," said Gretchen, absently patting the colorful quilt blocks draped over her arm and taking a seat at the sewing machine next to Sarah.

Sylvia was too surprised to reply. All she had done was hire Gretchen for the faculty of Elm Creek Quilt Camp, a position Gretchen had rightly earned, and the arrangement was mutually beneficial. Perhaps it was just a simple figure of speech and not something Gretchen truly believed, but it puzzled Sylvia that Gretchen would think that any part of their professional or personal relationships was a debt that needed to be repaid.

Sylvia began pinning the blocks into pairs, replacing them carefully rather than undoing all of her hard work by mixing up the blocks. She had just finished pinning the last pair in the second row when the cordless phone rang from the top of the fireplace mantel where Gretchen had left it after Bonnie's call. Agnes was the closest, so she quickly set her Christmas stockings aside and answered. "Summer, dear," she cried happily. "So lovely to hear from you."

Gwen immediately perked up and began digging herself out from beneath the folds of fabric and batting. "Hand it over," she said to Agnes as she rose, stabbing her needle into the quilt and setting the hoop on her chair.

"Let me wish her a Happy Thanksgiving first," Agnes admonished her mildly. "Happy Thanksgiving, Summer. Is it snowing where you are? Are you making time to sew on this quilter's holiday?"

"This could take awhile," Gwen muttered, glancing from Agnes to her chair as if regretting that she had set her quilt aside even for a moment. Or perhaps she regretted not insisting upon a mother's prerogative to speak to her daughter first, no matter how dear the friend who happened to answer the phone. Fortunately, Agnes kept her conversation brief and soon handed the phone to Gwen, who settled down on the dais on the opposite side of the room for a private chat with her daughter. Sylvia caught the occasional encouraging phrase and wistful wish that they were spending the long holiday weekend together, and no one there could have failed to overhear Gwen's occasional bursts of laughter. Gwen and Summer were closer than any mother and daughter Sylvia had ever known, and she knew that Sarah wished she and her own mother got along so well. As for Carol, she kept glancing up from her work to study Gwen with puzzled curiosity, as if Gwen must possess some secret knowledge that Carol could learn in time.

After a time, Gwen crossed the room and handed Sylvia the phone. "Summer would like to speak with you."

"I'd be rather disappointed if she didn't." Sylvia gladly took the phone and strolled over to the fireplace to warm herself while they chatted. "Hello, Summer, dear. How is your quilter's holiday going? Have you begun any new Christmas projects?"

"Not a one, I'm afraid," said Summer. "It's not much of a holiday for me. I have so many papers due before the end of the term that I can't afford a day off, and that's even without the research I've been doing on my own for fun."

"Surely you'll find some free time to spend with Jeremy."

"Yeah, I should probably call him and wish him a happy Thanksgiving. He left a message on my cell yesterday but my roommates and I had a houseful of starving graduate students to feed and I never found a minute to return it."

Sylvia couldn't even tacitly encourage Jeremy to talk on his cell phone while he was driving in such dreadful weather. "I suppose at this point you might as well wait a few hours and tell him in person. I hope the storm isn't as bad on the turnpike as it is here."

Summer fell silent for a moment. "What do you mean?"

"I didn't mean to worry you," said Sylvia,

detecting concern in Summer's measured question. "Jeremy left here quite early in the morning after dropping off Anna and he may have been well into Ohio before the worst of the storm struck us."

"Jeremy's on his way to Chicago? Today?"

"Why, yes. Since you were too busy to get away, he decided to come to you." Suddenly Sylvia understood. She threw Gwen a helpless look, and then Anna, but they were busy with their sewing and didn't notice her distress, nor would they have been able to rescue her if they had. "I'm so sorry. I've clearly ruined Jeremy's surprise."

At that, Anna's sewing machine clattered to a stop and she twisted around in her chair to shoot Sylvia a look of utter incredulity. Sylvia shook her head and shrugged, and Anna returned an almost identical gesture. Clearly Anna hadn't known Jeremy intended to surprise Summer, either.

"Believe me," said Summer. "I'm surprised."

Sylvia wondered why Summer didn't sound pleased in the slightest. "I'm sure you'll be glad to see him," she said, no longer sure at all.

"Of course I will, but I really don't have time for company. I'm swamped with work."

Sylvia didn't point out that Summer had taken off the previous day to entertain a houseful of graduate students, which suggested that her schedule was apparently somewhat flexible. "Knowing Jeremy, he's brought along a backpack full of books and his laptop. You can work together and still enjoy each other's company. I doubt he expects you to entertain him."

"If he did, he should have given me some advance notice. Now I'll have to clean up this place, and shop for groceries, and hope my roommates don't mind that we're having company again—" Summer broke off. "But it'll be fine. Thanks for the warning."

"Warning?"

"You know what I mean. Speaking of which—are you sitting down?"

Sylvia was so surprised she laughed. "Not at the moment."

"Maybe you should sit."

"Do you have bad news?"

"Quite the opposite."

"Then consider me sufficiently forewarned. What is it?"

"I've dug around in some online indexes to California vital records and voter registration lists and I think I may have tracked down one of Elizabeth's descendants."

"What?"

"Elizabeth and Henry had three children—Eleanor, who appears on the 1930 census form I sent you; Thomas, two years younger; and Sylvia, who was born in 1934 and is your namesake, or so I'm guessing. I lost track of the daughters and I assume that they married and changed their last names. Thomas, on the other hand, shows up a few times in the historical record."

Sylvia's head grew light. "I think I should sit down." Gretchen barely had time to swing her feet out of the way before Sylvia sat down hard on the ottoman.

"It's almost scary how much information you can find on the Internet," said Summer, but a tone on the phone line drowned out the last syllable. "Are you sitting?"

"Yes." Sylvia threw a reassuring smile to Gretchen, who watched her anxiously. The tone sounded again, and Sylvia instinctively raised her voice. "What did you discover about Thomas?"

"He spent most of his life in the Arboles Valley, but— Is that your call waiting?"

"Yes, but whatever it is, it can wait." It couldn't be as important as what Summer had to say, and if it were, the caller would leave a message once the voicemail system kicked in after the fourth ring.

"Okay, if you're sure. Anyway, Thomas Nelson lived in San Diego for a few years before moving back to the Arboles Valley."

Sylvia waited impatiently for the tone to sound a fourth—and blessedly final—time. "To the Jorgensen farm?"

"No, a different address." Sylvia heard the rustle of paper. "I'll mail you the printouts—or rather, I'll send them back with Jeremy. You'll get them sooner that way."

"Is Thomas—" Sylvia steeled herself. "Is Thomas still living?"

Summer hesitated. "I'm afraid not. I found his death record in a Social Security database. He passed away five years ago. But as far as I can tell, his son and daughter are still living in Southern California."

Sylvia's heart thumped. "He had children?"

"Yes, unless I've mixed up two Thomas Nelsons from the area. That's possible."

But not likely, as thorough and meticulous as Summer was—unlike some researchers. "The private detective I hired after my sister passed away concluded that I had no living blood relations. He told me quite emphatically that I was the last descendant of Hans and Anneke Bergstrom."

"In that case, you might want to ask for a refund."

Sylvia clasped a hand to her forehead. "I don't believe this." But even at the time, she had wondered how the detective reached his conclusion so quickly, and how out of all the cousins and second cousins she had played with in childhood, not one had left a son or daughter behind. "What can you tell me about Thomas's children?"

"Hold on a sec." Again paper rustled in the background. "His son, Scott, was born in 1961. Scott's current address is for Newbury Park, California, which is near the Arboles Valley though not in it. Thomas's daughter was born in 1965, but I couldn't find her in any online directories so my guess is that she married and changed her last name, too. I wish women didn't do that. It's very inconvenient."

"Did you say you had a current address for Scott Nelson?" said Sylvia.

"An address and a phone number," said Summer. "Would you like them?"

Sylvia laughed, for she had already bounded to her feet and was hurrying to the nearest classroom for a pencil and paper.

CHAPTER FOUR

Anna

ANNA COULDN'T EXPLAIN why she didn't want the other Elm Creek Quilters to know she was making Jeremy a quilt for a Hanukkah gift. It wasn't because she was afraid they would give away the secret, for she was certain she could trust them. It wasn't even because she didn't want them to know how much Jeremy meant to her, since the "Best Friend" quilt block she was making in his honor would make that evident enough. Maybe she hesitated because she worried that if her friends knew she was making Jeremy a quilt, which every one of them considered a gift of great significance, they would completely misunderstand the situation and think that she and Jeremy were more than just friends, which was simply absurd because Jeremy was crazy in love with the gorgeous, brilliant, talented Summer Sullivan, someone Anna admired and considered a friend. All of that made the thought that Anna might be attracted to her longtime across-the-hall neighbor absolutely, laughably ridiculous.

Still, there was no need to make a big deal out of the quilt and give anyone the completely wrong idea that she wanted to be more than friends with Jeremy. Even though she didn't—and though she knew Jeremy would burst out laughing at the very thought of the two of them, Jeremy and Anna, a couple—the suspicion that she *might* have a crush on him could make things awkward for her around the manor. The Elm Creek Quilters weren't a gossipy bunch, but Summer was a founding member whereas Anna was a newcomer, and she knew where their loyalties would fall.

Anna wasn't even sure if she would be able to finish the quilt on time or that she would definitely give it to Jeremy if she did. She had already devoted every evening of the past three weeks sketching her design, finding the perfect blue and gold fabrics, and figuring out the complicated math of six-pointed stars when Jeremy mentioned during the drive from their apartment building near Waterford College to the manor that Hanukkah was actually a relatively minor holiday. "It's not the Jewish Christmas," he explained as they rumbled down the rough gravel road through the Bergstrom estate. "Religiously, it's not as significant as Passover or Rosh Hashanah, for example. It's arguably our best-known holiday among non-Jews because of its proximity to Christmas, but best-known doesn't necessarily equal most important."

"But you do celebrate Hanukkah, don't you?" Anna asked, thinking of the hours she'd already devoted to the quilt and the pieces of fabric she'd already cut.

To her relief, he did. "Stop me if you've heard this one," he said, misinterpreting her question as curiosity about the holiday's origins. "In the second century BCE—"

"You mean BC?" Anna interrupted.

Jeremy threw her a wry glance. "No, I said BCE. Before the Common Era."

"It's the same date though, right?"

"Yes, but considering the topic, I thought it would be more appropriate to use BCE."

Anna folded her arms and regarded him. "You know who you sound like?"

"If you say Gordon," Jeremy warned, "I'm going to turn this car around and you can find your own way to Elm Creek Manor."

"You'd turn around when we're almost there?"

"I'd be tempted, if you compared me to your pompous, didactic, arrogant boyfriend. Remember when he tried to pass off that sonnet by Sir Phillip Sydney as his own composition in your honor?"

Of course Anna remembered. No one had ever written her a love poem before—and as Jeremy had soon proven, Gordon hadn't either. "Ex-boyfriend," Anna shot back. "Very ex."

"Ex-boyfriend. I never liked him."

"Then why didn't you say something at the time? You might have opened my eyes earlier and spared me months of misery."

"I did say something," protested Jeremy.

"You dropped strong hints," Anna acknowledged, "but you could have been more forthcoming."

"What could I have said that wouldn't have prompted you to defend him?" said Jeremy, and although Anna wouldn't admit it, she knew he was right. "I never thought he was good enough for you. If I weren't—"

"What?" asked Anna when he didn't continue. "If you weren't a peace-loving liberal, you would have punched him in the nose?"

"No." Jeremy paused to turn the windshield wipers up higher. "I was going to say that if I weren't dating Summer, I'd ask you out."

Anna's breath seemed to flutter in her chest—until she reminded herself that Jeremy had met her before Summer, and if he had wanted to ask her out, he could have. "Oh, really," she said archly. "So Gordon isn't good enough for me, but you are."

Jeremy frowned slightly. "That does sound arrogant, doesn't it?"

"Just a bit."

"Well, I'd definitely treat you much better than he did, so I'm closer to good enough for you than he is."

"Fair point." Anna shifted in her seat, warmed by his words despite the storm. "Where were we?"

Jeremy thought for a moment. "Second century BCE. At that time Antiochus IV was oppressing the Jews—erecting an altar to Zeus in the Temple in Jerusalem, further desecrating the Temple by sacrificing pigs upon it—"

"Pigs? Aren't the Jewish people anti-pig?"

Jeremy guffawed. "Or very pro-pig, considering that we don't eat them. Anyway, Antiochus virtually outlawed Judaism, even going so far as to massacre Jews. Eventually the Jewish people revolted, overthrew the monarchy, and liberated the Temple, which they then needed to cleanse and rededicate. Unfortunately, they discovered that the Greeks had defiled almost all the consecrated oil used to fuel the eternal flame in the Temple, which was supposed to burn throughout the day and night."

Anna nodded, chagrined that she knew so little and had never asked him before, although some of the details were vaguely familiar. "But they found enough, right?"

"That's where the miracle comes into it.

They found enough consecrated oil for a single day and night, and yet, somehow, that single day's supply kept the Temple's menorah burning for eight days and nights, which gave them enough time to prepare a fresh supply of oil."

"So that's why you light eight candles over the span of eight nights."

"Exactly," Jeremy said. "There's also a ninth candle, the shammus or servant, which we use to light the others and usually place in the center of the menorah. We add one new Hanukkah candle to the menorah each night, placing them from right to left, but we light them from left to right, to honor the newest one first. We recite prayers and give gifts, but not like the huge mass of presents you'd find under your Christmas tree."

"Are you speaking of my family in particular or is that your universal Christian 'you'?" Anna asked.

"The latter."

"We were lucky if we had two presents for each kid," Anna told him.

"But given the sheer number of kids in your family—"

"Yes, you're right. That often added up

to a huge mass of presents. I just didn't like the insinuation of greed."

"I didn't mean to imply that you or anyone else in your family was greedy," Jeremy said, just as the car left the woods and came upon the bare-limbed orchard. The engine whined as the wheels momentarily lost traction with the gravel road. "I know that's not what Christmas means to you. Look at that. The sleet's starting to freeze already. In another hour, this road will be a sheet of ice."

Uneasily, Anna watched the icy drops splash against the windshield. "Maybe you should reconsider driving all the way to Chicago in this."

"I'll be fine. I'll stay ahead of the storm."

"No, you'll be heading right into it."

"Maybe I'll pass through it before it gets too severe."

"Maybe."

Jeremy grinned. "You don't sound very optimistic."

Anna wasn't, but Jeremy knew the forecast and was still determined to go. He missed Summer and no storm was going to keep him from spending the long holiday weekend with her. Anna imagined them happily curled up together beneath a quilt on the sofa in Summer's Hyde Park apartment, books and pens and papers scattered around, laptops idle on the coffee table, snowed in but perfectly content since they were together. Of course Jeremy would brave a blizzard to be with the woman he loved; the only real surprise was why he hadn't left the day before, or the day before that, to beat the storm. He could have celebrated Thanksgiving with Summer and her friends instead of Anna and the manor's permanent residents, but he'd said that nothing could compel him to miss Anna's magnificent feast, especially since Summer planned to serve a mock turkey concocted out of tofu and mushrooms.

"You eat latkes for Hanukkah, right?" Anna asked, gripping her seat with both hands as the car swerved past the barn and rumbled over the bridge. "And serve them with either applesauce or sour cream?"

"That's right. I'm impressed a Catholic girl like you knows that."

He shouldn't have been. If Anna remembered any details about a holiday, they would be the ones about food. "I guess I'm not completely ignorant."

"Not even close." Jeremy brought the car to a shuddering halt in the parking lot behind the manor. "Maybe you should have brought a suitcase. You could be spending the night."

Anna unfastened her seat belt and pulled up the hood of her coat. "If the city cancels bus service, I'll catch a ride home with Gwen or Diane."

"If bus service is canceled, your friends shouldn't be driving either."

"Oh, so it's not safe for us to drive a few miles to downtown Waterford, but it's safe for you to drive hundreds of miles across three states?"

Jeremy shrugged, sheepish. "Do what I say, not what I do."

"Except you're not the boss of me." Anna climbed out of the car and slung her tote bag over her shoulder. "Drive safely, all right? Will I hear from you?"

The look her words inspired suggested that Jeremy had rarely heard such a bizarre question, and that was saying something since he had taught Introduction to

World History to college freshmen. "Of course."

"Of course," she replied, and then she shut the door and waved as he drove away. How was she to know whether he'd be in touch while he was gone? Yes, they saw each other mornings and evenings before and after work even when Jeremy didn't drive her to the manor, and they usually spoke on the phone once or twice in addition to that, and they texted back and forth throughout the day, but she didn't expect that to go on when he was spending time with Summer. Obviously he'd rather talk to Summer, but when Summer wasn't available, Anna would do.

Anna watched Jeremy's car round the bend and disappear behind the red barn built into the side of the hill, and she caught herself sighing disconsolately. That's what she was: a friend to joke around with and spend time with when the woman Jeremy preferred wasn't around. But it was fine. Summer was the girlfriend, and Anna was just a friend. It was the way things were, and she was okay with it.

Most days, anyway.

Anna had liked Jeremy from the start,

from those first perfunctory greetings they exchanged when they happened to leave their apartments at the same time to the numerous occasions he had held the outside door for her when he was leaving the building and she was returning with her arms full of grocery bags. She didn't learn his name until that day a few years ago when she had taken some of his mail to him after it had been erroneously delivered to her mailbox, and they had spent a good twenty minutes chatting about the weather, their landlord's terrible record on maintenance issues, and the ridiculous rent increase he had recently announced.

Over time, she learned more about Jeremy in quick, casual conversations whenever they crossed paths in the hallway or the lobby, like picking up crumbs from a tablecloth. He had written his master's thesis on the Battle of Gettysburg, he taught two undergraduate classes each semester, and he had recently passed the candidacy exam to be accepted as a Ph.D. student in the Department of History. She considered asking him over for coffee some evening for a study break, but she lost her courage when she realized how stupid that sounded, considering that she was a university employee rather than a student and therefore had no studying from which she needed a break. Hoping a better, less obvious invitation would occur to her, she contented herself with accidental meetings in and around their building—until one night, completely unexpectedly, Jeremy knocked on her door.

"I hope this isn't too late," he said, shifting the weight of a large cardboard carton he carried. His brown eyes were warm and friendly and the exact color of melted chocolate behind his round, wire-rimmed glasses and, as usual, his curly dark brown hair tumbled into his eyes.

"Not at all," said Anna, although she had been seconds away from slipping into her pajamas and dragging herself wearily off to bed. Her alarm woke her at five o'clock each morning so that she could do the breakfast prep work for the faculty cafeteria.

"The Waterford College Key Club is collecting nonperishable food items to make Thanksgiving baskets for needy families in the Elm Creek Valley." Jeremy offered her a familiar, endearing, lopsided grin. "You probably saw the flyers posted in the lobby."

"Oh, I think I did," she said, opening the door wider, unsure if he wanted to come in. "On the light blue paper?"

"Next year they should use bright orange," he said. "Apparently not many people noticed them because the cartons by the mailroom were almost empty."

"That might not be the only problem," said Anna, wincing. "I think I might have seen that guy from the first floor—you know, the one who chains his bike to the emergency exit—taking a box of cereal and a plastic bottle of apple juice from the carton."

Jeremy rolled his eyes. "Great. That explains a lot. I might have to explain the principle of giving to the needy a little more clearly to him."

"Be careful. He's in great shape from all that biking and I don't think he's very nice."

"Someone has to stand up to bullies or they'll take over the world. Anyway, the cartons are due to be collected tomorrow and I don't want to endure the shame of knowing we're the only building on College

Avenue that turned in only—" gesturing to the meager contents of the carton, he continued, "a few boxes of pasta, a canister of raisins, and a package of granola bars."

"That would be embarrassing," Anna agreed, smiling. "So you've taken it upon yourself to collect door to door?"

"Exactly, and after what you've told me, I'm also appointing myself Guardian of the Carton, which means I'll keep it in my apartment and leave a note telling the Key Club where they can pick it up."

"That's very decent of you."

He gave her a self-deprecating shrug. "Anyone could have done it. I just thought of it first. And, when I thought of who might have food to give away, I naturally thought of you."

Her heart sank. Of course he had naturally thought of her, the plump girl, because big girls always had food stashed away and ought to be all too happy to have someone carry it off before they gorged themselves. Flustered, she smiled, beckoned him inside, and had almost persuaded herself to just let the innocent insult go when she heard herself say, "Why did you think of me?"

"Because you're always bringing home bags full of organic produce from the natural foods market way over on Campus Drive rather than shopping at the convenience store across the street like almost everyone else around here." He spotted the table in her tiny kitchenette and set the carton upon it. "Also, you told me you're a chef for College Food Services, so you probably have a well-stocked pantry with extra staples in reserve. And lastly, anyone nice enough to sign for as many packages for an across-the-hall neighbor as you have without demanding a tip is surely generous enough to share some of those extra staples with the less fortunate."

She hoped she wasn't blushing. "I bet you say that to all your neighbors you beg food from."

"No, just you." He raised his eyebrows, hopeful. "So, what do you say?"

So charmed was she by his altruism and humor that she was inclined to give him as much of her pantry as he could carry away, but instead she settled for giving him two boxes of pasta, a canister of oats, and some other staples of which, as he had guessed, she had extras. Jeremy seemed alternately fascinated and amused by the more exotic items on her shelves, and after she found herself passionately defending her expensive imported extra virgin olive oil and Belgian dark chocolate, he began opening various cupboards, pulling out three items at random, and asking her what she could make using all three. The whole-wheat chocolate cappuccino brownies she suggested on his fifth attempt to stymie her sounded so tasty that they decided to make some, right then and there, and Anna had to laugh at how impressed Jeremy was that she invented a recipe on the spot. While the brownies were baking, she accompanied him on his rounds through the three-story apartment building collecting items for the Thanksgiving baskets. Later, they enjoyed the brownies in all their warm, tasty, chocolate-cappuccino goodness right from the pan as they watched *A Charlie Brown Thanksgiving* on television, sitting cross-legged on her sofa, licking chocolate from their fingertips, as comfortable as if they had been friends for ages.

From then on, their accidental meetings in the hall usually turned into lengthy conversations unless one of them was running late, and at least once every two weeks Jeremy came over for dinner or dessert. They met less frequently after Anna began dating Gordon—Jeremy thought Gordon was a pompous blowhard and Gordon didn't like Anna to pay attention to anyone but him—but they still talked almost every day.

Anna had been involved with Gordon for more than a year when Jeremy mentioned meeting a beautiful girl at the library, so the sting of jealousy caught her completely off-guard. A few months later, when the stunning, auburn-haired beauty moved in with him and turned out to be as friendly, kind, and interesting as she was gorgeous, Anna silently chastised herself for not being more delighted for Jeremy, her friend. When Summer moved out about two months later, Anna naturally assumed they had broken up, but apparently they were still a couple even though Summer had decided to stay at Elm Creek Manor until her departure for graduate school. It was Summer who helped Anna land the chef's job, Summer who encouraged Jeremy to drive her back and forth to the manor on days the bus ride would be too inconvenient. But it was Jeremy who seemed the most relieved and satisfied when Anna broke up with Gordon, and Anna who was secretly delighted when Summer's absence gave Jeremy more free time—which he seemed very glad to spend with her. Their old companionship resumed, stronger than ever, and Anna had come to think of Jeremy as her best friend, although he probably thought of Summer as *his* best friend. It didn't matter. She was simply glad he was a part of her life, in whatever way that was possible.

Entering through the back door of the manor, Anna left her coat and boots in the hall closet and went to the kitchen, still fragrant with spices from the Thanksgiving feast she had prepared the day before. The sight of the gleaming new appliances, granite counters, cozy seating areas, and spacious, well-organized workstations delighted her anew every time she entered. The blank wall above the nearest booth awaited the quilt she and Sylvia were collaborating on, piecing together scraps from a favorite but worn gingham tablecloth and the salvageable fabric from Sylvia's great-aunt's feedsack aprons. They had set the quilt aside recently to work on holiday projects, but when it was finished, it would boast an appliqué still life in the center framed by blocks that reminded them of the kitchen: Broken Dishes, Cut Glass Dish, and Honeybee, among others that they had not yet chosen.

Taking a crisp white apron from the hook on the back of the pantry door, Anna tied it on and noted a few signs that someone had come downstairs to breakfast earlier: The coffee pot was a quarter full and keeping warm, a few crumbs had fallen on the counter near the toaster, and Andrew's favorite coffee mug sat drying upside down on a towel beside the sink. Anna smiled. No matter how often she and Sylvia encouraged him to put his dishes in the dishwasher, when he had but a single cup, he preferred to wash it by hand. Old habits were difficult to break in a man his age, she supposed.

Working from memory, Anna gathered the ingredients for her favorite ginger pumpkin bisque soup. As she set a large copper stockpot on the stove, she thought about the two days earlier that autumn when she and Sylvia had emptied all the cupboards and drawers in preparation for the kitchen remodel, sorting tools and pots and pans in good condition from others long past their usefulness. Sylvia had entertained Anna with stories of her family's holiday traditions, including the history of the cornucopia centerpiece and the tale of the famous Bergstrom apple strudel. Anna planned to surprise Sylvia with a scrumptious apple strudel on Christmas morning, and she was toying with the idea of introducing some of her favorite dishes from her own family's holiday celebrations, perhaps the *panettone* recipe handed down through her mother's side of the family or the *pangiallo* from her father's. She still remembered standing on her tiptoes to peer over the counter while her father's mother, whom she called Nonna, mixed the dough for the sweet bread, which despite its name—"yellow bread" in English—was not yellow at all but dark, rich, and full of nuts, fruits, and bits of chocolate.

Anna loved to hear Nonna's stories of the holidays she had enjoyed as a girl back in her village in the mountains of Abruzzi, before she married Nonno and came to

America. Instead of decorating the home with a Christmas tree like those in American homes, Nonna's father would build a *ceppo*, a wooden pyramid with several shelves and a frame wrapped in festive garland. Upon the bottom shelf, Nonna's mother would arrange the family's cherished Nativity scene, a wedding gift from a beloved uncle and a symbol of the gifts from God. On the center shelves she would place greenery, nuts, fruits, and other small presents, symbolizing the gifts of the earth and of humankind. At the very top of the *ceppo* she would set an angel, a star, or a pineapple, representing hospitality. Lit candles on the shelves' edges illuminated the scene and gave the *ceppo* its other name, the "Tree of Light."

In years gone by Anna had listened, entranced, as Nonna described the elaborate Nativity scenes or *presepi* displayed throughout villages across Italy, life-size tableaus in front of churches, businesses, and residences of the wealthy, and smaller but no less beloved figures at homes of people of modest means. The figures resembled the Holy Family and the shepherds, wise men, angels, and animals that had attended them, and sometimes also the people of the town—fishermen, merchants, farmers, whatever trades were most prominent. Often the wealthy paid artisans handsomely to create figures for their *presepi* that resembled the members of their own family, and one of Nonna's uncles, a talented woodcarver, had earned a nice living doing so. The much smaller figurines he had carved for Nonna's mother had become one of the Del Maso family's most cherished heirlooms.

On Christmas Eve, Nonna's family would fast all day and, since their Catholic faith forbade them to eat meat on *La Vigilia,* they would feast upon fish instead, seven dishes to symbolize the seven sacraments, the seven days of creation, or the seven virtues of faith, hope, charity, temperance, prudence, fortitude, and justice. Nonna could describe the Christmas Eve dinners of her youth in mouth-watering detail: baked baccalà, a type of salted cod; roasted eel; shrimp; sea bass roasted with garlic, thyme, and rosemary; fried calamari; octopus sautéed in lemon, oil, and parsley; and her favorite, linguini in clam sauce. Afterward, the children might entertain the rest of the family with poems and songs they had learned in school, or the family might pass the hours before Midnight Mass playing *tombola,* a gambling game that sounded to Anna something like Bingo, but with a colorful board of ninety squares, each marked with a number and a picture.

Anna smiled to herself as she stirred the fragrant soup and remembered the Christmas Eve when she was fifteen and tried to re-create the feast from Nonna's childhood. The linguini in clam sauce, sea bass, and shrimp had turned out perfectly, but the calamari and octopus had been rubbery and tasteless, and she had not even attempted the eel and baccalà since she had been unable to find them in her neighborhood grocery. With culinary school and years of experience behind her, she knew she would enjoy a much different result if she ever attempted the meal again. She should, and soon, as a Christmas gift for her Nonna.

"Good morning, Anna," Sarah suddenly greeted her from the doorway. "You'd better not be making breakfast! Sylvia strictly forbade it."

Anna threw her a quick smile over her shoulder. “Don’t worry. This is for lunch. I’m only here early because the bus is running a limited holiday schedule, so Jeremy dropped me off on his way to Chicago.”

Sarah nodded. “Yes, I heard. He’s going to see Summer.”

Not even the first major winter storm of the season would have kept him away. Anna turned back to the stockpot and explained that since Summer couldn’t—or wouldn’t, although Anna kept that suspicion to herself—come to Jeremy, he was going to her. He probably would have made the thousand-mile-plus round trip every weekend if his academic schedule and aging car would permit. Instead, he made do with Anna’s company, which Anna enjoyed, so she really shouldn’t complain. Why did she feel like complaining now, when the situation had never bothered her before?

Anna and Sarah had been chatting only a few moments when Anna felt her cell phone buzz in her back pocket. “Would you mind keeping an eye on this while you have breakfast?” she asked Sarah, gesturing to the stockpot with her spoon, knowing whom the caller must be. “I still have a few more seams to go on my quilt block for the cornucopia. This is my first day-after-Thanksgiving as an Elm Creek Quilter and I want to get it right."

When Sarah agreed, Anna quickly untied her apron and hurried into the hallway to answer the phone before it went to voicemail.

"Dreidels," said Jeremy, by way of a greeting. "I forgot to mention dreidels."

Anna smothered a laugh as she picked up her bag of quilting supplies and went to the ballroom. She intended to finish her block just as she had told Sarah, or her excuse would be a lie. "You called me to talk about a Hanukkah game?"

"You know about it? I'm impressed."

Anna nudged open the ballroom door with her hip, wishing his approval didn't please her so much. "You should keep both hands on the wheel in this weather—unless you've already slid off the road into a ditch so you're not technically calling and driving?"

"Relax. I'm using the hands-free headset. I admit it's worse out here than I thought it would be."

Anna felt a pang of worry as she stepped

into the nearest classroom, one of several created in the ballroom by tall, moveable partitions. “Maybe you should hang up and concentrate on the road.”

“I will, after I tell you about dreidels.”

“Okay. Dreidels.” Holding the phone to her ear with one hand and reaching into her tote bag with the other, she set the pieces of her Best Friend block, almost complete, upon the nearest table. “Those are those little squarish top thingies, right?”

“Well said.”

“Thanks.”

“Yes, dreidels are tops with four sides, each bearing a Hebrew letter—*nun, gimel, hey,* and *shin.* The letters represent the phrase *Ness Gadol Haya Sham,* which means ‘A great miracle took place there.’ ”

Jeremy went on to explain that the letters also stood for the Yiddish words *nit, gantz, halb,* and *shtell,* which meant *nothing, all, half,* and *put,* respectively. To play the game, all players put a coin into the pot and took turns spinning the dreidel. If the dreidel landed on *nun,* nothing happened and the next player took a turn. If it landed on *gimel,* the player won the whole pot. If *hei* came up, the player claimed half of the pot, and if *shin,* the player put one coin in. Whenever the pot was emptied, every player put in another coin. The game ended when one player claimed all of the coins.

"Sometimes we played with candies or poker chips instead of coins," said Jeremy. "Especially when we were kids."

"That sounds like fun," said Anna, plugging in an iron.

"It was. Okay, your turn."

"My turn for what?"

"To tell me a holiday story from your childhood. Please? I have a long drive ahead of me and I'm bored."

Anna rummaged through her tote bag for the small plastic box of pins she was sure she had packed. "What's the matter, have you already heard all of Summer's stories, or didn't she answer her phone?"

"I haven't called her."

"And you don't think that's odd?"

"What's odd?"

That Jeremy called Anna and not Summer when he wanted company on a long drive. That Anna hadn't wanted Sarah to know Jeremy was calling her, even though a friend ought to be able to call another friend any time without provoking curiosity in a third friend. That none of this bothered her much until recently.

"Nothing," she said.

"So do I get my holiday story? With or without Santa Claus, I'm fine either way. Or do you not feel like talking at the moment?"

She always felt like talking to Jeremy. Conversation came so easily with him, so effortlessly. He made her laugh, when he wasn't talking all starry-eyed about Summer, and she made him laugh, too. "My Nonna used to tell me the story of La Befana."

"Nonna is your dad's mother, right?"

"Right." Anna sat down in a folding chair beside the ironing board and closed her eyes, remembering her grandmother's voice, her comforting smell of rosewater and face powder and basil. "In my grandmother's village back in Italy, the children weren't visited by Santa Claus on Christmas Eve. Instead, if they were very good, an old woman called La Befana brought them gifts on January sixth, the Feast of the Epiphany. Children would hang up stockings the night before, and in the morning they would be filled with oranges, chestnuts, coins, candy, or small toys—or coal, if the child was naughty, like you, and talked on the phone when they should have been paying attention to the icy roads."

"The driving age must be pretty low in Italy," Jeremy remarked. "I've never heard of La Befana."

"I read somewhere once that La Befana means the Christmas Witch, although she wasn't a witch in the stories Nonna told me and the other grandkids. Legend tells that long ago, La Befana was busy with her housework when the three Wise Men knocked on her door and explained they were searching for the newborn child who would become the King of Kings. They asked for her help and invited her to join them on their journey, but she was skeptical and sent them on their way, declaring that she had floors to sweep and dishes to wash."

"Talk about a missed opportunity."

"Yes, she eventually figured that out. Later, maybe after folding laundry and dusting lost their charm, she had second thoughts. She tried to catch up to the Wise Men and help them find baby Jesus, but they were long gone. So instead she gave gifts to all the children she could find, hoping that one of them was the child Jesus. Every year she resumes her search, leaving gifts for little Italian boys and girls along the way."

"So instead of a fat man in a red suit, you have a confused old woman who thinks the baby Jesus was born in Italy. Didn't the Wise Men mention that they were heading for Jerusalem?"

"You're ruining my Nonna's story for me, you know."

She could tell he was grinning when he said, "I didn't mean to."

"Sure." Suddenly Anna heard noises on the other side of the partition, the sounds of furniture being moved across the parquet dance floor. "Listen, I have to go. Drive safely, okay?"

"If you insist. Talk to you later."

"Okay." She hung up the phone and left the classroom to see who had joined her in the ballroom, only to find Matt and Joe moving tables from one of the classrooms closer to the fireplace, setting up for the quilting bee. She offered to help, but they assured her they had everything under control, so she returned to the classroom to finish her quilt block for the cornucopia, wondering what she would do with it after the ceremony. Traditional piecework wasn't really her thing, so she doubted her Best Friend block was the first of enough to make a full quilt.

She had just finished pressing the completed block when her cell phone vibrated, buzzing loudly on the folding chair where she had left it. Jeremy had sent her a text: "Maybe one of these years, Santa could bring La Befana a good map."

He was the only person she knew who texted with perfect grammar and spelling. "Don't text and drive!" she fired back, smiling as she returned the phone to her back pocket. She put away her sewing things and returned to the kitchen, where Sarah, Gretchen, and Sarah's mother, Carol, were busily preparing their dishes for the potluck feast. Anna thanked Sarah for keeping an eye on her ginger pumpkin bisque, which had simmered to perfection in her absence.

Sometimes it was okay to let things simmer untended. Some flavors took time to develop and rushing a dish to completion would ruin it. The best chefs, like the best quilters, cultivated creativity and patience—even when they didn't want to.

BEFORE LONG GWEN arrived, and her cheerful announcement that the storm might worsen so much that they would all have to spend the night in the manor did nothing to lessen Anna's fears about what Jeremy might face on the turnpike. Soon Sylvia, Diane, and Agnes joined them, and Anna tried to put visions of car accidents out of her mind as the Elm Creek Quilters settled down in the ballroom to spend the rest of the morning quilting. She had finished half of the six-pointed stars she planned for Jeremy's gift when her cell phone vibrated in her pocket again. "Brrr!!!!" Jeremy had texted.

Fortunately, she was at the ironing board with her back to her friends, so she could discreetly slip out of their conversation and text him a reply: "I told you not to text and drive!"

"I'm not driving," he promptly texted back. "I stopped for gas and a cup of coffee. It's brutal out here."

She felt a pang of worry, but she breezily replied, "I warned you but you went anyway. Don't complain to me. Tell it to Summer if you want some sympathy."

She didn't know why she wrote it and she regretted it the moment she pushed Send. But it was too late. The message had been sent. She waited an anxious few minutes for his reply, and when it came, her heart thudded in her chest.

"I'd rather tell it to you," he had written.

After a moment's pause, she sent back a single question mark, their code for a request for further explanation. When twenty minutes passed without a reply, she decided he had left the gas station and was on the road again, for once taking her advice and keeping his hands on the wheel instead of his phone.

All through the morning and potluck lunch, Anna wondered what Jeremy had meant by his last, cryptic text. Why would he rather write to Anna than to Summer? Did he mean that he preferred Anna on this specific occasion because she could always tease him out of a bad mood? Or did he mean that Anna was the more sympathetic of the two, since she was just a friend and not as demanding as a girlfriend might be?

Or did he mean that she was the person he preferred to talk to just as a general rule?

Could that be it?

Had he, too, finally realized what had slowly dawned upon her in recent days, that even though they had never talked about it, they had become very close, closer than mere friends, and that the day hadn't begun until they greeted each other with a text across the hallway that separated their two apartments, that the day didn't feel properly concluded until that last, late-night goodnight phone call? Had he finally noticed that he spent more of his time and attention upon the friend who happened to be a girl than his girlfriend, and had he begun to ask himself what that meant? Was he really so unaware of what Anna felt when they sat at her kitchen table sampling a new dessert she had created, when they rode side by side in his car cracking jokes about corrupt politicians and so-bad-they-were-good movies? Had he not figured out that she repeatedly turned down Sylvia's invitations to move into a comfortable suite in the manor, with no rent to pay and easy access to the kitchen of her dreams, because she would miss him if he weren't living right across the hall? Did he not suspect, as she did, that he had begun describing them as "good friends" so often and so emphatically because he was afraid that he had begun to feel more for her than that?

She didn't know. At that moment he was on his way to see Summer despite the storm, and that said a lot. But, as he himself had admitted, he would rather talk to her.

He was concerned about hurting Summer. So was Anna. She didn't like to think of herself as someone who would steal a friend's boyfriend, but Summer had been pulling away from Jeremy for months, beginning with the day last spring when she had moved out of his apartment and into the manor. Moving to Chicago and discouraging him from visiting too often seemed, to Anna at least, another way to distance herself. But Jeremy was determined to make it work, even though he surely had feelings for Anna, feelings that she only now could admit that she shared.

Didn't he?

Maybe he did, Anna thought as she sat at the sewing machine feeding blue and gold pieces of fabric beneath the blur of the needle, trying unsuccessfully to drown out the voices in her head with its industrious clatter. Maybe he did have feelings for her, but his feelings for Summer were stronger. Maybe he did, but he doubted Anna felt the same. Maybe he did, but he cherished their friendship so much that he wouldn't jeopardize it for anything, even the chance for something more, something deeper.

Anna would never know unless they talked about it, and Jeremy was probably halfway to Chicago and his girlfriend, as inconveniently out of reach as he could possibly be. A heart-to-heart talk would have to wait for his return.

Resigned, Anna resolved not to think about Jeremy and to instead lose herself in the enjoyment of her friends' company. It was difficult not to think of him, though, when every stitch she put into her quilt was another stitch for him.

Later Bonnie called from Hawaii to wish her fellow Elm Creek Quilters a happy Thanksgiving and to share in their celebration of their quilter's holiday. Then Diane abruptly announced that she intended to head for home before the storm worsened, rushing off before any of them could convince her to stay. Everyone wanted to be with the people they loved at the holidays, Anna thought wistfully as she heard the distant, muffled sound of Diane's car starting in the parking lot behind the manor. She wondered if anyone would ever love her so much that he would brave a snowstorm to be by her side. If anyone did, she suddenly realized, she wouldn't want him to take the risk. She would want him to stay where he was safe and warm and happy, even if that meant greater loneliness for herself.

Jeremy loved Summer, and Anna knew it. She should hide her feelings and let them sort things out on their own. If Jeremy and Summer weren't meant to be, they would figure it out eventually and part ways, but Anna couldn't be the wedge that drove them apart.

Jeremy probably thought of her as no more than a friend anyway.

She deliberately shoved all thoughts of him out of her mind and rejoined the quilting party chat—just as her cell phone vibrated in her back pocket, startling her so much that she almost leapt out of her chair. She stammered an apology to her friends and read Jeremy's text: "This was a bad idea."

"What?" she quickly texted back. "Driving in a blizzard? Texting while driving?"

A pause, and then a reply: "Are you saying you don't want any more texts from me?"

"You know that's not what I meant," she texted back. "And don't dodge the question."

Again she waited, but he didn't write back.

He confounded her thoughts. He made her happy and anxious, content and worried, at peace and yet embattled with her own feelings. With a sudden rush of dismay, she realized that she had quite accidentally fallen in love with him—and in the worst fashion, unrequited and unwanted. Unless . . . unless it wasn't.

As the afternoon passed, Anna moved from sewing machine to fireside to cutting table, joining in her friends' discussion of pregnancy symptoms, the Christmas Boutique at Sylvia's church, and the best layout for the Master Quilter's lovely Star of the Magi blocks. All the while her thoughts were on Jeremy, wondering if she should tell him how she felt, and if so, what she would say, or if pouring out her heart to him would only make things worse.

The phone rang on the fireplace mantel. Instinctively Anna reached for her cell even though the manor's cordless phone sounded nothing like hers, which was on silent in her pocket. She shook her head, exasperated with herself. Could she be any more of a mess, jumping at the ringing of a phone, analyzing Jeremy's every casual phrase for deeper meaning?

Summer was on the line, calling to wish everyone a belated happy Thanksgiving and an enjoyable quilter's holiday, although it sounded as if she had been too busy to celebrate with any quilting that day. She wouldn't find any more time once Jeremy arrived, Anna thought with a sudden jolt of jealous misery. As Gwen cheerfully took the phone to the other side of the ballroom to enjoy a private chat with her daughter,

Anna settled back down at the sewing machine, wishing that she had caught a ride home with Diane. She no longer wanted to finish Jeremy's gift or share the company of her friends but to hide away in her own small apartment with a good book, a comforting quilt, and a pan of dark-chocolate cappuccino brownies.

Her back to her friends as she worked at the sewing machine, she blocked out the rest of the party as well as she could, but she couldn't help noticing when Sylvia took the phone from Gwen. She hoped they wouldn't pass the phone around or put Summer on speaker as they had done with Bonnie when she had called from Hawaii. Anna liked Summer and hated herself for envying a friend who had never been anything but thoughtful and generous to her, but she couldn't bear to hear Summer tell one and all how happy she was, awaiting her boyfriend's arrival.

She tried to close her ears to Sylvia's voice, but suddenly a telling phrase cut through: "I'm so sorry. I've clearly ruined Jeremy's surprise."

Anna brought her sewing machine to an abrupt halt and turned in her chair to find

Sylvia shooting her a look of utter dismay. Sylvia shook her head and shrugged, and baffled, Anna mirrored the gesture. Jeremy's surprise? What surprise? Hadn't Jeremy— Had he really gone to Chicago without—

"I'm sure you'll be glad to see him," Sylvia continued, her voice suggesting a profound lack of certainty. She offered a few hesitant pleasantries about how Summer and Jeremy would surely have a lovely weekend, even if all they did was study, but Anna barely heard a word of it. Mechanically, she rose and left the ballroom for the grand foyer, crossing the black marble floor as she took her cell phone from her pocket, coming to a stop at one of the two tall windows flanking the front double doors, pressing her free hand and forehead to the cold glass, the sound of wind filling her ears.

She waited, but before common sense could catch up with her whirling thoughts, she dialed Jeremy's number.

He picked up almost immediately. "Hey, Anna. Did you call to scold me about texting while driving or to entertain me with another holiday story?"

"Neither," she said numbly. "I know why you called me instead of Summer."

"What are you talking about?"

"You don't prefer to talk to me. You just couldn't call Summer without her figuring out that you're on your way."

Jeremy was silent so long Anna thought the connection had broken. "Anna, I wouldn't call you if I didn't like to talk to you. You're my best friend in Waterford. Maybe my best friend anywhere."

She laughed shortly, tearfully. Yes, that's what she was, a friend. It's all she would ever be to him. "Why didn't you tell Summer you were coming to see her?"

"I wanted it to be a surprise."

Maybe the other Elm Creek Quilters would believe that, but Anna didn't, and she doubted Summer would either. "This is me, Jeremy. Are you sure that's the story you want to go with?"

"If you know why I didn't tell her," said Jeremy, his voice rising in agitation, "why ask?"

"Because I want to hear it from you."

"I didn't tell her because I thought she'd ask me not to come."

"Then why would you go to her? Why would you drive hundreds of miles through a storm to be with someone who doesn't want you, when someone who does want you is right here?"

She regretted the words as soon as she spoke them.

"Anna." Jeremy's voice was almost drowned out by the storm just beyond the windowpane. "What are you trying to say?"

"Nothing," said Anna quickly, and again regretted her words. "No, wait. There's something. When you come back—"

"What?"

"I can't be your fallback girl anymore."

"My what? What are you talking about?"

"I can't be that girl you call and text and spend time with because you can't be with your girlfriend. I can't be that loyal best friend you ditch when the woman you prefer decides to pay attention to you. I was okay with that for a long time, but now it hurts too much, and I need to back off."

"Anna, that's not fair. I've never ditched you for Summer. Ever. If anything, I spend more time with you than with her."

"Exactly." Anna shivered in the cold and

stepped away from the window. "Shouldn't that be telling you something?"

"It tells me that you're my friend and I care about you. I don't understand why you want to bail on our entire friendship just because—" He sighed, frustrated. "I don't know, because you think I'm keeping you in reserve in case it doesn't work out with Summer. Is that what you think?"

"Something like that, yes."

"What does that say about me, that you think I treat people like that? That I would treat you, of all people, like that?"

"That's not really the issue. I'm not questioning your character."

"Actually, you kind of are."

Anna sat down heavily on one of the marble steps. "Jeremy, don't turn this around. This isn't about your insult and injury."

"Then what is it about? I don't understand why you're doing this. You don't want to be my friend anymore because I have a girlfriend? That doesn't make any sense. If one of your women friends had a boyfriend, would you stop being her friend?"

"It's not the same."

"How is it not the same?"

"I'm not in love with any of my women friends."

There was a long pause. Anna frantically searched for something to say to put a different spin on her words so they would mean anything other than what she had all too clearly said, but nothing, nothing came to mind.

"Anna—"

"I've got to go," she said, rising from the step.

"Anna, wait—"

"Drive safely, okay? Good-bye, Jeremy."

She hung up the phone, flooded with a painful sense of loss. She had ended the most important, fulfilling friendship of her life, all because she didn't think she could bear being a friend and nothing more. How would she feel in the weeks and months and years to come, when she would be even less than that?

She pressed a hand to her lips, blinking back tears. He'd expected a scolding and had hoped for a holiday story, and instead she'd blindsided him. It had felt necessary, but was it right? Couldn't she have learned to accept her limited place in his life—and was it really limited, considering all they shared? Why reject what they could have because it couldn't be everything she wanted?

She took a deep, shaky breath. It didn't matter. If she called him back to tell him she'd made a terrible mistake, that she'd spoken without thinking, that she wanted to be friends, he might forgive her and agree, but he would still know how she truly felt. Awkwardness would fill the spaces between them, the discrepancy in their feelings obliging them to tread carefully and measure their words. The days of their easy companionability were behind them, and she did not know what, if anything, they could move toward.

Jeremy had wanted another holiday tale. She could have told him a different version of the legend of La Befana, a variation on the charming children's tale Nonna had saved until Anna had grown old enough to fully grasp it. In that other, starker account, La Befana was a young mother who lived in Judea in the days of King Herod. When the Three Wise Men's search for the infant Jesus led them to Bethlehem and they told the king of their quest, Herod ordered the execution of all children under the age of two rather than risk losing his throne to the newborn usurper. La Befana's son was among the holy innocents murdered. Devastated, she could not accept that her son was dead but gathered his belongings in a sack and went out in search of him. Grief aged her overnight, stooping her back, graying her hair, wrinkling her skin. At last she found a baby boy so poor he slept in a manger, and to Him, the infant Jesus, she gave her son's possessions. Every year since, the grief-stricken woman would resume her journey, offering gifts to other children, caring for them as she longed to care for her own lost child.

The merriment of every holiday story seemed tempered by loss. The miracle of Hanukkah had followed war and the defilement of the Temple; the gifts of La Befana had begun as the outpouring of nurturing love from a grieving mother. Anna's loss was not as great as these and some good would yet come of it, though she ached when she thought of the void Jeremy's absence from her life would leave.

Heavy hearted, she turned away from the entrance to the ballroom and sat down on the bottom step of the oak staircase, trying to will her sadness away, to compose herself before returning to the gathering of friends. Their warmth and laughter suddenly seemed as remote to her as Jeremy had become, thanks to a single decision that she already regretted. Every minute that passed put more than miles between them.

CHAPTER FIVE

Gretchen

GRETCHEN DIDN'T MEAN to eavesdrop, but it was impossible not to overhear Sylvia's conversation with Summer and to deduce that Summer was displeased by the news of Jeremy's surprise visit. Gretchen wondered if someone—Anna, perhaps, since she was his closest friend among them—ought to warn him that he might not receive a cordial welcome.

As the newest Elm Creek Quilter, Gretchen scarcely knew Summer, who had participated in Gretchen's job interview but had left for graduate school only a few weeks after Gretchen and her husband,

Joe, had moved into the manor. Gretchen had no idea how long the two had been dating, but she believed that they had lived together for a time, until some disagreement or another had compelled Summer to move out of Jeremy's apartment. She wondered how any young couple could rebound and resume a normal dating relationship after living together, but she had seen couples with extraordinary devotion overcome even greater obstacles. She wasn't sure, however, if Summer and Jeremy were one of these. They were both delightful young people, but that didn't mean they were perfectly matched.

She and Joe, on the other hand—well, she could not have found a better, more loyal, or more loving husband if she had submitted a list of the qualities she most admired to the Lord above and had him made to order. They had met at church when Gretchen was an aspiring teacher, two years into a home economics and elementary education program at a small college that had awarded her a scholarship; Joe a machinist at an Ambridge steel mill outside Pittsburgh. He was a wonderful dancer, polite and respectful to her parents, and handsome enough to inspire envy in all but her closest friends, who loved her so much that her happiness was their own. On their wedding day, she had considered herself the luckiest woman alive, and after forty-six years of marriage she still believed that, even though life had not turned out as she had expected.

Their newlywed years had begun promisingly enough. Gretchen earned her degree and found a job teaching at a Catholic primary school, and she supplemented her modest income and Joe's wages by picking up occasional housecleaning work from the same family that had employed her mother and grandmother as domestic help. Joe was too proud to bear this easily, so he worked long hours and accepted as much overtime as he could, determined to have Gretchen end her association with the privileged family that had employed hers for three generations. Inevitably, as soon as the couple got a little bit ahead, the car broke down or the furnace went out or the roof needed to be repaired, so they committed themselves to frugality and found their happiness within each other, hopeful that more prosperous times would come their way.

But all their hopes were shattered on the morning Gretchen's principal came to her classroom and somberly informed her about a terrible accident at the steel mill. Joe had been taken to Allegheny General Hospital, unconscious and with a broken back. He was not expected to live.

When Joe survived that first night and woke the next morning with no memory of the steel beam that had pinned him to the floor for an hour before his friends could free him, Gretchen deliberately ignored the doctors' grim predictions that he would never walk again. Trusted friends urged Gretchen to convince Joe to accept the doctors' diagnosis rather than encourage false hope, but Gretchen refused. Let the rest of the world condemn him to a wheelchair; she would believe in him. Joe needed her to believe in him.

In the long, slow, painful months of his recovery, Gretchen quit her job so she could stay home to care for him. Their modest savings quickly disappeared, but Gretchen made ends meet on a small monthly stipend from Joe's union. And, against Joe's wishes, she convinced her former employer to hire her on permanently as a housecleaner on Saturday mornings, when she could arrange for a neighbor to check in on Joe from time to time.

Gretchen knew Joe blamed himself for the misfortune that had forced her to give up teaching, which she loved, for back-breaking labor in the home of a spoiled princess of a woman who felt entitled to Gretchen's loyal service thanks to their intertwined family histories, but Gretchen didn't blame him. It was an accident of fate, no one's fault, but he refused to see it that way, and instead redoubled his efforts to recuperate. Within months he could sit up in bed unassisted, and soon after that he could move from the bed to the chair on his own; within a year, he could stand. From the kitchen below she would hear him attempting slow, shuffling steps across the bedroom floor above, but she resisted the temptation to dash upstairs to watch, knowing his pride would suffer. For Joe, it was bad enough that she had to work to support them, a fact of their married life they accepted but did not discuss. If he did not want her to watch him struggle to walk, she would leave him alone until he was ready.

But their limited means and his limited mobility meant an end to Saturday night dances and Sunday matinees with friends. Instead, they entertained themselves in the evenings by listening to the radio or reading aloud to each other. Most often, Joe would read aloud while Gretchen quilted. His voice, as strong and deep as before the accident, comforted her, and the piecework drew her attention from the shabby furniture, her made-over dresses, the diminishment of their expectations, the loneliness and isolation of their lives. Gretchen's scrap quilts brought warmth and beauty into their home, allowing them to turn the thermostat a little lower or to conceal a sagging mattress and threadbare sofa cushions. She quilted to add softness and color to her hard, muted life, to give purpose to her hours, and to distract her from the unfairness of fate.

Although Joe defied his doctors' expectations and learned to walk again, he never fully recovered his old strength, and any accidental jolt made him grimace from pain. Eventually he had no choice but to abandon his plans to return to his old job, his old life. For many long, bleak months he sank into depression, but Gretchen refused to go down with him. Since Joe no longer needed her constant attention, she found a new job as a substitute teacher, and while it was not steady work, it helped pay off some debts and got her out of the house.

Eventually, impressed by his wife's indomitable resolve and intrigued by the solace she found in creating objects of comfort and beauty, Joe took up refurbishing old furniture when a chance discovery of a broken antique rocking chair inspired him to fix it and sell it for a twenty-dollar profit. Next he restored a bureau and matching chest purchased for a few dollars at a yard sale, and sold both to a shop in Sewickley, netting fifty dollars. Within months, neighbors and strangers alike frequently stopped by the garage to browse through the finished pieces on display or to schedule an appointment to drop off worn or damaged furniture for him to refurbish. Joe made a sign and hung it above the entrance to the garage: JOSEPH

HARTLEY: FINE FURNITURE REPAIRED AND RESTORED. He worked when he felt able, resting when the strain on his back and legs became too much. He taught himself cabinet making and woodworking from library books and soon began designing and building his own original pieces.

As his reputation grew, Joe took on almost more work than he could handle, but he set everything aside upon receiving a special request from Gretchen's grandmother. Her church, a Croatian parish in Pittsburgh, needed a skilled restorer to repair ornate cabinetry in the sacristy, someone who knew how to properly care for the old wood but who wouldn't cost them a fortune. Joe promptly accepted the job free of charge, which delighted Gretchen's grandmother and prompted her to exclaim that Gretchen had married "a treasure."

"He'll make a wonderful father someday," she told Gretchen privately, patting her arm affectionately. Gretchen could only smile and agree that she thought he would, too. She didn't add that she and Joe had been trying again, having postponed starting a family during Joe's long convalescence, but month after month, the blessing of a child was denied them. Gretchen ached to hold a child of her own, but she had begun to fear that she never would.

The repairs in the sacristy of Holy Family Catholic Church took Joe several weeks, and whenever Gretchen had a day off from teaching, she would spend the morning with her grandmother and bring Joe a sack lunch to share at noon. One day, when the restoration was nearly complete, the pastor, Monsignor Paul, examined Joe's work thoughtfully before remarking that he knew of another worthy organization that could benefit from his talents. "They won't be able to pay," the priest told him frankly, "but you're a faithful steward of your talents, and I think you'll find the work has other rewards."

Gretchen knew Joe was eager to resume his paid work, but he could hardly refuse the monsignor's request when phrased in such terms. He quit work early for the day so the priest could escort him to the other site, a few blocks away. Gretchen accompanied them, and as they left her grandmother's neighborhood, the small but well-kept bungalows gave way to row houses in disrepair—broken windows, trash in the gutters, graffiti on walls and telephone polls, crumbling stoops leading to front doors boarded up with plywood, children in tattered clothing playing unattended in the alleys. Gretchen remembered her grandmother remarking that the neighborhoods surrounding hers had "gone downhill" in recent years, but she had not expected so dramatic a decline. Nor had she expected the monsignor to lead them to a three-story Victorian house with peeling paint and a front yard entirely taken up by a vegetable garden and a rusty swing set. An elderly white man pushing a shopping cart stuffed full of discarded bottles and newspapers and a thin African-American woman a few years younger than Gretchen browsed through two card tables set up in the driveway, one stacked with canned goods, the other with used clothing. A neat, hand-painted sign above the front door announced that they had arrived at Abiding Savior Christian Outreach.

As the monsignor knocked on the front door, Gretchen and Joe exchanged a wary look behind his back, but they both quickly masked their feelings when the door swung open to reveal a barrel-chested African-American man in a brightly colored tunic, black slacks, and sandals. "Good to see you, Father," he greeted the monsignor before his gaze lit upon the Hartleys. "I see you brought some company. What a pleasure."

"This is the man I told you about," Monsignor Paul said, resting his hand on Joe's shoulder. "Joe Hartley, the carpenter who's restoring our sacristy so beautifully. This is his wife, Gretchen. Gretchen and Joe, I'd like you to meet Louis Walker, my good friend and a true servant of Christ."

"I'm glad you can help us," said Louis in a deep voice flavored with a Southern accent, shaking Joe's hand and then Gretchen's. He beckoned them to follow him inside, into a small front room with shabby sofas and chairs lining the walls and a table covered in parenting magazines in the center. Upstairs an infant squalled, and from somewhere closer but yet unseen came the voices of young women engaged in heated conversation punctuated by laughter. The floorboards creaked beneath worn carpeting as Gretchen trailed after the men, past a dining room with a long table set with at least a dozen mismatched chairs and into a kitchen where the smells of fried chicken, scorched oil, and boiled greens lingered in the air.

"You can see the problem right here," said Louis, rapping on the door to a cabinet under the sink. "The folks who owned the place before us knew how to cut corners better than they cut wood."

Even Gretchen could see that the cabinet doors were too large and banged into each other rather than closing properly. A quick glance around confirmed that all of the other cupboards were similarly poorly constructed. Joe tested the door of the nearest cabinet and could open it only a third of the way because the hinges had been set too far from the edge.

Joe looked around, shaking his head. "All of these doors need to be replaced."

"That's a little out of our operating budget," Louis replied dryly. "Any way you can fix these so they hang right and shut tight enough to keep the mice out?"

Joe ran a hand over his jaw, considering. "I could remove them, sand 'em down, and reset the hinges, but I think you're going to need all new hardware. Most of these are rusted through."

"One of my parishioners has a son who owns a hardware store," said Monsignor Paul. "I could probably arrange a donation if you tell me what you need."

"Let me look around and I'll make a list," said Joe. "But I don't need to wait for the hinges to take care of the sanding. I can start as soon as I finish the work at Holy Family."

Gretchen hung back as Louis and Joe discussed the project while the priest looked on in satisfaction. At the sound of voices, she scooted out of the doorway just as three teenage girls, one in the later stages of pregnancy, one carrying an infant, burst into the kitchen chatting and teasing one another. Their demeanor became more reserved at the sight of the priest, whom they greeted respectfully, but lightened when they saw Louis.

"What you girls up to?" Louis asked. "Shouldn't you be studying?"

"We finished," piped up the smallest of the three, an African-American girl who wore her hair in tight cornrows with red beads on the ends. She looked to be about fifteen, Gretchen thought, trying not to stare at her rounded abdomen.

Louis's eyebrows rose. "What's your teacher going to say when I tell her you got all that work done in an hour?"

The girl carrying the baby glanced at her companions and shifted the baby to her shoulder, patting her gently on the back. "What Alicia meant was that we're *almost* done. We're going to go over our math problems one more time. We were just taking a break."

"Uh-huh," said Louis, skeptical.

The third girl, her thin blond hair slipping out of its braid in wisps, avoided Joe's eyes as she stepped around him to take a glass from a cupboard above the stove and fill it at the sink. Her tummy bore only the slightest tell-tale bulge but worry had already carved a notch between her brows.

Abiding Savior Christian Outreach, Gretchen realized, was a home for girls in trouble, as her grandmother might have phrased it. She wondered where the girls' parents were, where the fathers of their children were.

"What time do we eat?" Alicia asked, reaching for the refrigerator handle.

"Five o'clock, same as every day," said Louis, his warning look enough to prompt her to reluctantly release the door. "If we let them eat between meals, there isn't enough left for meals," he explained after the girls each helped themselves to a drink of water at the sink and left the kitchen. "My wife portions things out so that everyone gets an equal share, adjusted for how far along they are, of course, and she makes sure that everyone eats plenty of vegetables whether they like 'em or not."

"How many girls stay with you here?" Gretchen asked.

"Only six at the moment. Usually we have about ten. Most we've ever had is the most we can fit, twenty."

"Where do they come from?"

"Pittsburgh, mostly," said Louis, leaning back against the counter and folding his arms over his broad chest. "Some come to the city from small towns in Ohio and western Pennsylvania after their parents throw them out. When they end up on the streets, homeless folks and shelter workers know to send them our way."

"Their parents throw them out?" echoed Gretchen, bewildered. "So young, and—and in their condition?"

"A pregnant, unmarried daughter is a huge disappointment to some families," said Louis. "Their anger gets the better of them and they think throwing the girl out is a suitable punishment. Teach her a lesson."

"What lesson is that?" said Joe, horrified.

Louis shrugged. "If they break the rules and shame the family, it won't be under their roof. Sometimes homeless girls get pregnant. Sometimes pregnant girls get homeless."

"The lucky girls end up here," said Monsignor Joe. "The *very* lucky girls marry the fathers of their babies and go on to live good lives."

"He has to say that," said Louis, tossing the priest a wry glance. "Marriage works for some of these young mothers, but it's not always the best solution for our residents."

The monsignor spread his hands as if to suggest that they had long ago agreed to disagree. "The lucky girls end up here," he repeated, "where Louis sees that they have a safe place to stay, enough to eat, medical care, and parenting classes."

Gretchen, who longed for a child of her own, could not imagine throwing a precious daughter out into the world in so vulnerable a state. "Do the girls—your residents—do they give up their babies for adoption?"

"Some of them do," Louis acknowledged, "but we try to teach them to be good mothers so they can care for their children right themselves, keep them. If they don't want to or can't, well, there aren't a lot of places for these babies to go, you understand."

Gretchen nodded wordlessly, thinking of the young mothers little more than children themselves, taking parenting classes to learn what they had probably been unable to observe in their own childhood homes. She wondered about the tables set up in the driveway, the garden plot in the front yard, and she suspected that Louis Walker ministered to a wider community than the young expectant mothers who had found shelter beneath his roof.

In the weeks to come, the stories Joe brought home from Abiding Savior Christian Outreach confirmed her hunch. To Joe's surprise, Louis assisted him in his work rather than leaving him to it, and Joe quickly realized that Louis wanted to learn all he could so that the next time repairs were necessary, he would not need to rely on anyone else for assistance. "The Lord provides," he told Joe, "but He's also mighty keen on self-reliance."

His Southern accent came from the state of his birth, Mississippi, where he had lived for his first eighteen years. He told Joe harrowing stories of growing up in the segregated South—the humiliating forced deference to whites, the segregated drinking fountains and entrances to buildings, the inadequate schools, the threats of violence that were too often actualized, the ramshackle houses in impoverished neighborhoods that lacked running water, streetlights, and paved roads. What chafed an outspoken youth like Louis most in those days was the lack of voice, the inability to improve his people's situation, despite their ostensible right to vote, a right they were too often prevented from exercising.

His passion for justice caught fire the first time he heard Dr. Martin Luther King, Jr., preach at his church. With inspiring eloquence, Dr. King asked them to practice nonviolent civil disobedience in order to win the civil rights that had been too long denied them. Louis marched with Dr. King, participated in Freedom Rides to challenge segregation in public transportation, and organized peaceful student protests in pursuit of equal access to education. His parents feared for his safety after he was attacked by a gang of white thugs outside a post office, and they begged him to withdraw from the movement after a cross was set aflame in their front yard, but Louis could not, would not, abandon the cause that he believed God had called him to serve.

Then one afternoon as he, his girlfriend, Alice, and his best friend, Thomas, were leading a student march through the streets of Jackson, singing protest songs to drown out the angry jeers of white folks lining the sidewalks, a gunshot went off. As the students scattered, the police swept in and arrested as many as they could apprehend on the grounds that they were marching without a permit. Louis, Thomas, and twenty other young men were taken to a maximum security prison, where they spent five nights in cells with the furnace blasting despite the sweltering summer heat, were prodded awake with billy clubs every time they drifted off to sleep on the hard concrete floor, and were force-fed laxatives. Louis emerged from the ordeal shaken but more committed than ever to the cause of justice for all.

He knew he had made enemies, but he had not counted on their bloodthirstiness, nor could he have imagined on that Saturday morning when he let Alice borrow his car to take her mother to the dentist that someone had planted a bomb beneath it, or that in an instant he would replay again and again in his nightmares for years to come, that it would kill his first love, the woman he had intended to marry, and to love and cherish and honor all the days of his life.

Anguished, he swore to find the murderers, but his younger brother begged him for their parents' sake to flee before the culprits realized they had missed their intended target. Louis packed a single bag and took the next train out of town, spending all but ten dollars to go as far from Mississippi as he could afford to go. The money in his pocket could take him as far as Pittsburgh, so that was where he went.

His ten dollars soon was spent. With no prospects and no family to take him in, Louis ended up on the streets, sleeping in doorways, taking meals at a soup kitchen, finding odd jobs where and when he could. He dared not write home to his parents out of fear that the men who had tried to kill him would track him north, or that they would take their rage out on the loved ones he had left behind.

As the hard days stretched into months, as he grew thin and bone-weary and began to wonder if maybe it would have been better to risk his life in Mississippi than to endure the harsh, friendless existence in a northern city, he prayed to God to deliver him from his misery, and he vowed that if he could get on his feet again, he would devote himself to serving others in need.

Little by little, he made his way. A minister at a Methodist church helped him find a job as a dishwasher in a restaurant and a cheap room to rent. As he regained his strength, he took classes and earned his GED. His dreams of college not forgotten, he enlisted in the Marines, served in Vietnam, and attended Duquesne University on the GI Bill, earning a degree in Social Work.

Louis never forgot how his prayers had been answered or the vow he had made. Shortly after graduation, he worked for a nonprofit organization serving the homeless in Pittsburgh, but he grew frustrated with bureaucratic obstacles that prevented immediate help for the people who needed it most and a short-sighted focus on short-term solutions instead of the more arduous task of addressing the root causes of poverty and homelessness. Conferences where well-meaning activists discussed how to fund and operate more homeless shelters irritated him. "These people don't need shelters, they need homes," he griped to a like-minded woman, Andrea, who had served with him on several committees. "Otherwise we'd call them the 'shelterless.' "

Frustrated, he severed ties with official

government agencies and went off on his own, determined to spend every cent he earned buying abandoned properties in the inner city, restoring them to habitable shape with the help of volunteers, and giving them to the people who needed them most. The restoration of a three-story Victorian house near a Croatian immigrant neighborhood was well underway when Andrea, an obstetrics nurse who volunteered at a local free clinic, alerted him to the plight of homeless expectant mothers. As soon as the bedrooms and the kitchen were finished, Louis scrounged up donated beds, mattresses, and sheets and took in the first residents. The Abiding Savior Christian Outreach ran entirely on donations, and although Louis occasionally butted heads with representatives from government agencies who preferred people to work within the system, he knew his mission made a difference in his community. Now, five years later, he and Andrea were married with two children, and he had raised enough money to purchase a four-story apartment building a few blocks away, which they intended to remodel and rent out apartments at a dollar a year to people who would otherwise have nowhere to turn. Louis had already renamed the building "Thankful Abode" in remembrance of his gratitude for prayers answered years before.

Gretchen listened, fascinated, each time Joe came home with a new tale about Louis Walker's mission, his marriage to Andrea and their children, and their plans for the future. "I told him you were a teacher," Joe said one day, "and I could almost see his ears prick up."

"Did you tell him I'm only a substitute home economics teacher?"

"There's no 'only' about it," said Joe, indignant. "You have a lot to teach those girls, and to Louis, your flexible schedule is a bonus."

A few days later, Gretchen began volunteering at the mission, teaching the young mothers and mothers-to-be how to prepare simple, nutritious meals, how to sew, how to do laundry, how to keep a house clean and safe for a toddler, how to keep a household budget and balance a bank account—something a few of the girls claimed they would never need to know, since they would never have enough cash to open a bank account, never enough left over at the end of the month to save. "You should and you shall save something for a rainy day," Gretchen told them firmly.

"Maybe that works for you," a resident told her once. "But it's always the rainy season for us."

"Except when it's snowing," another chimed in.

So Gretchen told the girls how no one had imagined a life for her other than to become a housemaid as her mother and grandmother had, but that she had worked hard in school and earned a scholarship, and now she was a teacher. "But I'm not finished," Gretchen told them. "I have other dreams, too, plans that I'm saving for, and someday I'm going to fulfill them. You can, too. Your first duty is to your child, of course, but if you work hard, live frugally, and save, you can make a better life for yourself. I can't do it for you, but I can give you the tools you'll need—and that means learning to balance a checkbook, even if you don't have a bank account yet, because someday you will."

Some of the girls still looked dubious, but they settled down to their studies, and in some of their eyes, Gretchen thought she glimpsed the light of possibility dawning.

Gretchen also taught the girls to sew, certain that every mother needed to know how to sew on buttons, patch worn trouser knees, and mend torn seams. Most of them had never held a needle before, so to practice and perfect their stitches, their first projects were small, scrap Four-Patch quilts for their babies. Even the most ambivalent about motherhood warmed to the project, and as they sewed squares of cotton and poly blends together, they spoke about their hopes and fears for the future. Andrea, passing through the cramped front room on her way to the kitchen or the office, overheard bits of their conversations, occasionally lingering in the kitchen doorway to hear a shy girl express her most private fears about what might happen to her and her baby once they left Abiding Savior. Later Andrea told Gretchen that she marveled at her ability to get the girls to share so openly. “It’s not any of my doing,” Gretchen said, embarrassed by the undeserved praise. “It’s the craft. Quilters talk when they're gathered together, even beginning quilters. They always have."

In due course, Joe finished the kitchen project and resumed the work that had been accumulating in their garage, but Gretchen continued to volunteer at Abiding Savior at least two days a week, unless she was occupied with an extended substitute teaching assignment within the public schools. The girls Gretchen observed in the classrooms and passed in the halls were, for the most part, happy and well-adjusted, with plenty to eat, decent clothes to wear, and a caring adult at home to love and guide them. And yet she knew that some of the residents of Abiding Savior had possessed all the outward trappings of comfortable, secure, middle-class lives before they had ended up on the streets, and she wondered which of the girls who attended her classes and always turned in their homework felt unloved at home and contemplated escape through running away or through fleeting affection in the back seat of a boyfriend's car.

A world away at Abiding Savior, she taught the young mothers domestic skills and held their newborn babies when they were desperate for a few uninterrupted hours of sleep. Often, frightened and alone when the first labor pains began, they begged Gretchen to come with them to the hospital and stay with them until it was over, their babies in their arms. In the evenings at home with Joe, Gretchen would stitch quilts for new residents, gifts of love and comfort they would use during their stay at the mission and take with them when they departed, requiring the continuous replenishment of her supply. As the years passed, she saw many young women come and go, taking the quilts she had made them and their few belongings, their babies swaddled in bright quilts they had made with her guidance. But always they left, the difficult young women who balked when she tried to teach them to cook, the acquiescent ones whom she feared might need the outreach center's services again within a year, the babies who squalled all night and left all the residents weary, the sweet ones whose adorable smiles belied their circumstances.

"Doesn't it ever make you too sad to go back?" Joe asked one evening when she told him about a young woman who had been working the streets but had sought sanctuary at Abiding Savior when her pimp beat her for getting pregnant. Two days after delivering a stillborn baby boy, she had fled into the night, taking nothing with her but a few dollars' worth of change kept in a jar in the kitchen.

"Most of their stories don't end so tragically," Gretchen said, thinking of how she and Andrea had held each other in the kitchen and cried when they realized the girl was gone, most likely reunited with her pimp and back working the streets.

"I know," Joe said, "but day after day, meeting all these girls who never wanted babies, and in the meantime, you and I . . ."

His voice trailed off, and Gretchen reached for his hand and held it. Yes, in her more selfish moments, she wondered why God had blessed those frightened youngsters with children and withheld them from her and Joe, but then she thought of the many, many babies she had rocked to sleep at the mission, how many bowls of rice cereal she had mixed and diapers she had changed, how many young women she had consoled and advised, and she could not consider her life empty or herself barren. She had loved so many children, and she was thankful for every life it had been her privilege to touch.

Every Christmas, the parishioners of Holy Family treated the residents of Abiding Savior to a celebration rich with the flavors of their Croatian traditions. Monsignor Paul would have a pair of young men of the parish haul a *badnjak*, or yule log, to the outreach center, which he would sprinkle with holy water as they set it in the fireplace, reciting a prayer of blessing for the household. Louis and his eldest sons would set up a small Christmas tree in the front room, which the ladies of the parish would adorn with *licitarska srca,* gingerbread hearts decorated with colored frosting. On Christmas Eve, Gretchen's grandmother or one of her friends would give the residents a round pastry called a *krstnica,* a cake inscribed with a cross adorned with a pastry bird at the end and a hole in the center into which a candle was placed. Gretchen, who had heard her grandmother explain the symbols many times, would tell the residents that the cake represented the world;

the cross, redemption; the candle, Christ as the light of the world; the four birds, the Four Evangelists, Matthew, Mark, Luke, and John. The residents always wanted to know why they had to keep the cake on the table and not eat it until the first day of the New Year, but Gretchen's grandmother had never given her any reason other than it was tradition. Although not all the residents of Abiding Savior were Catholic, Monsignor Paul encouraged everyone to celebrate Midnight Mass at the church, and afterward, the women of the parish served a favorite traditional meal of baked ham, *kolbassi,* potato salad, horseradish, nut roll, and cookies. They sprinkled straw beneath the table to remind everyone of Jesus's humble manger, a tradition that never failed to amuse the girls.

On Christmas morning, thanks to the generosity of the parish, the residents enjoyed sweet, flavorful apple strudel for breakfast and gifts beneath the Christmas tree. But despite all the merriment, Gretchen sometimes detected wistful longing in some of the girls' eyes, as if they were missing their families or remembering the Christmases of their childhoods, as they were or should have been. She offered these girls extra hugs and a shoulder to cry on, if they needed it, or time alone away from the festivities if that was what they preferred. But for the most part, the holidays offered the girls a welcome respite from the cares of ordinary days, a time when they could enjoy luscious treats and joyful music, prayers and the warmth of the fireside. Winter would settle in around them soon enough, but the spirit of Christmas held it at bay for a little while.

Over time, perhaps because Abiding Savior reminded Gretchen daily of how richly she and Joe had been blessed despite the hardships they had faced, the hope and optimism of their newlywed years gradually returned. Gretchen began teaching quilting to neighborhood girls, their mothers, and then to their mothers' friends as a quilting revival swept the nation. She traveled to quilt guilds in Ohio, West Virginia, and throughout Pennsylvania to lecture and teach, and—as she had hinted to the young residents in her first weeks at Abiding Savior—she nurtured a dream of opening a quilt shop. Eventually she fulfilled a version of that dream, obliged by economic necessity to go into business with her on-again, off-again housecleaning employer. They enjoyed a long, successful run until her partner's unquenchable need to have her own way in everything tarnished Gretchen's dream—and then, just as she was wondering how she could keep her chin up and make the best of it indefinitely, she spotted a quarter-page ad in *Quilter's Newsletter Magazine* announcing that Elm Creek Quilts needed two new teachers to join their accomplished circle of quilters.

What a lovely, enchanted place Elm Creek Quilt Camp had seemed to Gretchen five years before when she and her partner had visited, although their trip was more of a spy mission than a vacation. Gretchen's business partner had heard about the marvelous success of the Elm Creek Quilters and was toying with the idea of creating a similar quilters' retreat in Sewickley. Gretchen had enjoyed her week at quilt camp tremendously, but she was neither surprised nor disappointed when her partner had concluded that they could not possibly reproduce the Elm Creek Quilters' achievement. "If I had inherited an enormous mansion in the middle of the countryside, I could do it, too," Gretchen's partner grumbled as they drove home. Gretchen refrained from pointing out that she had indeed inherited something very much like it, along with an impressive trust fund. What she lacked was a group of close quilting friends she could rely upon to help run the business as Sylvia had in the Elm Creek Quilters.

How wonderful it would be, Gretchen thought wistfully, to become one of the lucky applicants invited to join that elite circle of quilters. Well, why couldn't she? The more she considered the idea, the more she realized that the job had come along at precisely the right time and could be an answer to her prayers. She could leave the tarnished dream of the quilt shop shared with an unbearable partner and yet remain at the center of the quilting world. The ad mentioned that a live-in arrangement within the manor was possible, which would fulfill Joe's fond wish of retiring to the country. The estate was large enough that they could surely find a place for him to set up a woodworking shop—perhaps in the caretaker's red barn between the manor and the orchard.

But moving would mean leaving behind cherished friends and their home of several decades—and the end of Gretchen's days at Abiding Savior.

As much as it pained her to think of leaving, she assembled her application packet with her résumé, letters of recommendation from favorite quilting students, sample lesson plans, and photographs of her very best quilts. She murmured a prayer as she took them to the post office and sent them to Elm Creek Manor. Six weeks later, Sarah called to invite her for an interview, and before she knew it, she was offered the job.

It was a dream come true, a prayer answered, and yet she could not move away from Ambridge without regret.

As the summer ended and moving day approached, Gretchen prepared herself for her last day at Abiding Savior, for tearful good-byes and promises to keep in touch, and for photographs with Louis, Andrea, and their children. Joe planned to take the day off to accompany her and offer moral support as well as to offer his own farewells. Gretchen took comfort from the assurances of a former resident, now a teacher herself, who had promised to take over Gretchen's responsibilities and enlist the help of other teachers from her district to carry on her unfinished endeavors. Still, even though it comforted Gretchen to know that she was not leaving Louis understaffed, she expected her last day at Abiding Savior to be bittersweet.

What Gretchen had not expected was to round the corner and see the front porch, yard, and driveway filled with women and children, a richly diverse palette of skin tones, their ages spanning twenty years, accompanied by children of all ages. It was, she realized as they greeted her warmly, a reunion of former Abiding Savior residents whom she had taught through the years.

Overwhelmed, she listened as they told the stories of their lives after they had departed the mission, the trials they had faced and hardships they had overcome thanks in no small measure to Gretchen and all she had taught them. "You were the first person who ever believed I could make something of myself," Alicia told her, a sentiment that Gretchen was to hear again and again throughout the day. "When you believed it, I was able to believe it."

Later, when he caught her alone, Joe noted the surprising number of teachers in the group, all of whom claimed Gretchen as their inspiration. His face beamed with pride as he kissed her. At the end of the celebration, her former students presented her with a beautiful Album quilt, each block signed with a heartfelt message of gratitude for all she had done for them when they were most alone and in need.

Gretchen stammered out her thanks and tried to explain that they were praising her too much. All she had done was to spare a few hours a week to support the mission Louis had begun. Everyone teased her good-naturedly and assured her that they knew how much of herself she had given to them even if she didn't, and she deserved every expression of their thankfulness, and more.

As the party broke up, Gretchen lingered to bid one last farewell to Louis and Andrea. Embracing them both in turn,

Gretchen was suddenly inspired to say, "I'll still make quilts for your residents just as I've always done. I'll mail them to you."

"I'm afraid I can't let you do that," said Lewis. His hair had gone white since the day they had first met, but his deep voice had lost none of its warm accent.

"Can't let me?" Gretchen echoed. "You don't mean you'd refuse my donations?"

Louis scratched his head, stalling for time. "I wouldn't have put it in those words, but I guess it's fair to say that's exactly what I mean."

"Why?" Gretchen protested, astonished. "It's no trouble. I enjoy making the quilts, and we all know how much the residents appreciate having something warm and comforting to call their own. If you're worried that my new job will keep me too busy, I promise you I won't be working any more hours a day than I did at the quilt shop."

"It's not that," said Andrea, glancing at her husband and drawing closer to him as he put his arm around her shoulders. "You've blessed us with so many wonderful gifts, but now you're moving on, and the time has come for you to share your talents with some other worthwhile group."

"Your former quilt guild has volunteered to provide us with as many quilts as we could ever need," Louis explained. "I'm sure you'll find a worthy cause in your new community that needs your gifts—both material and of the spirit. If you don't find them, they'll find you. You're a good steward of your talents and the Lord will send someone who needs you your way."

Speechless, Gretchen nodded, wondering if the faint echo of Monsignor Paul's words from so long ago was a sign.

SHE WONDERED STILL as she sat among her new friends at Elm Creek Manor, enjoying the warmth of the fireside and the pleasure of their company, pinning together colorful fabric pieces to sew into whimsical stars. When Sylvia had explained that their quilter's holiday was meant to give them time to work on Christmas projects, Gretchen had instinctively begun a new crib quilt, the same size and style as she used to make for the youngest residents of Abiding Savior. She had caught Sarah giving her work sidelong glances, and she was sure the younger woman wondered why Gretchen made baby quilts when she had no children or grandchildren of her own. Little did Sarah know that Gretchen also had two completed crib quilts lovingly folded and put away upstairs in her bedroom, until she could decide what to do with them. She could send them to Louis—despite what he had said, he wouldn't waste money mailing them back—but he wanted her to find a worthy cause in her new community to support, and sending him the quilts would be an admission of failure. Surely someone in the Elm Creek Valley needed her quilts, perhaps the Holiday Boutique at Sylvia's church.

Suddenly, standing nearby with the phone pressed to one ear, Sylvia groped for Gretchen's ottoman, and Gretchen quickly swung her legs out of the way just before Sylvia sat down. "Are you all right?" Gretchen asked, but Sylvia only gave her a trembling smile that was probably meant to be reassuring. Sylvia's conversation with Summer had evidently shifted from Jeremy's unexpected visit to something about someone named Thomas, a private detective, and the whereabouts of someone named Scott Nelson. Gretchen tried to parse out the details, but with only Sylvia's half of the conversation to work with, she soon gave up. Then, as suddenly as she had sat down, Sylvia laughed, rose, and briskly crossed the parquet floor on her way to the portioned classrooms, leaving her friends staring after her.

"What was that all about?" asked Carol.

"I have no idea," Gretchen replied. "It seemed like bad news about Jeremy, then surprising news about . . . something, but it seems to have ended well."

Carol looked bewildered. "Do all quilting bees at Elm Creek Manor take such unusual turns?"

"Usually," said Gwen, frowning in puzzlement. "Why wouldn't Jeremy tell Summer he was coming for the weekend? She doesn't like those kind of surprises."

"Maybe Anna knows," offered Agnes. They all looked to the sewing machine the chef had been using recently, and only then realized she had not returned from—wherever she had gone.

Gretchen tried to remember how long Anna had been absent, but her curiosity swiftly shifted to Sylvia as she reappeared clutching a scrap of paper in one hand and the phone in the other. "What did Summer say?" Gretchen asked. "Is it good news?"

"Possibly." Sylvia seated herself on Gretchen's ottoman again. "It's certainly promising."

"What's promising?" asked Agnes eagerly. "Goodness, don't keep us in suspense."

"Summer may have found a descendant of my cousin, Elizabeth Bergstrom Nelson."

A chorus of gasps and exclamations went up from the circle of quilters. "Isn't Elizabeth the one who went to California in the 1920s and vanished off the face of the earth?" asked Sarah from the ironing board where she was pressing the seams of the two rows she had joined together. Her expression showed strain, but some instinct told Gretchen it had nothing to do with the weight of the twins.

"I wouldn't have put it with such dramatic flair, but yes, she is indeed." Or rather, she *was.* "Thanks to my friend Grace Daniels, I was able to give Summer a place to focus her search of historical records, and now—" Sylvia held up the scrap of paper with a flourish. "I have the name, address, and phone number of Scott Nelson, who may be Elizabeth's grandson."

"Are you going to call him?" asked Gwen.

"Of course."

"What are you going to say?" asked Sarah.

Sylvia hesitated. "I don't know."

"It doesn't really matter what you say," said Carol. "He'll be thrilled to hear from a long-lost relative."

"Perhaps." Sylvia studied the scrap of paper. "On the other hand, it's entirely possible he's never heard of me, or of Elm Creek Manor, or of any of the Bergstroms. Elizabeth broke her ties to this family decades ago. How likely is it that she passed down any stories of us to her grandson?"

"You can be the one to tell him," said Gretchen. "Think of what a marvelous gift that would be, to restore a missing piece of his family history."

"Even so, it may come as quite a shock to hear from a first cousin twice removed that he never knew existed." Sylvia appeared to mull it over, but then she placed the phone on the table beside Gretchen's chair. "I'll need to think this over carefully and plan exactly what I want to say."

"You could write him a letter instead," suggested Agnes. "Sometimes when you have something difficult to say, it's easier to express oneself in writing."

"Now you tell me," said Anna, returning to her sewing machine, cell phone in hand. She flicked a switch on the side and tossed it into her bag. "If I reach for that thing again, I want someone to smack me."

"Let's not resort to violence," said Gwen. "Hey, Anna, do you know why Jeremy didn't tell Summer he was coming to visit?"

Anna was picking up fabric pieces from the table, and to Gretchen it appeared that she was packing up for the day. "He thought she would tell him not to come."

"Why would she do that?" asked Gwen, bewildered. "Why would he think she would?"

"It's a mystery," said Anna shortly, folding the sections of her unfinished quilt and tucking them into her bag. "I've lost interest in this project. Does anyone want help?"

"It's a shame Diane left," said Agnes,

glancing out the windows at the swirl of blinding white. "She would've gladly taken you up on the offer."

"I hope she's made it home by now," said Sarah, shaking her head and adjusting her partially completed quilt top on the ironing board.

"If no one needs me here, I'll be in the kitchen," said Anna, setting her stuffed tote bag out of the way so someone else could use the sewing machine. "I'll put on a fresh pot of coffee and see what I can throw together for supper, since it looks like we'll all be spending the night."

"Are there any leftovers from our Patchwork Potluck?" asked Sylvia.

"Leftovers of leftovers?" asked Gwen, dubious.

"Never fear," said Anna. "I'm well practiced at turning nothing into something."

"Whatever you make will be delicious, I'm sure," said Sylvia, giving the scrap of paper one last look before folding it and slipping it into the pocket of her cardigan.

"Let me help," said Carol, setting her quilt aside and rising. "Sarah was such a picky eater as a child that I learned a few tricks to make a tempting dish out of a bit of this and a bit of that. Besides, it's her fault you have so few leftovers to work with."

"I'm sure Anna already knows anything you might show her, Mom," said Sarah, an edge to her voice.

"But I'd still welcome the help," said Anna quickly. Shooting her daughter a perplexed frown, Carol rose and followed Anna from the ballroom. Moments after they left, Anna's purse buzzed—or rather, not her purse, but the phone inside it.

"Should we answer?" asked Agnes. "What if it's important?"

"They'll leave a message," said Sarah. "If Anna wants us to hit her rather than let her answer her phone, I think she'd prefer to let the call go to voicemail."

They resumed sewing and waited for the insistent buzzing to cease. Sarah rubbed her lower back and took her freshly pressed rows from the ironing board to the parquet dance floor where the others lay in place. Gretchen watched as she carefully eased herself to the floor and reached for a new row to pin to those already sewn together, when suddenly her foot knocked her plastic box of pins over and sent them scattering.

Quickly Gretchen set her quilt aside and hurried over to help. "I'm so clumsy," Sarah glowered, straining to reach a pin that lay just beyond her fingertips.

"Let me get those," said Gretchen. "You get the ones within easy reach."

Together they picked up the pins and returned them to the box. Sarah spoke not a word, but her cheeks were flushed and her eyes shone. Gretchen had seen that same look of quiet distress on the faces of many young women through the years, and she knew at once that something was troubling Sarah, something more than the storm, her mother's careless insults, and the scattered pins.

"Is something wrong, Sarah?" she asked, touching her on the shoulder.

"I'm just tired."

Gretchen tucked her skirt beneath her and sat down. "I'm sure you are, but I don't think that accounts for everything."

"Well—" Sarah hesitated and glanced at the fireside, where the remaining Elm Creek Quilters were engrossed in conversation. "It's—it's probably nothing, and I didn't want to say anything in front of everyone and have everyone analyze and speculate. You know how it is."

Gretchen nodded, but she suspected that when Sarah said "everyone," she meant her mother. "I won't say a word to anyone. Promise."

Sarah flashed her a quick, tearful smile of thanks. "It's Matt," she said. "Ever since college—no, before that, even when Matt was still in high school—his father has made it clear that he expects Matt to take over his construction company someday."

Gretchen studied the blue, tan, and burgundy Log Cabin variations Sarah was assembling into a top, row by row. "This quilt is a Christmas gift for him, isn't it?"

Sarah laughed shortly. "Ironically, yes. All the while I've been working on this quilt for him to try to give him a sense of Elm Creek Quilts as a wonderful, thriving, creative place, he's been redoubling his efforts to convince Matt to take over the family business."

"But Matt enjoys working here, doesn't he? He's contributed as much to Elm Creek Quilt Camp as any founding Elm Creek Quilter."

"I agree completely, and yes, he does enjoy his work here, but he's also very loyal to his father."

"I would imagine that he's more loyal to you," said Gretchen. "You have a life here. Matt wouldn't ask you to give up Elm Creek Quilts."

Sarah hesitated. "No, at least, he hasn't yet."

"But you think he might?"

"His dad injured his back a few years ago, and when it's at its worst, as it is now, he can't work."

"That's a shame. Is early retirement an option?"

"It wouldn't even be early, but no, he can't afford to retire. I also think it would break his heart to see a company he's devoted his life to simply dissolve." Sarah pressed the back of her hand to her forehead. "I understand how he feels. I certainly hope Elm Creek Quilts will endure long after I retire, but—" She patted her abdomen. "I'm not going to expect the twins to take it over for my sake."

"And that's what you suspect he wants Matt to do?"

"Suspect? I'm sure of it. I don't mean I

think he's faking the back injury, but when it's acted up in the past, he simply took on fewer jobs and asked Matt to help him on weekends. Now he says he needs Matt all winter."

Gretchen had already guessed the answer, but she asked, "What did Matt tell him?"

"He agreed to do it. He didn't even ask me first."

"Oh, Sarah." Gretchen shook her head. "He should have discussed it with you."

"That's what I think, but once he'd made up his mind, what else could I do but go along? Like he said, the orchard and gardens are dormant for the winter and camp is closed for the season. Winter is the one time of year Elm Creek Quilts can spare him."

"But what about you?" asked Gretchen gently. "Can you spare him, for his father's sake?"

"I don't want to," said Sarah tearfully. "I'm sorry if I sound like a spoiled brat, but we have so much to do before the babies arrive—childproofing the manor, decorating the nursery, taking childbirth classes, going through all those prenatal doctor's appointments—and I want Matt with me for all of it."

"Of course you do." Gretchen put her arm around Sarah's shoulders. "That's perfectly understandable."

"On the other hand, I don't want his dad's business to fail. It would be my fault for not allowing Matt to help him, and they would never forgive me."

Gretchen thought the fear of resentment a poor reason for Sarah to agree to the arrangement against her wishes, but she kept that to herself. "How long will Matt be away? He'll return in time for the birth, right?"

"He assures me he will, but—" Sarah pushed the quilt rows away, frustrated. "What if he changes his mind? What if after the babies are born, he decides that his father can't get along without him? What if he gives up his job here to take over his father's business after all? What if he expects me to follow him?"

"That's a lot of 'what ifs,' " said Gretchen. "You don't know if any of that will happen. There's no sense in worrying."

Sarah didn't seem to hear her. "I won't leave the manor. I love Elm Creek Quilts.

I'd miss quilt camp. I'd miss my friends. I couldn't do it. He'll have to commute, but then the twins will hardly ever see him, and what kind of life is that?"

"Sarah, dear," said Gretchen, cupping Sarah's face in her hands. "You're getting yourself all worked up over possibilities that may never occur. Take a deep breath, honey."

To her relief, Sarah did. She took one deep, shaky breath and let it out, and then another. "I don't want to go through this pregnancy alone."

"You're not alone," Gretchen told her firmly. "I know you want Matt by your side every moment, and if not for his father's troubles, he would be. But you won't be alone. Agnes has been beside herself wanting to help you decorate the nursery; she would have offered before but she didn't want to intrude. Joe can childproof the manor; he's brought far more treacherous buildings than this up to code. And as for your childbirth classes, I know it's best to have your husband along, but if Matt can't be there, I'll go with you."

Sarah was so surprised that she choked

out a laugh. "You would? You'd do that for me?"

"Of course. I'll coach you with your breathing and feed you ice chips and take care of anything else you might need." She had accompanied frightened girls little more than half Sarah's age through the birthing process and had witnessed nearly every possible complication. "I'm not as handsome as Matt, but I'm far more experienced, and I promise you, you'll be in good hands."

As Gretchen explained how it was that a woman with no medical degree and no children of her own had acquired so much experience helping new mothers, she remembered Louis Walker's prediction that a worthy cause needing her support would find her, if she did not find it first. Sarah was surrounded by people who loved her, and if Gretchen had not offered to attend childbirth classes with her, her mother or one of the other Elm Creek Quilters would have, but Gretchen knew there were other women who had no friends to turn to, who could not make quilts to keep their children warm.

Since moving to the Elm Creek Valley, Gretchen had spent far too little time beyond the borders of the Bergstrom estate, too little time exploring her new community and discovering where she could best contribute.

If she were to remain a good steward of her talents, it was time to look beyond the walls of Elm Creek Manor and seek a greater purpose.

CHAPTER SIX

Gwen

I DIDN'T HAVE A lonely Thanksgiving," Summer assured Gwen. "Our apartment was full of starving graduate students from all around the world. It was a veritable feast of international cuisine."

"And afterward you all hit the books?" Gwen inquired, delighting in the sound of her daughter's voice, even over the phone. She would be content to sit and listen to Summer recite the University of Chicago Winter Quarter Course Catalog if they had nothing better to discuss, but they never ran out of conversation.

"Actually, afterward we attended the

Day of Mourning rally on the Midway sponsored by the Native American Students Association. It was powerful and moving. You would have loved it."

Gwen probably would have, but she couldn't help teasing, "So you celebrated the holiday, and then you denounced it?"

"Not quite," said Summer. "There's a difference between gathering with loved ones to express gratitude for one's blessings and endorsing the official national holiday of Thanks-giving, which ignores the tragedy of the Pilgrims' early encounters with the indigenous peoples."

Summer was preaching to the choir, but Gwen didn't interrupt as her daughter explained that the official holiday, meant to commemorate the Pilgrims and Native Americans sharing the harvest in peace and harmony, was instead a painful reminder of genocide, the theft of native lands, and the unrelenting, ongoing assault on native culture. At the rally, students of Native American heritage had accompanied chants with drums and denounced the atrocities their people had endured ever since the Pilgrims landed at Plymouth Rock. Until American schoolchildren were taught an accurate version of the Puritans' treatment of indigenous peoples, their fishing and hunting rights were restored, the hundreds of treaties made with the United States government were fully observed, and Native Americans were granted complete self-governance would Thanksgiving truly be a day to express gratitude rather than shame.

"I have no problem with marking an official day devoted to expressing thankfulness," Summer clarified, "but tying it to sanitized versions of the colonization of the American continent is problematic. Plus, as a vegetarian, I'm troubled by the militant demand that we all sit down to a huge turkey dinner. The tofu version tastes just as good."

"I can only imagine what your grandparents said when you told them how you'd spent the day. You did remember to call them, didn't you?"

"Of course I did, but I stuck with the theme of the holiday and gave them the expurgated version of my day," said Summer, laughing. "I focused on the international feast with my roommates and friends and left out the rally."

"So none of your friends went home for the holiday weekend either?"

"No, we all stuck around. Shane's graduating next month, it's too far for Maricela to travel, and Julianne has her candidacy exam in two weeks. None of us could afford the time away."

"But you're still planning to meet me at Grandma and Grandpa's for Christmas?"

"I wouldn't miss it."

"Even if you have a ton of work to do?"

"I'll definitely have a ton of work to do, but I won't let it keep me away. It wouldn't be Christmas without you, Mom."

Gwen blinked away tears. "Nor without you, baby girl."

"Oh, please don't cry, Mom," said Summer, dismayed. "You can't cry on a quilter's holiday."

"Why not? It happens all the time. Sometimes this manor is a veritable waterworks." Gwen glanced out the window at the sound of ice scouring glass. "A frozen waterworks today. I hope the weather's better where you are."

"We had snow showers this morning but they've tapered off. It's not enough to keep me from making it to the library on foot. Speaking of research, which I indirectly was, is Sylvia around? I have some news for her."

They said their good-byes, with promises to chat again soon. Gwen quit the dais on the far side of the ballroom, passed the phone to Sylvia, and returned to her seat by the fireside, carefully lifting the folds of the quilt so they wouldn't catch on the armrest or the tiny screw holding the slender wooden hoops in place. She stretched her hand and flexed her fingers before she slipped on her thimble and took up her needle again, listening with only half her attention to Sylvia's side of the conversation. Summer had been helping the matriarch of Elm Creek Quilts research her family history, and she had apparently discovered a new lead. "That's my girl," she murmured, thinking how alike they were in interest and temperament, although Summer was far more sensible than Gwen had been as a young woman, a blessing worthy of enormous thanksgiving despite anyone's concerns about the origin of the national holiday.

As a young woman, Gwen had been proud of her reputation as a brainy nonconformist in her home town of Brown Deer, Kentucky, west of Lovely about halfway between Pilgrim and Kermit, population 1200, home to six churches and no movie theaters. From the age of ten, Gwen had longed to escape that dull, stifling, provincial backwater, and eight long years later, college 170 miles away in Lexington brought her intoxicating freedom. Perhaps too much freedom, and definitely too much intoxication. At the end of her sophomore year, Gwen decided to leave school and find herself. She set out with two friends, hitchhiking across the country, crashing wherever they were offered a bed, smoking or swallowing whatever promised enlightenment, joining a commune in Berkeley, protesting the war, and falling passionately in infatuation with Dennis, a long-haired, strung out, unwashed pale young man whom she was certain was her soul mate. He was not, however, someone even a habitually tolerant flower child in an altered state of consciousness would want as the father of her child. That was why several months later when Gwen discovered she was pregnant, she left Dennis and hitchhiked her way back to Brown Deer.

Her parents were thankful and relieved to see her again, for she had not kept in touch from the road and for months they had not known where she was, or even whether she was living or dead. She never understood how much and how unconditionally her parents loved her until they welcomed her home without a word of recrimination and cared for her in the months leading up to her child's birth. Gwen was their daughter, and despite her mistakes they staunchly stood by her, insisting she eat well, see her doctor regularly, and venture out in public rather than cower inside ashamed of herself—although as an unmarried, pregnant, former valedictorian, lapsed Catholic, college dropout, she figured she had good reason to be.

Several months after her return to Brown Deer, Summer was born, a healthy, beautiful girl with a thick shock of auburn hair the same color as her mother's. When her daughter was fifteen months old, Gwen returned to college, having never lost her love of learning. In the three years Gwen worked to earn her degree in history, Summer lived in Brown Deer with her grandparents, and Gwen drove home to be with her on weekends and school holidays. It grieved Gwen to spend so much time away from her precious daughter, but she knew she would make a better life for them both if she completed her education. Summer was a happy, affectionate child, the light of her grandparents' lives, and Gwen often found herself overcome with thankfulness for the way they had welcomed her home, cared for Summer so lovingly, and given Gwen a second chance to pursue her dreams.

Her mother cried tears of joy and pride at Gwen's graduation, and even her father's eyes shone to see her in her cap and gown. A few months later, Gwen and Summer left for Cornell, more than six hundred miles away, where Gwen had been accepted into the graduate school. Excited, happy, and yet as apprehensive as if she had never been on her own, Gwen moved them into a small apartment in Ithaca, settled Summer into the nursery school program on campus, and threw herself into her work and motherhood as only someone who had learned not to take either for granted could.

The early months were not without mishaps. Gwen had never taken care of Summer entirely on her own, and sometimes, such as when she didn't know the words to Summer's favorite lullaby or when Summer took only a few polite nibbles of the frozen waffles that bore only a passing resemblance to Grandma's made from scratch, Gwen felt frustrated, inadequate, and wholly unprepared to raise a child on her own. And although Summer delighted in having her mother all to herself, sometimes she woke in the middle of the night sobbing, homesick for her grandparents and her familiar room in their cozy house. After a Christmas visit to Brown Deer, Summer balked when she discovered that they had not come home to stay and refused to get in the car until Gwen's mother promised to visit soon. But by spring, Summer had settled into a pleasant routine of nursery school by day and playtime with Gwen in the evenings, and when Gwen felt sleep-deprived and pulled in twenty different directions, she reassured herself that she was investing in their future and setting a good example of hard work and perseverance for her daughter.

She earned her Master's degree in two years and sailed into the Ph.D. program with the highest marks in the department and the promise of a four-year fellowship that offered a modest stipend and full tuition waiver. Several of her professors encouraged her to specialize in their fields of research and offered to serve as her thesis advisor, but Gwen waited as long as she could before committing herself to one path. A few months into her third year of graduate school, she decided to specialize in nineteenth-century American history with an emphasis in Women's Studies. Not only did she find the era fascinating, but she was also eager to study under Dr. Victoria Stark, a Rhodes scholar and Harvard Ph.D. whose depth and breadth of historical interests and uncanny ability to unearth rich veins of primary source materials from dusty, mostly abandoned archives had earned Gwen's admiration. What impressed Gwen as much as her professional credentials and accomplishments was that Victoria was only eight years her senior and the single mother of a ten-year-old boy. Seeing Victoria succeed in a demanding profession while raising a child on her own gave Gwen hope that she could, too.

Before long, their meetings to discuss Gwen's academic progress became the highlight of her week, and later, when Victoria offered her a newly funded teaching assistantship, Gwen gladly accepted. In her first semester as a TA, Gwen led a small discussion group associated with one of Victoria's large lecture courses and helped grade papers and exams, but her students' evaluations were so positive that the following semester Victoria would ask her to teach the lecture class occasionally if she were called away on some other university business. Gwen enjoyed leading classes as much as conducting research, and knowing how competitive the job market was likely to be by the time she graduated, she was grateful Victoria trusted her enough to give her the opportunity.

Eventually she completed her course requirements and was able to focus on her thesis topic, the experiences of women who had disguised themselves as men so that they could serve in the military during the Civil War. Delving into late-nineteenth-century newspaper accounts and diaries,

Gwen searched for common threads that united the women as well as the unique differences setting each woman apart. Whenever her research stalled, Gwen dealt with her frustration by hashing out the problems with Victoria over coffee, playing with Summer, or rekindling her creativity through quilting. She had joined the Tompkins County Quilt Guild out of longing for the friendships she had left behind in Kentucky, and their monthly meetings brought her respite from the academic grind.

But despite the occasional frustration, her days were rich and full, her future bright, her daughter happy and thriving. Victoria assured her she was progressing well and encouraged her to accept more responsibilities, to submit papers to journals, and to present her research at conferences. One day, she summoned Gwen to her office to announce that Gwen had been invited to participate in a graduate school research conference. Only the best and the brightest doctoral candidates in the country were asked to speak at the prestigious annual gathering, an honor that would serve Gwen well when she completed her degree and began her job search.

"As another nice perk, you'll be able to spend three days and two nights in Boston," Victoria told her, glancing up from the paperwork to smile at Gwen. Her imposing manner belied her short stature, and her curly, salt-and-pepper hair tumbled loose to her shoulders. She had the dry voice of a former smoker, and she often absently held one earpiece of her glasses between her fingers as if it were a cigarette. "You can finally explore those archives you've been talking about."

"Two nights away?" echoed Gwen, dismayed.

"I'm sure Nancy or Peter would take over your classes for you," said Victoria. "Or you can give your students a take-home exam. I've been remiss if I haven't taught you a few of those tricks over the past few years."

"It's not that," said Gwen. "It's my daughter. I can't leave her, and I can't bring her along either." She imagined Summer trailing after her from lecture hall to library, sporting her pink backpack full of books and smiling up at the astonished academics. Summer would probably thoroughly enjoy herself, but Gwen wouldn't be able to concentrate on either conference or research with Summer in tow.

"Oh, of course." Victoria removed her glasses and studied Gwen, a furrow appearing between her brows. "How old is she now?"

"She's eight."

"Second grade?"

"Third."

"Hmm," Victoria mused. "You don't have any family nearby, isn't that right?"

"My closest relatives are my parents in Kentucky."

"And your daughter's father . . . He's not in the picture?"

Gwen laughed shortly. "No, and I'd like to keep it that way."

Victoria sighed, slipped on her glasses, and smiled regretfully. "I know from experience that the university doesn't offer any overnight childcare programs. Apparently it isn't meant to be, not this time. It isn't easy to balance work and family, but you have to set your priorities so that you'll have no regrets later. Don't be discouraged. You'll have similar opportunities in the future, and the invitation itself proves that your potential has been recognized."

Gwen nodded and thanked her, but her heart sank. She could have put the conference presentation on her CV, but not a mere invitation. She knew, too, that it would reflect badly upon Victoria that her prized student had turned down such an honor, and yet Victoria accepted her refusal with easy grace.

Gwen vowed to make it up to her, somehow.

THE CONFERENCE CAME and went, without Gwen, but she took consolation in the excellent progress of her research, which she had already begun to shape into a rough outline for her dissertation. One day, she was heading to Victoria's office to consult her about a possibly apocryphal memoir of an Alabama woman soldier who had been captured by the Union at Vicksburg when she saw a group of undergraduates milling around outside Victoria's door. They looked up at the sound of Gwen's approach, and she knew at first glance that they were displeased.

"Do you know where Dr. Stark is?" one of the younger women asked. "She never showed up for lecture."

"Then it looks like you get the day off," said Gwen cheerfully. "Enjoy yourselves."

"She was supposed to review for our midterm," said one of the men, clearly disgruntled. "I was out for two weeks with mono and if I don't get the review, there's no way I'll pass."

For a moment Gwen feared that Victoria had asked her to fill in and she had forgotten, but Gwen's scrupulously maintained calendar, one of her many survival mechanisms, was legendary in the department. She would not have forgotten to record something so important. Frowning, she knocked on Victoria's door, ignoring the student who muttered not quite under his breath that they had already tried that.

"Does this mean that the exam'll be postponed?" asked another student. "That's only fair."

"I wouldn't count on it," said Gwen. She excused herself, went down the hall, and knocked on the door of a professor she knew well who allowed her to borrow his phone to call Victoria's office. She heard the phone ringing through the closed door, but no one picked up. No one answered at Victoria's home either. Concealing her worry, Gwen thanked the professor and returned to the students waiting in the hall. "Tina, would you round up any of your classmates who might still be waiting in the lecture hall?" she asked. "Whoever wants to review for the midterm should meet me in the department conference room in twenty minutes."

Tina agreed, and the group broke up. Gwen hurried back to her cubicle in the graduate students' office, gathered her notes, and met about a third of the class for the impromptu review session, wondering all the while what had happened to her mentor. Gwen's substitution seemed to appease the students somewhat, although many left the room muttering complaints. Afterward, she tried again to reach Victoria by phone, but when that failed, she slipped a note beneath the professor's office door, explaining what had happened and asking her to be in touch.

Victoria stopped by her cubicle the following morning with a cup of Gwen's favorite coffee, profuse apologies, and many thanks for the way she had risen to the occasion. "My sister has been ill," she said, lowering her voice, mindful of the graduate students studying or meeting with pupils nearby. "She had to be hospitalized quite suddenly. I confess I completely forgot about the lecture. I have no excuse. We've been meeting the same day, same time all semester."

Gwen took in the dark circles beneath the professor's eyes, her haggard appearance. "Do you want to go somewhere and talk?"

Victoria hesitated as if she were on the verge of refusing, but then she pressed her lips together and nodded.

Over coffee at the Commons Coffee House, Victoria quietly and matter-of-factly explained that her elder sister had lymphoma, the same type that had taken the lives of their grandmother, mother, and another sister. The sisters knew that she faced a repeating cycle of illness, treatment, recovery, remission, and recurrence, and unless scientists discovered a breakthrough cure, eventually it would take her life. "The treatment is almost as bad as the disease," said Victoria, absently stirring her coffee, her gaze far away. "My sister is determined to fight it, but she's an oncologist at Johns Hopkins and knows better than anyone what she's in for. But that's not the worst of it."

Gwen dreaded to know what could be worse, but she felt compelled to ask, "What is?"

Victoria inhaled deeply and raised her coffee cup to her lips. "Her two daughters have been tested and they, too, carry the gene." She set the cup down and added, almost as an afterthought, "As do I."

She wasn't ill, Victoria hastened to assure her, but despite meditation to help her deal with stress and logical thinking that told her she was statistically more likely to perish in a car accident, sometimes she felt as if she were holding her breath, waiting like Damocles for Dionysius's sword hanging overhead by a single thread to fall.

Sick at heart, Gwen promised to do anything she could to help. Victoria thanked her and said she hoped it wouldn't be necessary. But as her sister's condition worsened, Victoria more frequently asked Gwen to take over her classes, to discuss her research over the phone instead of meeting in person, and to create exams and writing prompts. "I'm telling myself that I'm giving you valuable experience," Victoria told her one morning after a week away to settle her sister into a hospice center, "but I know I'm merely rationalizing how badly I'm taking advantage of you."

"Not at all," Gwen assured her. "If it gets to be too much, I'll tell you, but in the meantime, don't add any worries about me to the pile. I'm fine."

"You're a remarkable young woman, Gwen," said Victoria, and her weariness seemed to lift for a moment. "I'm thankful we met."

Soon after that meeting, Victoria's sister passed away.

Gwen took over Victoria's classes during the two weeks she spent in Baltimore for her sister's memorial service and the administration of her estate. A few days after Victoria's return, Gwen stopped by her office to offer condolences only to find her mentor emptying the contents of a manila envelope on her desk and studying the accompanying letter with bemusement.

"My sister's colleagues are creating some sort of memorial patchwork quilt in her honor," Victoria said, glancing from the letter to a white six-inch square of muslin. "Her friends, family, and colleagues have been invited to contribute a square to a quilt celebrating her life, which they plan to display in the medical school library."

"What a wonderful tribute," said Gwen.

"Indeed, and I'll be terribly disappointed to turn down their invitation, but regrettably, I have no idea how to make a quilt block."

"It probably doesn't have to be complicated." Gwen held out her hand for the letter, and Victoria's eyebrows rose as she handed it over. "Oh, I see," said Gwen, reading it through. "You can piece a traditional quilt block if you like, or appliqué shapes and symbols to the muslin, or draw on the fabric with colorfast fabric pens, or any combination thereof. The challenge, I would think, is coming up with an idea."

"I gather you've quilted before," remarked Victoria, as Gwen handed back the letter.

"I picked it up when I was expecting Summer," Gwen said, thinking of those months in Brown Deer where her mother's quilting guild, the Brown Does, had been her only friends. As the daughter of a Doe, she had been an honorary Fawn even before she took up the art—probably from birth.

"Perhaps you could offer me a few tips?" asked Victoria. "I'd prefer to participate if I could."

Gwen agreed, and after taking a few days to mull over potential designs, Victoria decided that she wanted to create a design of autumn leaves and acorns, since autumn had been her sister's favorite season. Gwen invited her to choose rich autumn hues from her fabric stash, showed her the best way to cut appliqué shapes, and demonstrated how to sew them to the white muslin square. Victoria finished the block by embroidering her sister's name and a verse from her favorite Emily Dickinson poem in the center, a needlework skill she had mastered as a girl.

"It's not likely I'll ever see the finished quilt in person," Victoria remarked wistfully after she sent her block to her sister's friends.

"You could make your own memorial quilt for your sister," Gwen suggested. When Victoria smiled and pointed out that the one small block had taken her weeks to finish and she could not possibly complete an appliquéd, embroidered version for herself within her lifetime, Gwen offered to teach her to make a traditional Autumn Leaf block, which was mostly pieced using simple, straight seams, with only the stem in appliqué. "Don't worry if you finish the quilt soon or ever," Gwen added. "A memorial of this sort is as much about the process as the product."

Victoria accepted Gwen's offer, and after a few lessons she thanked Gwen and said she would continue on her own. Except for an occasional question about fabric selections or tools, she said nothing about her quilt, and after a few months, Gwen assumed she had abandoned the project, unable to carve out the time from her busy academic schedule. Then, shortly after Spring Break, Victoria surprised Gwen at one of their weekly dissertation meetings by unveiling a completed quilt top, a forest of falling leaves in autumn hues from verdant greens and rich wines to blazing oranges and mellow browns, beautiful and yet melancholy.

"Perhaps you could guide me through the next steps?" Victoria asked after Gwen stammered out astonished congratulations. She had never expected the professor to accomplish so much with so little instruction, but of course Victoria always nonchalantly exceeded expectations. So Gwen taught her to make a "quilt sandwich" by layering the pieced top, soft batting, and backing fabric, to baste the layers with large stitches, to hold them securely within a hoop, and to unite top, middle, and back with small, meticulous quilting stitches, enhancing the beauty of the top by giving it depth and dimension.

"It's quite therapeutic," Victoria explained a few weeks later when Gwen inquired about her progress and marveled that she had accomplished so much so quickly. "I chose fabrics that I knew my sister would have loved, and with every stitch I think of her. Not as she was at the end, ill and suffering, but earlier, when we were children together and happy, when she was a young bride, when she graduated from medical school, when she first rode a bike and learned to swim, when she saved her babysitting money to buy me a typewriter for Christmas—so many years, so many memories. At her memorial service surrounded by our family and her many friends, I grieved. Alone, working on this quilt, I celebrate her life."

Gwen understood exactly what she meant.

Whenever Victoria mentioned her second quilt and all those that followed, which was rarely, she spoke self-deprecatingly, as if she found it amusing that an educated feminist should derive such pleasure from traditional needlecrafts. Gwen did not take offense. She had once deplored quilting as pointless busywork, a trivial distraction that prevented otherwise intelligent women from devoting their time and energy to work that might actually make a difference in the world. But then she had been drawn into the Brown Does' quilting circle and had discovered that quilting was a uniquely accessible art form that flourished when practiced with others. Working in isolation, Victoria would never discover the deep, enriching friendships that bound one quilter to another, but she repeatedly refused Gwen's invitations to visit her guild, so Gwen stopped pestering her. She knew the quilting community would welcome Victoria warmly when she was ready.

VICTORIA'S FIRST SYMPTOMS appeared a few months before Gwen's candidacy exam, but whenever Gwen hesitantly asked if she felt all right, Victoria dismissed her obvious fatigue and weight loss as the result of work stress and insisted that her upcoming vacation would cure her of all ills. Later, after she began her first round of chemotherapy, she confided to Gwen that she had known what was wrong with her, but she didn't want to admit that the disease that had claimed four women in her family, the disease she had eluded longer than anyone had expected, had come at last to claim her.

In the year that followed, Gwen organized the history department into a support system so that Victoria had meals delivered to her home several times a week, rides to and from chemo treatments, a rotating shift of graduate students to take care of errands, and a round-the-clock schedule of volunteers, who had agreed to be only a phone call away should any unforeseen circumstances arise. Later Victoria credited their support and the excellent medical care she received at the University Hospital for her successful response to treatment, but Gwen knew it was her mentor's indomitable resolve that pulled her through. By the time Gwen defended her dissertation, Victoria was in remission.

Throughout her mentor's ordeal, Gwen had often thought that Victoria might not be there to stand beside her when she received her doctorate. She knew she would be forever grateful when the glorious sunny May afternoon arrived at last and Victoria was present. Gwen would never forget the pride in Victoria's eyes at the department reception following the commencement ceremony, her words of praise, her hopes that they would collaborate on many projects in the future, and her predictions that Gwen would make her mark in the field and be a credit to them all.

Summer was ten years old when Gwen accepted a job as an assistant professor in the American Studies department of Waterford College, nestled in the Elm Creek Valley beside a small town that reminded her of Brown Deer. She kept in touch with

Victoria, and their plans to collaborate on a Women's History textbook were well under way when Victoria broke the terrible news that her cancer had returned.

"But you were in remission," Gwen heard herself say numbly. "You were doing so well."

Victoria sighed and reminded her that this was the way the disease had progressed in the other women of her family, and she had always known it was a possibility. This time Gwen had to follow Victoria's treatment from long distance, wishing she were there to help, relieved that other students and faculty had stepped in to support Victoria as she had before.

Months later, when Victoria announced that her treatment had succeeded and she was once again in remission, Gwen did not fool herself that the treatment had cured her entirely. But years passed without recurrence, and Gwen began to hope that perhaps she had been wrong. Her hopes lasted until Summer was in middle school, when Victoria's symptoms reappeared.

Gwen's mother came to Waterford to stay with Summer for two months so that Gwen could move into Victoria's guest room and care for her. "It's a good thing you already have tenure," Victoria interrupted as Gwen read aloud to her to distract her during a chemotherapy session. "You'd never be allowed to take so much time off otherwise."

"What are you talking about?" Gwen replied, feigning puzzlement. "I'm not taking time off. I'm on a research trip consulting with a respected colleague. That's my story and I'm sticking to it."

She was gratified when Victoria laughed.

One night, as Gwen was helping Victoria prepare for bed, she confided that she and her doctor had been discussing other options for her future care. "If I pull through this recurrence—"

"Not if," Gwen interrupted. "When."

Victoria allowed a small smile and nodded. "When I pull through this, and when I've fully recovered and have regained my strength, my doctor thinks I should consider a bone marrow transplant. It's a dangerous course of treatment, but he believes it's the only way I might avoid this recurring pattern of illness, treatment, remission, illness. I believe the opportunity for a complete cure would be well worth the risks."

At the time her mentor's words barely registered, so intent was Gwen on seeing her through the immediate danger. Responsibilities called her back to Waterford College all too soon, so it was again by phone that Victoria informed her that she was once again in remission. The blessed news was as welcome as ever, but each time Gwen accepted it with a diminishing measure of relief. She wondered how many more cycles of recurrence Victoria could withstand, how long she could hold body and soul together by little more than sheer force of will.

Over the years, Gwen fulfilled some of the predictions Victoria had made on her graduation day and had found herself thwarted in others. But although academia had not turned out to be as completely fulfilling as she had once envisioned, her life became enriched in other unexpected ways. Gwen joined the Waterford Quilt Guild but eventually left with a group of close, like-minded friends to form the Tangled Web Quilters. Summer began high school—beautiful, brilliant, kind, generous, her presence a constant blessing. Distant ties began to loosen as newer bonds formed, and Gwen eventually heard from Victoria perhaps only twice a year, enough to know that she was in good health, thankfully, and enjoying her promotion to Dean of the Graduate School.

Gwen had not spoken to Victoria for several months when they ran into each other at a conference and spent an evening catching up over supper. Eventually the conversation turned to Victoria's health and her thwarted attempts to have a bone marrow transplant. Her brother, long hoped to be a suitable donor, had recently been eliminated after more thorough testing revealed previously undetected incompatibilities. "Now my hopes ride on a response from the national registry," said Victoria. "If I remain healthy until a suitable match can be found, my doctor will proceed with the transplant. If I have a recurrence before a donor appears—" She smiled ruefully and shook her head.

Gwen felt a chill, but she declared that of course Victoria would remain perfectly healthy until a donor was found, which would certainly be soon. When Victoria smiled knowingly and said she hoped so, Gwen knew that her former mentor had seen through her false bravado, and she was ashamed. Victoria deplored perfunctory niceties and Gwen had always respected her too much to give her anything but the plain, hard truth. As they parted ways, Gwen silently chastised herself and resolved that she would never again resort to cheery platitudes and deny Victoria the truth, no matter how painful it might be.

Back in Waterford, troubled by the thought of Victoria's limited window of opportunity, Gwen searched the Internet for information about bone marrow transplants. What she discovered alarmed her even as it increased her respect for Victoria's courage. Once a donor was found, Victoria would undergo radiation treatments that would destroy her own bone marrow. The stem cells taken from the donor's bone marrow would be given to her intravenously, much like a blood transfusion. The donor cells would travel through her bloodstream into her bones, where they would engraft, or grow, and begin to produce healthy cells. She would have to take antirejection medication for the rest of her life and possibly endure a host of side effects, but if the transplant succeeded, her lymphoma would not return.

But the odds of finding a donor were daunting.

Suddenly Gwen knew what she must do to help her beloved mentor: She would volunteer to be tested and add herself to the bone marrow donor registry.

Intellectually, she knew that the larger the pool of donors, the more likely a match would be found. But more compelling than any calculation of the odds was her belief in fate. After all that Victoria had done for her throughout the years—teaching her, guiding her, setting her on her way—it would be only right and just if Gwen could help Victoria now.

The histocompatibility antigen test was simple, virtually painless. Gwen made an appointment at the Elm Creek Valley General Hospital, where a nurse cleaned the inside of her elbow with antiseptic, wrapped an elastic band around her upper arm, inserted a needle into the vein, and collected a vial of blood, just like any other blood draw Gwen had had through the years. As she waited several days for the results,

Gwen's certainty that she would be a match for Victoria grew. When she was identified as a suitable donor, it would not be an astonishing coincidence but rather the sign of a benevolent presence in the universe, guiding their footsteps, bringing them together for a great purpose. Gwen loved and admired Victoria and considered her a friend as well as a mentor. No sacrifice was too much if it would free Victoria from the cycle of recurrence, increasing the quality of her life as well as extending it.

Gwen's expectations had soared so high that when the news came that she was not a match for Victoria, she was sure that there had been some mistake, some mix-up in the lab, something. Told that the results were accurate, Gwen nevertheless had herself retested elsewhere—and was shattered to hear the same unhappy result.

"I'm sorry you can't help your friend," the nurse consoled her as she left the clinic. "Don't lose hope. New donors volunteer for the registry every day. A match for your friend is out there somewhere."

Gwen wanted to believe her, but as she returned to her office on the Waterford

College campus, she realized that she couldn't wait patiently for that someone to appear, not when time was of the essence.

After consulting with the Waterford College infirmary and the Elm Creek Valley General Hospital, Gwen enlisted the help of the college premed and prenursing programs and organized a campus-wide bone marrow donor registration drive. Hundreds of students, faculty, and staff scheduled appointments or dropped by the basketball arena between classes to be tested. Local businesses donated prizes to be awarded to the various fraternities, sororities, and dorms that brought in the most residents. Campus bands entertained the volunteers and potential donors throughout the day, and College Food Services supplied tasty refreshments. At the end of the long, triumphant day, Gwen thanked her volunteers with tears in her eyes and a heart full of gratitude. Surely someone tested that day would turn out to be a lifesaving donor for someone—if not for Victoria, then for someone else whose need was just as great.

But Gwen would leave nothing to chance. She wrote impassioned letters to the history departments of Cornell and Harvard,

Victoria's alma mater, to remind them of Victoria's heroic ongoing battle, and she encouraged them to organize their own bone marrow donor drives. To her delight, they took up the challenge in admirable fashion, arranging a friendly competition between the two universities to see which could register the most donors. Between the three schools, more than three thousand potential bone marrow donors joined the registry, offering hope for a transplant and renewed good health to patients across the country.

Gwen's intention at the outset was to find a donor for Victoria, but she celebrated each announcement that a match had been made—a student at Waterford College to a child in Michigan, a professor at Cornell to a young mother in Iowa, an executive assistant with the Department of Biology at Harvard to a teenage boy in Dallas. "We'll find someone for you," she assured Victoria, and then, remembering her vow not to paint bleak truths in rosy hues, she added, "If our drives don't turn up a donor, someone else's might."

And that was what finally happened. A month after the last results came back from those tested at the university events, a woman in Georgia participated in a donor drive at her church organized on behalf of a fellow parishioner. She was an ideal match for Victoria. As Gwen rejoiced for her friend, she hoped that a donor would be found for the Georgia churchgoer. That was how it usually worked, she had discovered. Volunteers who signed up hoping to help someone they cared about ended up helping distant strangers, keeping their hopes alive that someday soon a stranger would be found to help their loved one.

One part of Victoria's ordeal had ended and another had begun. She underwent radiation treatments to destroy her bone marrow and prepare her to receive the donor's stem cells. Gwen waited apprehensively for updates from Victoria's son during the long months of her hospital stay, wishing she could visit, but understanding the need to limit Victoria's exposure to germs while the donor stem cells rebuilt her immune system.

Again Victoria's indomitable spirit and optimism carried her through. As time passed, she regained her strength and was permitted to return home. After taking a year's sabbatical, she was able to resume her duties at Cornell. She attended her son's wedding and was present at the birth of her first grandchild. From time to time she returned to the hospital for brief stays to deal with anemia or perplexing infections, but her doctors said she showed no sign of rejection. The bone marrow transplant had cured her cancer.

Yet it seemed to Gwen that the battle waged on. She had not expected Victoria to be hospitalized so frequently so her doctors could track down the cause of a fever or unexpected fatigue. She had not expected Victoria to have to deal with inconvenient, uncomfortable side effects of her essential medications. But whenever she saw Victoria, active and self-assured, she took heart. Her mentor had been given a new lease on life, and she was clearly making the most of it.

As the years passed, Gwen grew accustomed to Victoria's wry emails announcing that she was in the hospital yet again. She was relieved when Victoria mentioned that she planned to retire soon, for she worried that Victoria had been pushing herself too hard to make up for time lost to convalescence. Victoria told Gwen she planned to resume quilting in her retirement, for the demands of academic life had prevented her from "nurturing her inner artist" for too long. Her first project, she told Gwen, would be a quilt for her bone marrow donor, whom she had met two years after her transplant and had quickly befriended. Victoria and Kathryn had met in person three times and spoke on the phone weekly. "It's remarkable how close we've become," Victoria remarked. "She's saved my life, and for that I'll be forever grateful, but she's also become as dear to me as a sister just because of who she is."

Victoria wanted to thank Kathryn for her generous gift of life, and she could think of no more perfect gift than a quilt she made herself. She was out of practice, but she thought with a bit of effort she would remember her old skills. She had found a perfect block, too, a pattern that resembled an unusual forked star superimposed upon a square and named after Kathryn's hometown, Augusta. If she applied herself, Victoria speculated, she might be able to finish the quilt in time for Christmas.

Through spring and summer, Gwen followed Victoria's progress with delight, enjoying the amusing reversal of their old teacher and student roles. With Sylvia's blessing, she invited Victoria to spend a week at Elm Creek Quilt Camp so she could work uninterrupted on her labor of love. She and Gwen spent so much time chatting and strolling through the lovely gardens of the estate that Victoria did not accomplish quite as much work as she had planned, but upon her departure, she declared that she had enjoyed herself thoroughly and might make Elm Creek Manor the spot for an annual getaway. Gwen, happy to have spent a week nurturing their long and enduring friendship, assured her she was welcome to return anytime.

But with autumn came news from Victoria's son that she had been hospitalized again, and something in his tone warned Gwen that this visit was not routine. Her lungs and kidneys were inexplicably shutting down, and her doctors were fighting to halt her decline. She drifted in and out of consciousness, her son said, his voice breaking, but she had asked to see Gwen.

Immediately Gwen arranged for a graduate student to cover her classes and raced to Victoria's side, painfully reminded of the many times she had covered for Victoria so she could be with her dying sister. But Victoria could not be dying, she told herself firmly as she drove through the rolling, forested Pennsylvania Appalachians, insensible to their breathtaking autumnal beauty. Victoria had survived the bone marrow transplant and countless infections and adjustments to her meds. Surely this was just another setback—more serious than the others, perhaps, but nothing she could not overcome.

On the day of her arrival, Victoria was too ill for visitors, but Gwen was permitted to see her the next morning. Donning scrubs, mask, hairnet, and booties, Gwen sat at her bedside and forced back tears as Victoria weakly questioned her about her research, her ongoing battles with her department chair to investigate subjects he considered beneath notice, and her plans for the next season of Elm Creek Quilt Camp. "I don't think I'll be able to finish Kathryn's quilt," she said, after Gwen had run out of things to say that avoided the obvious matter of greatest concern.

"Of course you will," said Gwen vehemently. "It's your quilt, your gift. You'll finish it on your own, and Kathryn will cherish it."

Victoria replied with a look of mild reproach, too exhausted to manage the words. Gwen understood: Even now Victoria loathed false pleasantries, especially now, but Gwen could not bring herself to say what they both suspected was true.

"You won't be able to finish the quilt in time for Christmas," Gwen amended. "Not unless they let you bring your sewing machine here." She frowned in mock disapproval and waved a hand to indicate the medical equipment surrounding her beloved mentor. "Frankly, with all these contraptions, I doubt there's a spare outlet to plug it in anyway."

Victoria smiled faintly. "Then you'll finish the quilt for me and give it to Kathryn with my gratitude and deepest affection?"

"I'll work on it while you're in the hospital to keep things on schedule," said Gwen. It was the most she could bear to promise. "It'll be finished by Christmas."

"Don't let Kathryn blame herself for my death," said Victoria. "The bone marrow transplant worked. I'm free of cancer. Her gift gave me more years, better years, than I would have known otherwise. I saw my son marry. I held my first grandchild. I won that NEH grant—"

Gwen choked out a laugh. "Well, thank goodness you lived to see that NEH grant."

Victoria smiled, clearly pleased at the return of Gwen's sense of humor.

"Don't give up," Gwen implored. "It's not done until it's done."

"You should know better than to think you need to tell me that," said Victoria. "I'm not one to stop fighting."

"I know," said Gwen. She reached out and held Victoria's hand, feeling her lingering strength and undiminished love through the thin fabric that separated them.

Gwen returned to the Elm Creek Valley, where she awaited news from Victoria's son and hoped for the best. Memories flooded her as she worked upon Victoria's gift for Kathryn—her first months as Victoria's student, their many discussions about history and jokes about department politics, the times Victoria had offered guidance as an experienced single mother, their ongoing professional relationship in all the years since Gwen left Cornell and forged her own path, their enduring friendship. Gwen couldn't imagine what her life would have been if Victoria had not been a part of it. She did not want to learn what it would be without her.

Victoria died at the end of October. Gwen took a week's leave of absence from Waterford College and told the Elm Creek Quilters she would be out of town to attend her mentor's funeral. They offered sympathy and comfort, as she had known they would, but although she had mentioned Victoria throughout the years and they had met her during her visit to Elm Creek Quilt Camp, they did not understand all that Victoria had meant to her or the depth of her loss. Even Summer did not fully understand.

She met Kathryn for the first time at Victoria's funeral. "She spoke of you often," said Kathryn after they had embraced and shed a few tears of grief and welcome. "You were her favorite student. She was so proud of you, as proud of you as if you were her own daughter."

At that, Gwen broke down again, and Kathryn held her comfortingly. When Gwen managed to regain some composure, she told Kathryn how grateful Victoria had been—how grateful everyone who loved Victoria had been—for her selfless gift of life. Kathryn demurred, saying that her pain had been minimal and her recovery swift. Then, suddenly, her own composure shattered. "What good did it do in the end?" she asked, glancing to the sanctuary where Victoria lay at rest.

"You did a great deal of good," Gwen insisted, and told her what Victoria had said at their last meeting. Kathryn seemed to take some comfort in the thought of the time Victoria had gained, and all she had put into those years. Kathryn's gift and Victoria's battle had not been in vain.

AS GWEN SAT by the fireside in Elm Creek Manor with Victoria's quilt draped over her lap, a wave of grief washed over her. She stroked the quilt and breathed deeply until it receded. The soft greens, warm pinks, and rich browns soothed her troubled spirit, and she knew that when Kathryn received the quilt, she would understand how thankful Victoria had been for her generous gift of time and hope. Even though she had not lived to a ripe old age, she had lived longer, more comfortably, and with greater appreciation of life because of Kathryn.

At the end of an elegant swirl of quilting stitches, Gwen tied a knot in the thread and popped it through the back of the quilt so it was hidden within the warm batting. Snipping the trailing end of the thread, she set the scissors aside, loosened the screw holding the slender hoops together, and carried quilt and hoops to a clear space on the parquet dance floor. She spread out the quilt, but before moving the hoops to a new section, she stood and admired Victoria's handiwork, not only what was displayed before her but also what had been left in the hearts and minds of all who had known her. Victoria had left behind a rich legacy of historical scholarship, had inspired thousands of students, and had instilled in Gwen a passion for intellectual inquiry. Victoria had been as proud of Gwen as if she were her own daughter, Kathryn had told her. Gwen could not have asked for any greater benediction.

"It's beautiful," said Sarah, looking over from her seat on the floor nearby, where she was piecing together rows of blocks for her father-in-law's quilt, Gretchen by her side. "Your quilting complements your friend's piecing very well."

Gwen smiled as her gaze traveled across the quilt, Victoria's final masterpiece. "We've always been good collaborators," she said, "and she's never failed to broaden my perspective. I wouldn't have chosen these colors or fabrics or even this block, but now that I've worked with them, I see the artistry I would have missed without her guidance."

Victoria was ever the teacher, but now it was up to Gwen to complete the unfinished work she had left behind, a gift of gratitude to comfort a grieving friend.

CHAPTER SEVEN

SARAH PINNED THE last row to the bottom of the quilt top, wondering how a gift begun with such good intentions could have so quickly turned into an empty gesture. The nearly finished top was turning out as beautifully as she had hoped, the cabins underneath the stars reminiscent of snug homes with fires on the hearth, of warmth and comfort on snowy winter nights. But she would not sleep soundly in the coming winter with Matt so far away.

She understood now that her father-in-law had never seen Matt's job at Elm Creek Manor as anything more than an interim position, something to occupy his time until he decided to settle down, return home, and take over the construction company. Perhaps Hank even believed that the approach of fatherhood would compel Matt to shoulder the responsibilities he had too long neglected.

But Matt had a home, a rewarding career, and many important responsibilities at Elm Creek Manor. Sarah could accept Matt's absence over the winter, especially since Gretchen had promised to attend childbirth classes with her, but that didn't mean she was happy about it, or that she would patiently endure his absence when the babies arrived and throughout all the days that followed. Nor would she give up the home, the friends, the life she had built for herself at Elm Creek Manor so that Matt could fulfill his father's dream for him, a dream that had never been his own.

Matt needed to know that before he made any promises to his father on her behalf, promises she could not fulfill.

GRETCHEN HELPED SARAH to her feet so she could carry the pinned quilt top to a sewing machine and attach the last row to her father-in-law's quilt top. Although Sarah's circumstances differed vastly from those of the young women Gretchen had known at Abiding Savior Christian Outreach, her need for support and for assurances that she was not alone at a critical time was the same. So, too, was the warmth and certainty Gretchen felt upon knowing that she could help someone in need.

There was just no getting around it, Gretchen thought, smiling to herself. She was happiest and most content with the world when she was helping others.

She had been so busy since joining Elm Creek Quilts that she had lost touch with this essential part of herself. It was time to regain that connection. Making a quilt for the Christmas Boutique at Sylvia's church would be a decent start, but it did not go far enough. Gretchen's heart instinctively went out to mothers and their children. Although she was new to the Elm Creek Valley, it shouldn't be too difficult to find a need she could fill within her new community.

We're all very busy, but we should never become too preoccupied with our own concerns to help those in need, Sylvia had said earlier that day, and the other

Elm Creek Quilters had agreed. Perhaps, as a Christmas gift to herself and her new friends, Gretchen could find a way for the Elm Creek Quilters to give back to their community.

IN THE KITCHEN, Anna and Carol took inventory of the refrigerator and pantry and discussed how to assemble a tasty meal for their impromptu dinner party out of the leftover leftovers. Anna welcomed the distraction. Her distress over her last conversation with Jeremy—and it could very well be the last—had only increased since she had hung up the phone. What kind of idiot admitted she had fallen in love with her best friend and then ended that friendship, all within a matter of minutes? Whenever they'd had misunderstandings in the past, Jeremy had always called or texted her to clear the air before things went too far awry. This time he was not reaching out to her, and she could only assume that she had either scared him off with her declarations of love or he had agreed that it was best to end their friendship since he could not feel for her what she felt for him.

She pressed the back of her hand to

her forehead, closing her eyes against tears. If only she hadn't called him. If only she had waited until she had cooled down and could have composed her thoughts rather than blurting out what she had felt in the moment. She didn't want to end their friendship, she just wanted—

She took a deep breath and let out a long, shaky sigh. What did she want? Only for Jeremy to think of her as more than a friend. Only for him to love her instead of Summer. Only the impossible. He had not intentionally treated her as his "fallback girl," or whatever Anna had called it. He had always treated her as a friend, and they could have remained very good friends if Anna hadn't wanted more.

"Are you all right?" Carol asked, a head of arugula in one hand, a package of bleu cheese in the other. "If you're worried about dinner, you really shouldn't be. We'll make some gourmet turkey sandwiches, toss a salad, and everyone at Elm Creek Manor will leave the table satisfied. We don't have to be extravagant. They want something quick and easy so they can get back to quilting, remember?"

"You're right," said Anna, managing a smile. "But what about dessert?"

Carol nodded toward the pantry. "You have a ton of apples in there. Matt really overdid it with the harvest this year. How about making that apple strudel Sylvia's family always served for Christmas?"

Anna couldn't help laughing. "That's an all day project—peeling the apples, stretching the dough—but I think I could put together a simple cranberry apple crisp. We might even have some ice cream to go with it."

Carol nodded in satisfaction, took the last remaining loaf from the breadbox, and started on the sandwiches. As Anna turned away, she let her smile fade. She had convinced Carol that all was well, but Jeremy knew her better, and he would read the heartbreak on her face the next time they bumped into each other in the hallway outside their apartments. She dreaded their first accidental meeting. Maybe she should reconsider Sylvia's offer and move into the manor rather than endure the awkwardness of living only a few feet away from her former best friend.

Anna tied on the holiday print apron Sylvia had given her, the pride of her great-aunt Lydia's collection, and forced Jeremy from her thoughts. She would have time enough to deal with her broken heart, to mourn the loss of her most precious friendship, and to figure out how she had let her feelings run away with her so wildly. For now, other dear friends needed her, and she would not let them down.

WHEN ANNA AND Carol called their friends to supper, Sylvia carefully set aside her work, brushed stray threads from her slacks, and joined them around the table for the second time that day. As much as she enjoyed their company, her thoughts kept turning to her dear cousin Elizabeth, lost and possibly found. She had borne three children, and if the Scott Nelson that Summer had tracked down was Elizabeth's grandson, Sylvia was not the last Bergstrom after all. She had family. Distant family, family she had never known, but family all the same. It was also possible that Scott Nelson and his younger sister had cousins, children, other siblings—more descendants of Hans and Anneke

Bergstrom, more relatives than Sylvia had ever hoped to find.

Surely they deserved to know about their heritage, assuming Elizabeth had not passed down the stories of her youth to her children and grandchildren. But how should Sylvia reach out to this newly discovered possible second cousin? An unexpected phone call might be too much of a shock for Scott Nelson and too unsettling for Sylvia, since she would not know until she spoke with him whether he welcomed the news of a long-lost relative or if he would have preferred to keep Elizabeth's severed ties as they were.

A letter would be best, Sylvia decided. Such news as hers required the reflection and thoughtful composition of a letter, not the haste of email or the sudden intrusion of a phone call from a stranger. After their quilter's holiday had ended and her guests had departed, she would sit down and compose a letter explaining her search for Elizabeth's kin and inviting Scott Nelson to contact her if he wished to learn more about his grandmother's side of the family.

In his place, Sylvia would have joyfully welcomed the discovery of a long-lost cousin, but she did not fully understand why Elizabeth had become estranged from her family back home in Pennsylvania, and thus could only imagine what she had told her descendants about the Bergstroms. Perhaps Elizabeth had had more reason than embarrassment about her apparent misfortunes in the Arboles Valley to sever ties. Sylvia vaguely recalled that Uncle George, Elizabeth's father, had been a drinker. Sylvia's mother had worried about him, although Sylvia's father had assured her that Uncle George was nursing invisible wounds from the Great War and would be fine if left alone. Sylvia wasn't supposed to know about Uncle George's problem, and in the decades that had passed, she had forgotten about it until her curiosity about Elizabeth had pushed the memory to the surface. Perhaps her cousin had kept other secrets long before she left Pennsylvania.

Sylvia would never know unless she contacted Scott Nelson. She would write him a letter, extend a hand—and hope that he took it.

NUMB FROM THE cold, Diane trudged down the icy road, wishing she had never left her car. Twice she had fallen, and the wind swept her breath away so that every step forward was a struggle. She should have stayed in the car and awaited rescue. She should have heeded her more cautious friends' warnings and never left the manor. If only she could start the whole day over, she would live it differently. She would live entire seasons differently.

A sudden gust of wind drove icy crystals into her face. She gasped and turned her back to the wind, dismay overcoming her as she saw the path she had broken already disappearing as it filled with the blowing snow. She had made so little progress since setting forth, but she knew she had no choice but to press on. She was halfway between the car and the barn, and with an equal distance to cover in either direction, her best bet was the barn.

Pausing provided her no rest, no respite. She bent her head to the wind and continued on.

Suddenly, a dim light faintly illuminated the trees ahead of her and she thought she heard the faint rumble of a motor beneath the wind. She strained her eyes, praying for a glimpse of Matt's truck, but when she saw nothing she realized the sound came from behind her. Stumbling off the road, turning around, she saw headlights approach. Tim had come for her, she thought wildly, but the dilapidated car was not her husband's. As it halted beside her, the driver lowered the window.

"Diane?" Jeremy shouted over the wind, astonished. "What are you doing out here?"

Diane was so relieved that tears sprang into her eyes. "The same thing you are, I think," she called out, trudging to the passenger side as Jeremy leaned over to open the door. "Getting myself back to Elm Creek Manor where I belong."

"I SEE HEADLIGHTS," exclaimed Agnes from the breakfast nook window as the Elm Creek Quilters tidied up the kitchen after supper. "There's a car coming over the bridge."

"I hope this means Diane came to her senses and turned back," said Gwen, visibly relieved.

"If you hadn't taken your bad mood out on her, she might not have left in the first place," said Agnes, with a hint of reproach.

Sarah joined Agnes at the window.

"Diane's been gone an awfully long time for it to be her."

Anna peered through the window over the sink, the glass partially obscured by wisps of snow. "That's not Diane's car," she said as the vehicle slowly made its way across the snowdrifted parking lot and shuddered to a stop. "It's Jeremy's."

"I suppose the storm turned him back," remarked Carol as she wiped a table with a damp dishcloth.

"Or Summer did," said Sylvia, exchanging a knowing look with Gwen.

Loading the dishwasher, Anna tried not to look out the window again, but she stopped short when out of the corner of her eye she glimpsed two figures struggling through the drifts to the back door of the manor. "Someone's with him," Agnes cried out from the breakfast nook, just as Anna recognized his companion. "Oh, my goodness, it's Diane!"

The Elm Creek Quilters set down dishcloths and dustpans and brooms and hurried to the entryway—all save Anna, who methodically finished stacking dirty plates in the dishwasher, filled the chamber with detergent, locked the door, and switched it on. Her heart pounded as she listened to her friends ushering Diane and Jeremy inside, their voices a cacophony of astonishment and concern. She overheard boots thumping on the mat, coat hangers jingling in the closet, and a hurried explanation of Diane's car stuck off the road and a bitterly cold struggle on foot back to the manor that Jeremy's timely arrival had mercifully cut short.

Anna put on a fresh pot of coffee as her friends returned to the kitchen, Diane and Jeremy at the center. Anna spared a glance for Jeremy, but her attention quickly shifted to Diane, who looked exhausted and frozen through. Gwen hurried off for quilts to throw around the newcomers, and at a questioning look from Sylvia, Anna assured her that hot coffee was coming right up.

Jeremy shrugged off the quilt Gwen tried to drape around him, explaining that he had been in a warm car most of the day and it was Diane who needed their attention. He kept trying to catch Anna's eye, but she couldn't bear to meet his gaze. Why had he come back so soon? In their amazement over Diane's story of her accident and rescue, no one had asked Jeremy how he happened to come along at that moment, and if the storm had deterred him from going to Chicago, why had he come to Elm Creek Manor instead of going home to his own apartment near campus.

"We should call your husband and let him know you're all right," said Sarah as Diane slowly warmed herself.

"Don't you dare call Tim," said Diane, alarmed, her hands still shivering as she clutched her favorite pink cappuccino mug. "He thinks I never left the manor. Why worry him now?"

"You're going to have to tell him about the car sooner or later," said Sylvia.

"Let's make it later." Diane sipped her coffee, closing her eyes. "I need to regain my strength."

"The car might not be as bad off as you think," said Matt, who had joined them in the kitchen when he saw Jeremy's car pull into the parking lot. "I'll check it out in the morning after the storm passes."

"I'll help," said Jeremy. "When I stopped to see if anyone was in the car, it didn't seem to me that it was seriously damaged, just stuck."

"I'd rather know for sure before I call Tim," said Diane, drawing the quilt tighter around herself. "He doesn't know I was in any danger. Why ruin his evening?"

Sarah picked up the cordless phone and handed it to Diane. "Call him. Let him know you're safe and sound. He'll be more upset when he finds out you didn't tell him right away."

Sighing, Diane reluctantly took the phone and dialed her home number. Anna was torn between staying to support her and leaving the room to give her some privacy, but when no one else left, she too remained and finished wiping the countertops. Diane's conversation was brief, and as far as Anna could tell, Tim cared only for Diane's safety and barely questioned her about the state of the car. He did seem surprised that Diane had left the manor in the first place, and that she had not mentioned her predicament during their earlier call, before her cell phone battery died.

"Lesson learned," said Diane as she hung up and handed the phone back to Sarah.

"Let's hope so," said Gwen.

Before long, Diane announced that she

felt much better and she'd prefer to finish warming herself by the fireside. As the Elm Creek Quilters set off for the ballroom to resume their quilting marathon, the men to watch football on TV, Anna found herself the last to leave the kitchen—and Jeremy waiting for her in the hall.

He waited for the others to round the corner. "You are not my backup plan," he said emphatically.

"I know," she said, looking away, pushing her long braid off her shoulder. "I'm sorry I said that. I was upset and I just blurted out stuff. It seemed right at the time, but now . . ." She took a deep breath. "If I could have this day to do over—" But it was too late. There was no going back, and she knew she had ruined everything.

He studied her intently. "Do you regret everything you said?"

"Well . . ." Anna hesitated. "Not everything." As unwise and untimely as her confession had been, it was the truth, and it needed to be said. She could have worded it as an expression of feeling rather than as an accusation, but she couldn't unsay it. "What I regret most is saying that I didn't think we could be friends anymore. I want to be, and I hope we can, but I'll leave that up to you."

She stepped past him and hurried off to join the other quilters.

THE ELM CREEK Quilters worked until late into the evening, but Gwen couldn't find a moment to speak with Diane alone until they were heading upstairs for bed. "How are you feeling?" she asked, pausing outside Diane's door on her way to the room Sarah had prepared for her.

"Warmer," said Diane from her seat on the bed, sorting through the bag of sample-size toiletries Sylvia had given her. "Stupid."

Gwen folded her arms and leaned against the doorframe. "I'll give you warmer, but I object to stupid."

Diane glanced up, surprised. "Really? You? I thought you'd be the first to agree."

"It's not stupid to miss your family and want to be with them."

"That's not the stupid part. The driving through a snowstorm when they would barely notice my absence is."

"Of course they noticed your absence." Gwen entered the room and took a seat on the bed beside Diane. They adore you. They couldn't function without you."

"Right," Diane scoffed. "They're getting along just fine, I'm sure."

"They'd rather have you at home with them."

"Yes, with my unwanted Thanksgiving Eve lasagna and my silly, age-inappropriate Christmas crafts."

Gwen had no idea what Diane meant about the lasagna, but she couldn't let the criticism of her Advent calendars pass unaddressed. "I'm sorry for what I said about your project. I think your boys will love them." Suddenly Gwen imagined Victoria Stark shaking her head in disapproval of the perfunctory nicety. "What I mean is, they may not appreciate the calendars now, but someday they will. Maybe you should wait until that time arrives."

"That's exactly what I thought," said Diane, absently tracing and retracing a lavender triangle patch on the Corn and Beans quilt spread over the bed. "Someday they'll appreciate all the traditions I've tried to pass along to them. I can't force it, but I can hope that understanding will come in time."

"Don't ever lose hope," said Gwen. "No matter what your misguided friends say. I was upset earlier today and I took my bad mood out on you."

Diane rolled her eyes. "Tell me something I don't know."

"It's no excuse, but I lost a good friend a few weeks ago."

"The way you treat your friends, it's a miracle you have any left."

"No, I mean lost her, lost her. She died. Remember? I went to her funeral—"

"Oh, I'm sorry," said Diane. "I didn't understand. I forgot. I wouldn't have made a joke if I'd—"

Gwen couldn't help smiling. "It's okay. Victoria had a great sense of humor. She would have laughed."

"Victoria." Diane seemed to search her memory. "Wasn't she your professor? The woman who came to quilt camp last summer?"

Gwen nodded. "She was my professor, but she was so much more than that to me. To many people."

"I wish I'd known her better." Diane reached out and clasped Gwen's hand. "Tell me."

Slowly at first, and then with increasing warmth and affection and liveliness, Gwen told Diane about her long-time mentor, how Victoria had taught and encouraged her, how she had battled her disease with courage and incredible inner strength, how her search for a bone marrow donor had led to the discovery of matches for so many others, and at last, one for herself. How Gwen intended to finish the quilt Victoria had begun for her donor, who in her grief seemed to think her generous gift of life had failed Victoria, when in truth it had granted her precious healthy years she might not otherwise have seen.

Diane held her when the flow of words dried up and her tears began to fall.

SARAH SIGHED WEARILY as she climbed into bed and drew the quilts over her, watching Matt as he set crackers and a glass of water on her nightstand. When she had thrown back the covers that morning, she had anticipated a pleasant quilter's holiday filled with fun and friendship, and for the most part she'd had that, but the day had also taken enough unexpected twists and turns to fill an entire month.

At least Diane and Jeremy had returned to the manor safely, her friends were comfortable and cozy in their guest bedrooms, and she'd finished her father-in-law's quilt top. Working on it had given her time to contemplate Matt's plans for the winter, as well as Gretchen's kindhearted offer to fill in for him where she could. Surrounded by loving friends, Sarah would be perfectly fine while he was away, but there were limits to how much time apart she would endure, and he needed to know that. They each had to change their expectations and meet in the middle upon common ground.

"Matt," she began as he climbed into bed beside her. "I understand that you need to help your father. I won't like having you away so much, but I accept it."

Matt rolled onto his side and stroked her from her shoulder to her elbow and back, resting his hand upon her cheek. "Thanks, honey. I know it's not the ideal situation, but I don't have any choice."

"You always have a choice," Sarah reminded him. "And in February when the babies come, I'll need you here."

"Of course. I wouldn't miss that for anything. You know that."

She knew his intentions were good, but if labor came on suddenly and he was three hours away, he might not make it in time. "I know you want to be here, and you'll plan to be here," she said. "That's what I want, too."

"Then we're okay, right?"

She wished it were that simple. "That's up to you, depending upon what you decide to do after the babies are born."

"I'm going to be here, obviously, with you and with them," said Matt. "We've talked about this."

"I need your word," said Sarah.

"You have it."

"Think it through before you promise, or it's an empty promise," she said. "Look, I don't see how you and your father can be certain that helping him through the winter will be enough to save the business. He can't know for sure whether his back will be better by spring."

Matt inhaled deeply. "Well, okay, you're right. There aren't any guarantees."

"If that happens, and if he can't return to work, what are you going to do? Save the business now only to watch it fail later?"

"That probably won't happen," said Matt.

"Let's not plan for problems that might never arise."

"We have to plan for it, Matt," Sarah insisted. "I know when the time comes, if the time comes, you'll be conflicted. We need to plan ahead what we're going to do if your father can't resume working when you have to leave. We need to decide how to handle it if he pressures you to stay longer."

Frowning, Matt sat up in bed and rested his elbows on his knees. "What do you want me to tell you, Sarah?"

"I want you to think it over carefully and be honest with me." And she had to be honest with him. "I am not going to leave Elm Creek Manor. I love the life we've built here together and this is where I want to raise our children. But I know you want to please your father, and when he tells you he needs you, you won't want to disappoint him."

Matt shrugged, helpless. "It's not simply a matter of disappointing him. It's sitting back and watching his livelihood disappear."

Sarah knew that, and it made what she had to say all the more difficult. "I understand, but if, after the babies are born, you decide to continue working for your father's business, I'm not coming with you."

Matt stared at her. "Are you serious?"

She couldn't speak. She nodded instead.

Matt sighed heavily and ran a hand through his curly blond hair. "Sarah, I'm in an impossible position here. I want to please you, and I don't want my father to lose his business. I'm trying to figure out a way to keep everyone happy and satisfied. Let me take care of the problem that's right in front of me before you ask me to tackle problems that won't come up for months, if ever, all right?"

It was not what Sarah had hoped to hear. She had wanted him to hold her and assure her that she and the babies would always come first, that he would never ask her to give up the life she loved so he could take over his father's business, that he wouldn't dream of leaving Elm Creek Manor if she weren't by his side.

But he couldn't or wouldn't tell her that, at least not yet.

"All right," she said quietly. "We'll cross that bridge if we come to it."

"And let's hope we never do." Matt

reached out to turn off the lamp, then lay down and pulled her closer to him. "Everything will work out. You'll see."

She hoped he was right.

"OF COURSE I'LL help childproof the manor," said Joe as he settled down in bed next to Gretchen. "But Matt should stick around to help me. He has no business taking off when his wife's expecting his babies. I thought better of him than that."

"His father's relying on him," said Gretchen. "Don't blame Matt for trying to take care of both his wife and his father. He's already torn. Let's not make things any worse by judging him. We don't know what we'd do in their place."

"Always the peacemaker," Joe said, kissing her on the cheek. "You have enough compassion for the whole world, my dear."

Smiling, she snuggled into her husband's embrace, but she lay awake long after he drifted off to sleep. Restless, thoughtful, she quietly stole from bed, put on her slippers, and drew on her robe. Easing the door open and closing it behind her with barely a sound, she left the bedroom and tiptoed down the hallway to the library, where she flicked on the lights, seated herself in the high-backed leather chair at the large oak desk, and tapped on the mouse to start up the computer.

Gretchen opened the web browser, typed "Quilting for good causes" into the search engine—and broke the silence with a laugh of joyful surprise when she was rewarded with almost a quarter million hits.

ANNA SLEPT RESTLESSLY, thinking of Jeremy sleeping only a few rooms away down the hall. He usually slept much closer than that, she berated herself when she finally gave up on sleep a few minutes after five o'clock. She shouldn't let his presence in the manor rattle her so. She probably wouldn't have, except they had left so much unsaid the evening before. She was not looking forward to facing him across the breakfast table, so she intended to stay on her feet most of the time, serving the meal. How she could avoid him on the ride back to their apartment building was another matter.

She showered, dressed, and went to the kitchen, where she put on a pot of coffee—and if she had a dime for every pot of coffee she had put on at Elm Creek Manor, she would have, well, a huge stack of dimes, but it was her job and she liked it, and she really needed to collect her wildly scattered thoughts before anyone else came downstairs—

She sat down in the breakfast nook and took a few slow, deep breaths. Jeremy would be coming down to breakfast soon, they would drive back to the apartment building together later, and for the foreseeable future, she would continue to live across the hall from him. She had to pull herself together and get through the initial awkwardness. He seemed willing to still be friends, despite knowing what he knew about her feelings for him, and that was a very good sign. If they both worked at it, their friendship could recover, and perhaps the broken places would knit together stronger than they had been before.

She rose and went to the pantry to collect flour, baking powder, and cinnamon, and by the time Sylvia and Andrew appeared in the kitchen doorway, she had squeezed a pitcher of fresh orange juice and had stacked the first batch of waffles on a platter. The couple set the tables and booths with enough places for all of their guests, who joined them one by one, filling the room with cheerful greetings and praise for the mouthwatering aromas that had enticed them from bed.

Anna's friends quickly thwarted her plan to busy herself with serving the meal, insisting that she sit down and eat, because they were perfectly capable of helping themselves to seconds and pouring their own coffee. Seated at one of the booths, Jeremy slid over and offered her the place by his side. After a moment's hesitation, she took it, and when he treated her no differently from any other day, she relaxed and became drawn into the conversation. The storm had passed overnight, and before coming to breakfast Matt had fastened the snowplow to his truck and cleared the parking lot and the back road as far as Diane's car. It was merely stuck upon a fallen tree, not damaged, he reported, and with Jeremy's help he was confident they could get it back on the road in no time.

Andrew joined Matt and Jeremy when they set out after breakfast. When the kitchen was restored to order, the Elm

Creek Quilters returned once again to the ballroom to stitch a few more seams or press a few more blocks before packing up for home.

"We'll certainly never forget this quilter's holiday," declared Agnes as she swept the floor free of snipped threads and bits of fabric.

"There are parts I'd prefer to forget," said Diane. Privately Anna agreed. She had resumed working on Jeremy's Hanukkah quilt since it looked like their friendship might survive the holiday, but the memory of that awful phone conversation still made her flush with embarrassment. She hoped that one day she and Jeremy would be able to joke about it, since forgetting it was unlikely.

It was late morning before the men returned from the woods, Matt and Andrew in the cab of the pickup, Jeremy following in Diane's car, which, except for a scuffed bumper, seemed none the worse for the accident. Diane hugged her friends goodbye, threw on her coat and boots, and raced outside, jumping into the driver's seat before anyone could remind her that she had promised Agnes her usual ride home.

"I'll drive you," Gwen said, repeating her offer from the previous night as the Elm Creek Quilters watched through the window as Diane's car crossed the bridge over the creek and disappeared around the barn.

"Let's leave soon," said Agnes. "If Diane gets stuck again, she'll need a ride, too."

Jeremy and Anna followed close behind. They drove in silence until they entered the woods, where Jeremy pointed out the place where he had picked up Diane the night before, and farther along, the site of the accident. Anna peered through the window at the churned up snow and the remnants of the fallen tree Matt had sawed apart to free the car, and shuddered at the thought of what might have befallen Diane if Jeremy had not passed by.

"Why did you turn around?" Anna asked him. "Were the roads really that bad?"

"They were bad enough."

"Why did you come to the manor instead of going home?"

He shrugged, keeping his eyes on the road. "I thought you might want a ride home."

In spite of herself, Anna laughed. "You

expect me to believe that? You never said a word about heading back out into the storm after you made it safely to the manor."

"It never occurred to me to leave after I found Diane along the way. Frankly, I think Sylvia and Agnes would have barricaded the door rather than let anyone else leave."

"Maybe, but that doesn't explain why you came back." After an awkward silence, she added, "Maybe it was just because of the storm."

"No, it wasn't." Jeremy shifted in his seat as they left the woods behind them and pulled onto the highway, which had been recently plowed and salted, the crystals sparkling in the bright sunlight. "I didn't turn around because of the storm. I could have made it to Chicago, but after you hung up on me, I called Summer."

"I didn't hang up on you," Anna said. "I said good-bye, and then I hung up. That's not hanging up on someone."

Jeremy threw her a weary glance. "Be that as it may. Summer and I had a short but long overdue chat. We decided it would be best if I didn't visit her."

Anna nodded. He had still come to the manor instead of going home.

"I called you to tell you I was on my way," Jeremy said after the silence had stretched out too long. "You didn't answer."

"I'd left my phone in the ballroom when I went to make supper," said Anna. "By the time I got back to it, you and Diane had already arrived." He hadn't left a message.

"There's something I need you to know." Jeremy kept his gaze fixed on the road straight ahead. "What happened between me and Summer, the way things ended—you are not the cause. I don't want you to think you split us up. We've been headed in that direction for a long time. I don't want you to feel any guilt about that."

Anna watched him. "Okay, I won't."

"Good."

They drove along without speaking. Few other drivers had ventured out that morning, but they encountered more as they approached Waterford. As they reached downtown, Jeremy held out his hand to her. After a moment's hesitation, Anna took it.

He laced his fingers through hers and drove on.

DIANE HAD BARELY pulled into the garage when the door to the mudroom opened and Tim, Michael, and Todd rushed out to greet her. She endured their teasing reprimands for allowing them to believe she was safe at the manor when she was actually in mortal peril—a charge she denied since she was never more than a mile from the manor—and for letting her cell phone run out of power yet again. They wanted her to promise she'd never leave the house without a full charge again, and although she rolled her eyes and said that a three-quarters charge would be good enough, she was secretly delighted by the attention. The boys hadn't come running to meet her since they were in elementary school.

The boys insisted upon carrying her things inside for her, although she didn't need the help since she hadn't planned for an overnight stay and had no luggage, only her purse and her quilting tote bag. Tim escorted her to the sofa, tucked a quilt around her, and brought her a mug of hot coffee as if she had come straight from the chilly, snowbound car rather than a comfortable suite at Elm Creek Manor. To her surprise, all three seated themselves nearby and asked her to tell them exactly what had happened. She agreed, but made an editorial decision to begin with pulling out of the parking lot rather than with the frustration that had compelled her to leave the manor.

Michael noticed the omission. "I still don't understand why you tried to drive in that storm. You've spent the night at the manor plenty of times. Why the rush to leave last night?"

Diane reached out, roughed his hair, and smoothed it down again. "I wanted to get home to my guys."

"You wouldn't have missed much time with us," Todd pointed out. "You're here now, and we'll still have most of the weekend together."

"I hadn't packed a bag," Diane made an excuse. "I didn't have my pajamas, my toothbrush, a change of clothes . . . Speaking of which, I need to change." She had showered at the manor, but putting on the clothes she'd worn the day before always left her feeling uncomfortably grungy.

She rose, and as she hefted her tote bag to her shoulder, intending to leave it in her sewing room on the way upstairs, one of the straps slipped and a few of the appliqués fell upon the coffee table.

"What's this?" asked Tim, who had a charming habit of always expressing interest in her quilting projects even though he still didn't grasp the difference between piecing and appliqué.

"This was a very welcome distraction while I was awaiting rescue yesterday afternoon. Honestly, I bet my friends still haven't checked the voicemail. When camp's not in session and there aren't dozens of calls to make . . ." Diane shook her head.

Todd picked up a piece of brown fabric that was meant to be the side of a log cabin. He found a few others and quickly assembled the cabin and the red, snow-covered barn beside it. Michael found a green piece cut in the shape of a pine tree, matched it to a brown trunk, and slid it in place beside the cabin. "This looks like that Advent calendar we used to have," he said, studying the scene. "Remember, Mom? You'd put candy or money in the pockets and we'd open one for each day of December leading up to Christmas."

Diane felt a thrill of delight. "You remember that?"

Michael shrugged. "Well, yeah. You never let us have candy except for Halloween, Easter, and Christmas. It was kind of a big deal."

"We used to argue over the prizes," Todd recalled. "Even though we took turns, Michael always ended up with the candy and I got the quarters."

"I did not," Michael retorted mildly. "You just thought I did. Anyway, back then, a quarter could buy more candy than I got in those pockets."

Todd grinned. "What did I know? I was a kid."

"Why did we stop using the Advent calendar?" asked Tim.

"It was cardstock," Diane reminded him. "It was falling apart. Half the pockets had fallen off."

"We still have it, though, don't we?" asked Todd.

Diane nodded. "It's tucked away with the rest of the Christmas decorations."

"Don't throw it out," said Todd, relieved. "It's an heirloom."

"Really," said Diane, staring at him. Had one of the Elm Creek Quilters phoned as she was driving home and put him up to this? "You think so?"

"We should start using it again," said Michael. "I can fix the pockets, and instead of candies and quarters, you can put tens and twenties in them."

"Inflation," added Todd, feigning regret. "You know how it is."

"Yes, I think I'm catching on," said Diane, smiling.

GWEN PULLED INTO Agnes's driveway, which was remarkably clear of snow. "Who shoveled your driveway?" she asked. "Magical yuletide elves? And can you send them to my house next?"

"My next-door neighbor has a snow blower," Agnes explained, gathering her things. "He's such a dear. He clears my driveway and sidewalk anytime we get more than an inch. I make it up to him with blueberry cobbler."

"Nice arrangement," Gwen remarked, noting that the neighbor had apparently salted Agnes's front walk, too. She waited until Agnes let herself in the house before pulling out of the driveway and continuing home.

Her own driveway was a mess, but Gwen managed to make it up the slope and into the garage. She carried her empty glass cake pan and purse inside, left them on the kitchen counter, and returned to the car for her sewing kit and Victoria's quilt, which she had removed from the hoop back at the manor, rolled into a neat bundle, and tucked into a pillowcase for ease of transport. Thanks to the storm that had kept Gwen at Elm Creek Manor—away from her books and computer—she had finished quilting all but a small corner section. She intended to finish the hand-quilting by Saturday afternoon and begin the hanging sleeve and binding on Sunday. If she stayed on schedule, she should be able to complete the entire quilt in time to send it to Kathryn for Christmas. She had promised Victoria she would, and she wouldn't let anything—exams, student conferences, or grading papers—stand in her way.

But first, she had to dig out her driveway.

She lugged the quilt, her sewing kit, and the slender bamboo hoops into the house and left them in the living room until she could resume her work. On her way to the hall closet for more appropriate winter outerwear, she passed her answering machine and noticed that the light was blinking. Summer probably hadn't left the message, since she usually called Gwen's cell. It was probably from a frantic student begging for an extension on a paper, she guessed, reaching for the button to play back the message.

"Good morning," an unfamiliar voice greeted her. "I'm calling on behalf of the National Bone Marrow Registry with an important message for Dr. Gwendolyn Sullivan. I'm pleased to inform you that you are a match for a patient in Arizona, and we're hoping that you're still willing and able to offer this gift of life. Please contact us as soon as possible so we can discuss the details, because as I'm sure you know, time is of the essence."

Gwen snatched up a pen and scrap of paper and jotted down the contact information, her heart soaring with thankfulness and hope. She knew that somewhere,

Victoria was celebrating the match. Perhaps she had even had a hand in it.

A CONTEMPLATIVE PEACE settled over the manor after their guests departed and all traces of the quilter's holiday were swept away from the ballroom. Gretchen had finished her Swamp Patch quilt, bright and cheerful in primary colors, and thanks to her late-night investigation on the Internet, she knew exactly what to do with it. And if Sylvia agreed to her plan, Elm Creek Quilts could contribute even more.

She waited until evening, when the day's work was finished and Sylvia had settled down in the formal parlor to relax with a book and a cup of tea. "How is your Star of the Magi quilt coming along?" Gretchen asked, lingering in the doorway, holding her own cup of tea. If Sylvia seemed to prefer her solitude, Gretchen would wait for a better occasion.

But Sylvia smiled and beckoned her inside. "I should have it finished in time for the Holiday Boutique, especially since my friend offered to machine quilt it for me. Sarah's been after me for months to purchase a longarm quilting machine for Elm

Creek Quilts, and at times like these when a deadline is fast approaching, the idea has a certain appeal."

"We had a longarm machine at Quilts 'N Things," Gretchen said. "Customers would rent it by the hour to quilt their tops, and my partner taught classes on how to use it. I resisted the purchase at first since I prefer hand-quilting, but soon I realized that my partner was right. The machine paid for itself within a year, and we were able to complete sample quilts to display in the shop much faster."

Sylvia nodded, mulling it over. "Perhaps Sarah and I should sit down and discuss whether we can fit a longarm quilting machine into our budget. We could certainly fit one into the ballroom. Would you join our discussion and let us benefit from your experience?"

"I'd be happy to. In the meantime, there's another subject I'd like to bring up at our next business meeting, if you and Sarah agree."

"What's that, dear?"

"I've been thinking over our conversation yesterday about your church's Holiday

Boutique, and how it's an important fund-raiser for the local food pantry. All the Elm Creek Quilters agreed that it's important for us to give back to our community, and I'd like to see us contribute as a group, as a circle of quilters as well as a company."

"I would, too," Sylvia remarked. "What did you have in mind?"

"I've always been drawn to causes that serve women and children," said Gretchen. "Last night I learned about an organization called Project Linus."

"Oh, I've heard of them," said Sylvia. "They provide quilts and blankets to children in need, everything from offering a comforting quilt to a seriously ill child at a hospital to providing a warm blanket to a youngster rescued by the fire department. Many of our quilt campers have mentioned that they participate in their local chapters. In my opinion, they do a great deal of good."

"I agree, but there's no chapter in the Elm Creek Valley," said Gretchen. "I think we should launch one, and let Elm Creek Manor become the drop-off spot for all our local quilters, knitters, and crocheters. We can distribute the donations throughout the Elm Creek Valley, wherever a need exists. There's the neonatal center and the children's hospital, the fire department, the food pantry—"

"What a wonderful idea," said Sylvia. "It perfectly suits the mission of Elm Creek Quilts."

"I'd be happy to contact the Project Linus national headquarters and find out what we need to do to make it official," said Gretchen. "I'd also take care of organizing the collection and distribution."

"With a team of Elm Creek Quilters to assist you, of course. We wouldn't let you do it on your own."

Gretchen knew she would need their help, and she welcomed it. "I'm thrilled that you like the idea, but . . ." She hesitated, wondering if Sylvia would think she had gone too far. "I know how we can do even more."

"You're on quite a roll, aren't you, dear?" Sylvia sipped her tea and regarded Gretchen expectantly. "Well, let's have it."

Before she could talk herself out of it, Gretchen plunged ahead. The quilter's holiday was a delightful tradition, but perhaps it was time to transform it into an even greater expression of thankfulness and giving. Why not create a winter quilter's holiday camp during which they and their campers would make quilts for Project Linus? All who attended would enjoy a delightful week at Elm Creek Manor free of charge, but rather than working on quilts for themselves, every quilt they created would go to Project Linus or another worthy cause in the Elm Creek Valley.

"I think quilters would be happy to make a quilt or two for children in need in exchange for a week's getaway at Elm Creek Manor, don't you?" asked Gretchen, studying Sylvia's expression for signs of approval or skepticism. "Anna's marvelous cooking alone would be worth the labor."

Sylvia sat very still for a long moment, and then she began to nod. "I like it," she declared. "A Quilter's Holiday Camp to make quilts for children in need, in addition to contributions to Project Linus all year long. We'll need to take it up with the other Elm Creek Quilters, but I'm sure they'll find the idea as intriguing as I do."

"I hope so," said Gretchen, smiling. "I know it will mean more work at a busy time of the year, but as you said earlier, we must never become too busy to help those in need."

"I must insist upon one thing, however." Sylvia smiled fondly. "I enjoy our quilter's holidays too much to end them. Let's continue to reserve the day after Thanksgiving for our circle of quilters so we may enjoy giving thanks and making holiday projects together. Diane would never finish a thing in time for Christmas if we end our tradition."

"We can't have that," agreed Gretchen. "How about this: Thanksgiving will be for family, the Friday afterward will be for the Elm Creek Quilters, Saturday will be a day of rest and preparation, and Sunday will be the first day of Quilter's Holiday Camp. What do you think?"

"I think I know what we'll do with the blocks we put in the cornucopia during our Patchwork Potluck from now on," said Sylvia, her eyes lighting up with anticipation. "We'll save them for our Quilter's Holiday Camp, stitch them together, and make the first of many warm, cozy, and comforting quilts for a neighbor in need. And you, my dear, will decide who receives it."

It was a duty Gretchen would happily accept.

SYLVIA FINISHED HER Star of the Magi quilt on the afternoon of December sixth, the Feast of St. Nicholas. As she folded it and set it aside until Matt could drive her to church to drop it off for the Holiday Boutique, she fondly recalled the St. Nicholas Days of her childhood. The night before, she and her siblings and whatever cousins happened to be visiting would each leave a shoe on the hearth of the ballroom fireplace. In the morning when they woke, if they had been good little girls and boys all year long, they would find their shoes filled with candy, nuts, fruits, and little toys. None of them had ever received twigs or lumps of coal, as naughty children were said to do, but Great-Aunt Lucinda often warned them that her brother had once received an onion, so such unpleasant deliveries were known to have happened.

Smiling, Sylvia made her way to the kitchen to fix herself a cup of tea just as the phone rang. She quickened her pace, but there was no need as someone else answered on the second ring. A moment later, Sarah appeared in the kitchen doorway carrying the cordless receiver. "It's for you, Sylvia," she said, covering the mouthpiece with one hand. "He asked for Sylvia Bergstrom-Compson-Cooper, so it might be a telemarketer. Or a tax collector."

Amused, Sylvia thanked her, took the receiver into the kitchen, and seated herself in the nearest booth. "Hello, this is Sylvia. May I help you?"

"Hi, yes, I sure hope so." The man, a bit nervous and around Sarah's age from the sound of it, cleared his throat. "My name is Scott Nelson. You wrote to me about my grandmother, Elizabeth Nelson."

"Oh, my goodness," exclaimed Sylvia. "Yes, Scott. I did indeed write to you. I'm delighted you called."

"Are you—you must be—are you the little cousin Sylvia my grandmother told me so much about? The one always getting into mischief?"

Sylvia laughed, tears of joy springing into her eyes. "Yes, yes, that would indeed be me."

"Every year on her wedding anniversary, she used to tell us kids how you didn't want her to marry our grandfather. She said you hid her mother's scissors so that she couldn't make Grandma's wedding gown, and you stole the keys to her trunk and threw them into the river so that she couldn't pack for her honeymoon."

"Yes, I was quite a charming little dear. Did Elizabeth—your grandmother—mention how I refused to try on my flower girl dress no matter how much my mother and aunts begged, and when that didn't work, I told the groom-to-be that I hated him and that everyone in the family wished he would just go away, but they were too polite to say it?"

Scott laughed. "She mentioned your dress, but not that last part."

"I should have kept it to myself, then."

"No, not at all," said Scott. "I think some people have kept too much to themselves all these years."

Sylvia smiled wistfully, thinking of the time lost, the once strong family ties broken. "I agree. There's so much I long to ask you about my cousin, what became of her after she left Pennsylvania. What else did she tell you about us?"

"Not much," Scott admitted. "She

mentioned a horse farm where the family used to gather for the holidays, and she had a few stories about the hotel her parents ran in Harrisburg. I'm ashamed to admit that I didn't always pay attention when she talked about her childhood. Now I wish I had, but it's too late."

"I understand," said Sylvia quietly. She often wished she had listened more carefully to her mother's stories. "Believe me, I do."

"Grandma's past has always been a bit of a mystery to us. She didn't pass down many mementos of the years before she came to California as a young bride, just a few photos and a patchwork quilt."

Sylvia gasped. "You have one of Elizabeth's quilts?"

"A few, actually, several she made after she and Grandpa settled in the Arboles Valley and one she brought with her. I don't know much about quilts, but this one has rectangles of light and dark colors wrapped around a lot of little red squares. She said it was a wedding gift from a great-aunt or a grandmother. I don't remember the relative's name, but she stitched it on the back of the quilt."

"Could it have been Lucinda?" asked Sylvia, although the quilt Scott described simply had to be the Chimneys and Cornerstones quilt Great-Aunt Lucinda had made for Elizabeth in the months leading up to her wedding. Sylvia clearly recalled standing at Lucinda's knee as she had stitched the blocks, explaining the symbolism of the pattern. The dark fabrics represented the sorrows in a life, the light colors the joys, and each of the red squares was a fire burning in the fireplace to warm Elizabeth after a weary journey home. Sylvia hoped the Chimneys and Cornerstones quilt and memories of home had comforted Elizabeth during the long years when she had allowed other ties to languish.

"Yes, Lucinda. That sounds right," replied Scott. "I could call my sister and ask her to check. And—" He hesitated. "I could show it to you next summer. We're having a Nelson family reunion at a park on the grounds of the old Triumph Ranch in the Arboles Valley—"

"Triumph Ranch?" cried Sylvia. "Do you mean it truly did exist?"

"Of course. Grandma and Grandpa founded it in the 1930s and raised their children there. One of my cousins still farms what remains of the old ranch lands. You can see for yourself when you come for the family reunion. My sister and I would like you to be the guest of honor. You're a part of our family, and you know more about our grandmother's heritage than any of us. We'd be very grateful if you'd come and celebrate her memory with us."

"I'd be happy to share what I know," Sylvia assured him. "Anything you want to learn about your grandmother as a young woman or the rest of the Bergstrom clan, I'd be delighted to share, in exchange for whatever you can tell me about her life after she left Pennsylvania."

"I'd like that, Mrs. Cooper. I'd like that very much."

"Please, call me Sylvia," she replied, her heart overflowing with thankfulness. "We are, after all, family."

The Best Friend

Prosperity

Nine-Patch

Swamp Patch

Grandmother's Delight

Signs of Spring